"Holly can be ready to go when you are."

Hawk rose forcefully to his feet. "That's *your child* you're calmly discussing giving away."

Leonie looked up with emotionless green eyes. "I'm not giving her away. She's your daughter."

"I've no intention of taking Holly away from you. Leonie, you almost *died* giving birth to her!" he said, trying to elicit some show of emotion. "I don't just want Holly. I want you, too. I want—"

"Hawk," she cut in quietly, "I don't want to marry you. I don't even want to be married again." She started toward the door. "Just tell me when you want Holly, and I'll see that she's ready." The door closed softly behind her.

She couldn't mean that. She couldn't mean to give up her child without a fight! There had to be more to it than that.

Books by Carole Mortimer

HARLEQUIN SIGNATURE EDITION
GYPSY
MERLYN'S MAGIC

HARLEQUIN PRESENTS
909—NO LONGER A DREAM
923—THE WADE DYNASTY
939—GLASS SLIPPERS AND UNICORNS
955—HAWK'S PREY
989—VELVET PROMISE
1005—A ROGUE AND A PIRATE
1019—AFTER THE LOVING
1037—TANGLED HEARTS
1050—TAGGART'S WOMAN
1069—SECRET PASSION
1083—WISH FOR THE MOON
1100—UNCERTAIN DESTINY

Don't miss any of our special offers. Write to us at the following address for information on our newest releases.

Harlequin Reader Service
901 Fuhrmann Blvd., P.O. Box 1397, Buffalo, NY 14240
Canadian address: P.O. Box 603,
Fort Erie, Ont. L2A 5X3

CAROLE MORTIMER

JUST ONE NIGHT

Harlequin Books

TORONTO • NEW YORK • LONDON
AMSTERDAM • PARIS • SYDNEY • HAMBURG
STOCKHOLM • ATHENS • TOKYO • MILAN

Our lovely boys,
Matthew and Joshua.

Harlequin Signature Edition published March 1988

ISBN 0-373-83206-0

Originally published in Great Britain in 1987 as *Witchchild*

Our lovely boys,

Matthew and Joshua.

PROLOGUE

LEONIE'S eyes widened on the man seated opposite her. 'Please don't feel you have to be in the least polite to me just because I only opened the door to my home and met you for the first time two minutes ago!' She gave him a wry smile.

His mouth tightened. 'Very funny, Miss Brandon,' he snapped. 'But I intend to make my feelings very clear about having a little gold-digger like you anywhere near my son!'

'Oh yes, Eagle, I think——'

'Hawk,' he cut in irritably. 'My name is Hawk, not Eagle,' he clarified, seeing her mystified expression.

Surely one bird of prey was much like another? She had told Laura that she hoped the name wouldn't be prophetic, but two minutes into her acquaintance with Hawk Sinclair, after he had verbally attacked her as soon as they reached the lounge, and she knew it was an understatement; *Shark* might have been more appropriate!

'Hawk,' she conceded lightly. Oh dear, they were going to have problems with this man, if his grim expression was anything to go by. 'I think you've expressed your feelings about that very plainly. However——'

'How much do you want, Miss Brandon?'

Leonie's mouth quirked with amazement. 'You're actually offering me money?' She absently tickled the pure white cat as it stroked against her denim-clad leg passing through the room on its way to the kitchen.

He nodded abruptly. 'In exchange for your leaving Hal alone.'

Green eyes lit up with amusement. 'No man has ever offered me money to leave him alone before!'

His mouth twisted with disgust. 'I'm sure plenty have paid you to stay *with* them!'

'You're getting nasty again now,' she reproved.

'Miss Brandon——'

'Can't you be a little less formal with the woman you're insulting?' she mocked. 'My name is——'

'I know your name, damn it!' He stood up forcefully, pacing about the comfort of the small lounge.

Even when he was so obviously angry with her this man was fascinating to watch, Leonie decided. He wasn't handsome, not in the way Hal was, more a power to be reckoned with, his movements all made with a leashed energy that drew attention to him even when he was standing still. And he had the most wonderful hair, gloriously thick and straight. It was a pity about his eyes; their cold greyness stopped him just short of being perfect, far from friendly as they looked at her. Oh well, maybe he thought he had good reason.

'Are you going to leave Hal alone or not?' he grated in a voice of rough velvet, his Texas accent, if he had ever had one, completely erased from the years of living away from his native State.

'Not. You see——'

He glared at her. 'I believe you should know right now that I never take no for an answer.'

Leonie was sure that was no idle threat, his business reputation having preceded him, at least. The Sinclair hotels were known worldwide for their exclusive luxury, and this man maintained complete control of them from his home in Manhattan, Hal had informed them ruefully. The occasional surprise visits his father paid to the individual hotels had been enough to put the fear of God into the staff until the next time he arrived unexpectedly. Having received one of those visits herself Leonie was beginning to understand the feeling.

'Hal still has a long way to go to learn the hotel business,' he rasped. 'And he's far too young to be thinking of marrying anyone——'

'Ah!' she pounced with satisfaction, absently stroking the long-haired tortoiseshell cat as it stood up in the chair it occupied, stretching before settling down to sleep again.

Dark brows rose over frankly impatient eyes. 'Ah?' Hawk Sinclair repeated, dangerously soft, his hands thrust into the pockets of his denims as he glowered down at her from his imposing height of well over six feet. To someone who barely scraped over five feet he just looked *huge*.

It was a pity she couldn't take notes of this conversation; she was sure she would never be able to convey all the nuances when she related it to Laura later. Those eyebrows, for example, expressed his feelings exactly every time he spoke.

'How old are you, Hawk?' she asked interestedly.

'How old——?' He looked ready to explode. 'What the hell does *my* age have to do with any of this?'

'A lot—if you're still young enough to be approaching your mid-life crisis rather than having already passed it.' She eyed him guilelessly.

In the next second he *did* explode, using all the swear words Leonie knew—and quite a lot that she had never heard before!

'Are you always this damned kooky?' he finally calmed down enough to ask. 'Hal needs his head examined——'

'*Hal* knows a good thing when he sees it,' she corrected chidingly. 'You haven't reached forty yet, then,' she guessed lightly, glancing sideways as Pop, a smoky-grey cat, strolled through the room to join the white cat in the kitchen.

'Hal's age is the one that's relevant here.' Silver eyes dared her to pursue whatever subject she might be leading up to with her questions. 'He's not even twenty yet, and you're already twenty-four——'

'Twenty-five last month,' she corrected pertly, her eyes widely innocent as he looked at her fiercely for interrupting.

'Too old—and too experienced—for Hal,' he rasped.

'Do you really think so?' Leonie sat forward on the edge of her seat, looking very youthful with her rich red shoulder-length hair curling loosely about her make-upless face, her green T-shirt moulding the slender delicacy of her childlike body, the tight-fitting denims making her legs look longer than they actually were.

'Not the way you look right now, no,' he conceded, his eyes narrowed with suspicion. 'Did Hal call you and let you know I'd probably be coming to see you today?'

She wished he had! 'The last time Hal mentioned your whereabouts you were in Nassau.'

'That was over a week ago!'

Leonie shrugged. 'To tell you the truth, Hal and I haven't really spoken a great deal.'

Hawk drew in a harshly angry breath, towering over her threateningly, his hands at his sides now, clenching and unclenching. 'Do you get some cheap thrill out of telling me you're too busy sleeping with my son to bother with conversation?' A nerve pulsed at his jaw.

'I realise you're having trouble accepting Hal's maturity because it makes you feel old, but——'

'The only thing I feel when I think of the two of you together is angry!' he grated.

'Because knowing your son is involved in an intimate relationship forces you to acknowledge that he's grown-up——'

'When did you qualify as a psychiatrist?' Hawk Sinclair demanded viciously.

Leonie relaxed back in her chair, lifting her feet up to rest on the cushion beneath her, her arms wrapped about her knees. 'I didn't,' she said without rancour. 'However, I am an observer of life.'

'Well, I wish you'd do your observing a thousand miles away from my son!' He glared at her.

She observed *him* curiously. 'Did you know you have the most expressive eyebrows? They define your every mood. They'd make a fascinating characteristic for one of the people in our books——'

'If I ever recognise anyone even remotely like

myself in one of your books you'll live to regret it!' he warned savagely.

Leonie sat forward eagerly, her chin resting on her knees. 'Have you ever read any of our books?' she asked.

'Fourth-rate detective novels aren't my favourite choice of literature,' he said with contempt. 'They obviously aren't making you a fortune either, otherwise you wouldn't need to take advantage of Hal's youthful naïveté in this way.'

'Hal was never naïve, not even in the cradle,' she dismissed reprovingly. 'He's too much like you.'

'Thanks—I think,' drawled Hawk Sinclair dryly.

'And our books aren't fourth-rate,' she defended indignantly. 'Leonaura Brandon is very popular.'

'You may well be,' he dismissed with impatience. 'Personally I can't stand books where everyone ends up getting murdered and the butler did it!'

Leonie shook her head. 'No one ever gets murdered in our books.'

'Then how the hell can they be murder books?'

'They aren't,' she shrugged. 'Not every detective investigates murders.'

He gave an irritated sigh. 'Miss Brandon, I asked you how much you want to get out of——Why the hell do you keep saying *our* books?' He gave a dark scowl at the realisation that his curiosity about her had once again diverted him from his purpose of buying her out of Hal's life.

'My sister and I co-author them,' she explained lightly. 'Leonie and Laura—Leon-aura,' she provided.

'Let's leave your sister out of this——'

'Oh, I don't think we can do that,' she told him thoughtfully. 'You see, *I'm* Leonie.'

Angry disbelief claimed the hard contours of his face, his eyes were silver slits. 'You mean you aren't—you're not——'

Leonie realised she was probably witnessing history being made, seriously doubting that Hawk Sinclair had ever before been rendered speechless. 'I mean you've been trying to buy off the wrong sister,' she confirmed ruefully. 'Laura is the one who's been dating Hal, as I'm sure you know.'

'You—I——'

'Why don't you sit down?' she offered as angry colour darkened his cheeks. 'Your blood-pressure——'

'There's nothing wrong with my blood-pressure!' he finally managed to burst out.

'Except that it's rising,' Leonie told him calmly. 'You really should learn to relax——'

'Relax!' he repeated harshly. 'I've been trying to reason with a child when I meant to bargain with a mercenary, and you tell me to *relax*!'

'Laura and I are twins,' she chided his reference to her age, bending to stroke Pop as he left the kitchen after eating his lunch.

Hawk became suddenly still and, if anything, more dangerous. 'You mean there's another one just like you running around loose somewhere?'

Her mouth quirked. 'Not quite.'

'How "not quite"?' He was eyeing her now as if he thought he might need to make an escape at any moment.

He really did look worried, poor man! 'Laura and I *are* identical. But only in looks,' Leonie added consolingly as he gave a pained groan. 'I'm the only kooky one,' she added mischievously.

He had the grace to look uncomfortable. 'I was angry when I said that.'

'And you aren't angry now?' she teased.

'Bloody furious, as you English would say,' he scowled. 'If your sister isn't here where is she?'

'Out. With Hal,' she revealed without guilt. 'They left early this morning.'

'Why didn't you say so when——Oh, what the hell!' He raised his eyes heavenwards. 'I'll talk to her some other time.' He turned to leave. 'When my blood-pressure is back to normal,' he muttered grimly.

'A nice cup of tea will help with that.' Leonie sprang to her feet. 'I'll go and make one and we can drink it while we finish talking.'

'I thought we had finished . . .' He was starting to look slightly dazed now.

Leonie had seen the same confused expression on the faces of most of the people she met. It usually faded once they had known her for a while, but Hawk Sinclair seemed determined this would be a brief acquaintance. A very brief acquaintance! Maybe he would change his mind once she had told him about Laura.

'I don't think so,' she smiled. 'We haven't really talked about my sister yet. I'm relieved the two of us met first,' she continued chattily. 'It means that most of your anger will have dispersed by the time you do meet Laura.'

'I wouldn't count on it!' He sank down weakly into an armchair, rubbing a hand over his eyes.

Leonie moved happily about the kitchen,

preparing the promised tea, confident she would be able to reason with Hawk Sinclair once he had calmed down enough to listen.

A kook, he thought. A one hundred per cent, fourteen-carat kook! And he had been trying to reason with it—her.

It had all seemed so straightforward when he had left the hotel this morning, enjoying the drive out into the country to this big rambling house that stood completely on its own on the outskirts of a small village. But that was before he had met *Leonie* Brandon!

Twenty-five. She didn't look anywhere near twenty-five. And what was all that rubbish about his age? Damn it, thirty-nine—well, almost forty—wasn't old. He certainly wasn't going through any crisis because of it. Hell, he was trying to justify his age to himself now! he realised with an inward groan.

God, if Laura Brandon was anything like her peculiar sister this was going to be more difficult than he could ever have imagined; Leonie seemed incapable of even taking an insult seriously!

When he had left New York yesterday he had been looking forward to being with Hal, and he had been shocked to the roots of his being when shortly after meeting him at the airport Hal had told him that he had met the woman he intended to marry. God, the woman was six years older than him, wrote flaky detective novels for a living—with her kooky sister; it was obvious she was more interested in what the Sinclair heir could give her than in Hal himself.

That surmise had been easy to make after Hal had told him all about Laura Brandon last night, just as it had been a simple thing to decide he would pay her off as she had obviously intended he should.

Fifteen minutes with Leonie Brandon and he wasn't even sure what he was doing here any more!

And how many more cats were going to come strolling through here? He had no patience with the creatures himself, thought they were totally hopeless as companions, never there when you wanted them, demanding when they were. Very much like a woman, in fact, and he had little time for them either, apart from their rather obvious attraction.

He turned sharply as Leonie Brandon came back into the room with the tea. My God, he thought, she looked so young. Or maybe he was getting old after all. He certainly didn't want any tea—a Scotch maybe, but not *tea*!

'Here we are.' She put the tray down on the coffee-table, smiling at him brightly.

She looked ten years old in that get-up and with that sprinkling of freckles across her uptilted nose, and yet the breasts beneath the T-shirt definitely proclaimed her a woman——Get a grip on yourself, Sinclair, he instructed himself impatiently. *That* was definitely a complication this situation didn't need!

He sat forward obediently to take the proffered cup of tea.

He had such strong hands, Leonie admired as she curled up on the sofa opposite him. He also looked totally ridiculous wrapping those long fingers about one of their delicate china tea-cups!

'Laura,' he prompted abruptly.

'No,' she smiled. 'I told you, I'm Leonie——'

'I meant you intended telling me about your sister,' he clarified in a controlled voice.

'Drink your tea,' she encouraged.

'Why?' he raised dark brows sceptically. 'Do you think it will leave me more open to the sad tale you're undoubtedly going to tell me?'

'It is only tea, Hawk,' she reproved. 'And what sort of sad tale did you have in mind?'

'Oh, something like Laura needs money for your old, sick mother, or father, or aunt, or——'

'There's only Laura and I,' she cut in quietly. 'And all Laura wants is Hal. She happens to love him very much.'

His mouth twisted scornfully. 'I'm sure she does,' he rasped. 'More to the point, Hal is sure she does,' he added harshly.

'You don't understand——'

'No, you're the one who doesn't understand,' he slammed his cup down impatiently. 'My son is nineteen years old, I'm not about to sit back and let him ruin his whole life by getting married far too young to a woman he barely knows!'

'Is that what you did?' she asked shrewdly. 'After all, to have a son of his age you must have married at nineteen yourself.'

'I was just twenty when I married,' he ground out, looking as if he would like to pick her up and bodily shake her. 'And the situation was entirely different. My wife and I grew up together, we always knew we would marry.'

'Okay, so it didn't happen this way for you, but that doesn't mean there isn't such a thing as love at first sight,' Leonie reasoned. 'Or that that isn't the way it happened for Laura and Hal,' she defended.

He sighed. 'I'm not denying that at this moment in his life Hal is sure he does feel that way about your sister, it's *her* feelings for *him* that I doubt,' he bit out grimly.

'Because your name is Sinclair and hers is Brandon, because you're rich and we're not so rich, because——'

'The reasons for my doubting the sincerity of her feelings are, as you are so ably proving, too many and would take too long to go into individually,' he told her impatiently. 'Besides which, Hal still has a long way to go before he knows the business as well as he'll need to to take over from me one day. He's going to be travelling extensively over the next few years.'

'Laura could go with him——'

'And no doubt she'd want to take her sister along too,' he sneered.

Leonie chewed thoughtfully on her bottom lip. 'Have you always been rich?' she asked at last.

'Always,' he admitted without apology for the fact. 'My father founded the Sinclair hotels, and by the time I was born they were already a world-wide concern.'

She nodded. 'Then I suppose you must have a pretty good idea of what it's like to be pursued just for your money.'

'Yes, I——I believe I was just insulted,' he drawled irritably.

Her eyes were widely innocent. 'Really? I can't imagine by whom.'

'Leonie,' he began reasoningly, 'I do not intend to let your sister marry my son.'

She grimaced. 'I was afraid you were still going to feel that way.'

Hawk eyed her suspiciously. 'Afraid?' he repeated slowly.

'Don't look so wary,' she chided. 'I'm not threatening you. Good gracious, do I look as if I could threaten anyone?' She looked down pointedly at her childlike body.

'It's the non-violent threats that are usually the most dangerous,' he replied.

She sighed. 'Well, I'm not making any kind of threat. I was just going to tell you that of the two of us Laura is the more practical one——'

'So practical she knew a meal-ticket when she saw it,' scorned Hawk.

Leonie gave him a censorious frown. 'When I get Winnie in a seemingly unsolvable situation Laura is always the one who——'

'I know I'm going to hate myself for asking, but *who* is Winnie?' he prompted irritably. 'Not one of your cats?'

She shook her head with a smile. 'The detective in our books,' she supplied. 'No matter how unlikely the situation—and believe me, I've thought of a few over the years——'

'Oh, I believe you,' he muttered.

Her eyes glowed with humour. 'Laura is always the one who comes up with the solution to the problem.'

'I'm surprised anyone reads your books at all;

it's difficult to relate to a man named Winnie—
even if you did once have one as Prime Minister
over here!' Hawk sneered.

She arched mocking brows. '*That* coming from
a man with a name like Hawk?'

'Henry Hawker Sinclair the Second,' he corrected
dryly.

She blinked at the length of the title. 'Then Hal
is . . .?'

'Henry Hawker Sinclair the Third,' he confirmed
softly. 'My father was called Harry, by his friends—
none of his enemies was ever brave enough to
come forward and say what *they* called him!' he
drawled. 'I was called Hawk to avoid confusion,
and now my son is called Hal for the same reason.'

'What's wrong with Henry?'

'About the same thing that's wrong with Winnie,'
he returned mockingly.

'Henry seems a good solid name to me,' she
shrugged. 'By the way,' she added as an after-
thought, 'Winnie is a woman. Now, about
Laura——'

'You write about a female detective?' he said
disbelievingly.

'Are you a chauvinist, Hawk?' she taunted.

'Not at all, Leonie,' he drawled. 'I was just a
little surprised. I don't know why I should have
been! Is Winnie as kooky as you?'

She smiled. 'Things—happen to her,' she nodded.

'I'll just bet they do,' he jeered. 'You were going
to tell me about your practical sister Laura,' he
reminded her dryly.

She sobered. 'Maybe that's the wrong word to
have used. Sensible might be a better way of

putting——'

'Believing herself in love with a nineteen-year-old boy is *sensible*?' scoffed Hawk.

'I doubt if Hal was any more as innocently gullible as you're making him out to be than he was naïve,' Leonie reproved. 'He gives the impression of having always been mature.'

The man seated opposite her gave a heavy sigh, his eyes narrowed. 'There's nothing wrong with bringing your child up to be independent.'

'I'm sure there isn't,' she soothed. 'I was just pointing out that Hal is hardly your typical nineteen-year-old.'

'No—he's a potentially very rich nineteen-year-old,' his father grated.

'You're going to upset Laura with that sort of talk, you know,' she chided. 'She's very sensitive about the age difference.'

'Not sensitive enough to stop seeing Hal!'

'That's the trouble,' Leonie sighed. 'She will if you ask her to.'

He gave an inclination of his head. 'Then I'll ask her to,' he drawled. 'End of problem.'

'You don't really believe that.' She shook her head. 'Laura will be heartbroken if you ask this of them—something I'm sure isn't going to bother you too much!—but Hal will resent your interference in his life.'

'He'll get over it,' his father dismissed harshly.

'Would you have "got over" loving your wife if your father had disapproved?'

Hawk gave an impatient frown. 'The situation never arose,'

Leonie stood up restlessly. 'Because the woman

you loved was suitable.'

'She came from a prominent Texas family, yes,' he admitted grudgingly.

'Rich,' Leonie drawled. 'Maybe we don't have a lot of money, but Laura is rich in such a lot of other ways—she's kind, totally loyal to those she cares about, and she cares for Hal so much. Oh, Hawk,' she went down on her knees beside his chair, her hands resting imploringly on his legs, 'don't break my sister's heart!'

He flinched back at her close proximity, the tension slow to leave his body. 'Leonie,' he sighed, 'I can't, in all conscience, approve of this marriage. They've only known each other three weeks, damn it!'

'You're getting over-anxious again,' she warned lightly. 'Would you give your approval if they'd known each other three months, six months, a year, say?' She looked up at him with excited green eyes.

He frowned. 'Why do I have the feeling I'm being set up?'

'Oh, come on, Hawk, answer the question,' she cajoled.

'Yes, I——' He gave an impatient shrug. 'I suppose any of them might be more encouraging than three weeks!'

'Twenty-four days,' Leonie corrected. 'I think Laura could even tell you down to the minutes and seconds if you asked her,' she said fondly. 'They met at the hotel Hal is managing over here at the moment, you know,' she added teasingly. 'There was a meeting of authors there, and Laura went along as one of the guest speakers.' She eyed him mockingly as he scowled. 'Thinking about having the conference facilities ripped out?'

'Thinking about it,' he acknowledged grimly.

'I shouldn't,' she patted his hand. 'They've met now. So what you're really afraid of is that their love for each other won't last?' she returned to their previous conversation without any loss of the intensity of the subject.

'What I'm *really* afraid of is that I seem to have lost control of this conversation,' scowled Hawk. 'I get the distinct feeling I'm being manoeuvred—and I don't like it.'

She could see that, she realised he was a man who liked to be in control at all times. It was only that she wanted to make things right for Laura and Hal, and this man had it in his power to destroy the beauty of their love. 'I wouldn't do that, Hawk,' she told him truthfully. 'I'm just trying to come up with a compromise that will make everyone happy.'

'I'd be happy if Hal never saw your sister again,' he drawled.

'No, you wouldn't,' Leonie shook her head confidently. 'Hal could make life very uncomfortable for you if he chose to do so.'

'I thought we'd already established that I don't like threats.' His eyes were narrowed.

'Just as we established that I don't *make* threats,' she nodded. 'I was just going to point out that Hal would naturally be unhappy——'

'And he would make my life hell,' Hawk acknowledged ruefully. Even as a kid Hal had been able to make his displeasure felt. And he was definitely no longer a child. If he had been this situation would never have arisen!

If only this little witchchild would get her hands off his thighs he might be able to think straight!

The jolt his body had received when she first touched him had had very little to do with surprise, more like shock, an *electric* shock that had momentarily rendered him helpless. And now that his equilibrium was returning he shifted uncomfortably, his denims suddenly uncomfortably tight. He didn't enjoy having to hide his arousal, because the woman he had been aroused *by* was the last one who should have evoked such a reaction within him!

Was she doing it on purpose, this little witchchild? The absolute candour in her sparkling green eyes seemed to say no.

Her fingers were lightly kneading his flesh now, and she seemed completely unaware of the turmoil she was causing inside him!

He stood up impatiently, feeling regretful as she overbalanced slightly at the abruptness of his movement, but leaving her to straighten without his assistance, knowing that he daren't touch her right now, that to do so could be his downfall.

Instead he attacked. 'How the hell many more cats are going to walk through here?' The incongruousness of the question struck him as much as it must her, but he knew he just had to talk about something that would take his mind off the throbbing ache in his thighs.

Leonie sat back on her heels, eyeing him curiously. 'How many have you seen?'

'Three—no, four,' Hawk corrected as he remembered the grey tabby he had seen stretched out in the hallway when he arrived.

She nodded. 'Then there are just two more. That's probably Daffodil and Pansy.'

'Who the hell has six cats?' he derided impatiently.

'I do,' she shrugged. 'Daffodil, Daisy, Tulip, Pansy, Rose, and Pop. That's short for Poppy,' she explained. 'I only found out after I'd named him that he was a boy.'

'You named *all* your cats after flowers?' He looked at her disbelievingly.

Her eyes widened. 'Why not?'

Why not indeed? Someone in a professional capacity could probably give him a lucid answer to that, but it was obvious there wasn't going to be one from this woman! Being in her company for too long was a little like being in a room with a bomb, unsure if it were active or not! She was strange with a capital S.

Then why did she intrigue him more than any other woman had for a very long time? If her sister was *anything* like her no wonder Hal was so enthralled with her; predictable this woman certainly was not! Boredom was always a problem with him with the women in his life; he doubted any man would have time to be bored with Leonie Brandon.

'They're all inside today, except Daffodil and Pansy, because of the rain.' Leonie took his silence to mean he wanted to hear more about the cats.

And damn it, she had piqued his curiosity! 'Why aren't—Pansy and Daffodil in too?' What stupid names to give those haughty creatures!

She shrugged. 'Because they like the rain.'

A stupid question deserved an equally stupid answer. Hell, he had better things to talk about than six oddly-named cats! Or their intriguing owner, he told himself sternly. Her twin couldn't be that innocent if she had enticed a nineteen-year-old boy into her net, but the woman in front of him, with her childlike body and guileless green eyes—how had he ever thought *she* could be the one involved with Hal?—was decidedly no match for the passion he would demand of her. She was probably still a virgin, and they were one breed he definitely avoided.

But an image of her kept flashing in and out of his mind, of her slender legs entwined with his, those pert little breasts crushed against his chest, the nipples nuzzling against him, her face flushed with ecstasy.

'We were talking about Hal and your sister,' he prompted harshly, his self-contempt at his thoughts chilling his eyes.

Leonie nodded, her bright red hair moving silkily against her cheek as she got gracefully to her feet. 'What if they leave it three more months before coming to any decision about marriage?'

'A year,' he insisted instantly.

'Six months appears to be the middle line.' She gave him one of those guileless smiles, her eyes wide and innocent.

He had been out-classed, out-manoeuvred, at a game at which he had always been considered an expert. And all because of a pair of wide green eyes—and a taut little bottom beneath tight denims, he acknowledged self-derisively. You *are* getting senile, Sinclair, he berated himself, when the mere movement of a woman's body against her clothes can distract you from your purpose!

He straightened. 'I told you, I don't want a gold-digger in my family,' he snapped insultingly. 'Six *years* wouldn't be long enough for me to accept that!'

'You may have to,' she told him heavily. 'Laura might be willing to accept any terms you care to make, but Hal has definite plans of his own, and he's the one you'll have to convince that you're only doing this for his own good.'

She was right, this little witchchild. Hal was his son all right, and there was no way *he* would have stood by and meekly accepted his father's interference in his life in this way, at any age. But he wasn't about to let Leonie Brandon know that he realised they might all have to compromise, him most of all!

'I'll deal with my son, Miss Brandon,' he said confidently. 'And when the time comes I'll deal with your sister too!' He turned to leave.

Leonie followed him out of the room. Even if she had made no sound as she walked, her perfume, the elusiveness of a spring flower, told of her presence; Hawk had never been so aware of a woman's perfume. He turned to face her all the more sharply because of that as she spoke quietly at his side.

'I'm afraid I still haven't introduced myself to you properly,' she shrugged as his eyes narrowed. 'My name isn't Brandon, it's Spencer.'

She was married! This witchchild was *married*? He glanced at her left hand, noticing for the first time the thin gold band on her finger that he had missed when he looked at her earlier. And he knew the reason he had missed it—he had been too intent on the beauty of the delicate hands, had imagined them caressing his body—Damn it, this couldn't go on! He could have his pick of women, he certainly didn't need to get mixed up with this strange, *married* one!

'It's *what* you are that matters to me,' he ground out. 'And as far as I'm concerned you're just the sister of the woman trying to trick my son into marrying her!'

Leonie stood shaking her head as she watched him leave. Laura and Hal were in love, genuinely in love, and the objection of Hal's father to that love could cause a rift between them all that might never heal.

She had to admit that she had been dismayed herself when Laura returned home, from speaking at one of the literary meetings Leonie took such pains to avoid, to drop into an armchair and dreamily sigh that she was in love. Laura had always been the level-headed one, the sensible one, and an announcement like that had to be taken seriously.

'But he's too young for me,' Laura wailed regretfully. 'A boy disguised as a man!'

A boy? Dear God, what did that mean? 'Tell me about him,' Leonie prompted softly.

'He's so tall and—and handsome.' Laura blushed. She was her sister's mirror image, except that her eyes were occasionally filled with an unspoken sadness. 'He was the manager of the hotel where we held the meeting, and——'

'Then he can't be *that* young,' Leonie said with some relief.

Laura's eyes rolled expressively. 'His family *owns* the hotel!'

Leonie became suddenly still. 'He's one of the Sinclairs?' Everyone had heard of the multi-millionaire family!

'Son of *the* Sinclair,' her sister nodded, her dismay reflected in sea-green eyes. 'Oh, Leonie, he's young, so much younger than I am, but when he looked at me I knew I loved him. And he said he felt exactly the same way!'

'You talked to him, then——Of course you talked to him,' Leonie chastised herself for her stupidity. 'Otherwise how would you know his name?'

'He said he's coming to see me tomorrow night,' Laura groaned. 'That we should start discussing our wedding plans!'

'He said *that*?' Leonie gasped at the speed with which the relationship had progressed. When Laura had left this evening she had been heart-free, yet a few hours later she was obviously deeply in love.

'Yes.' Her sister blushed again. 'Oh, Leonie, he asked me to marry him!'

And he had continued to ask every day since that evening three and a half weeks ago!

Leonie had liked Hal instantly; she had found him not to be the boy Laura had led her to believe, that he had been a man for some time, possessed of a confidence that had been inborn in him. And he was obviously deeply serious about his feelings concerning Laura, spending every moment that he could with her.

Hawk Sinclair wasn't going to find it at all easy

to 'deal with' his son!

Hawk's temper hadn't cooled in the least by the time he returned to the penthouse suite of the hotel.

Jake Colter, his assistant and friend for the last fifteen years, looked up from the contracts he had been working on, his blond brows rising over laughing blue eyes as Hawk let out a bellow for Sarah, his private secretary. 'How did the meeting with the mercenary author go?' he drawled.

Hawk's scowl deepened. 'It didn't! Sarah, where the hell are you?' he bellowed again.

The elegantly calm woman who had organised his business life for more years than he cared to think about emerged from her bedroom that adjoined the lounge, not at all perturbed by the chaos Hawk seemed to have brought back with him. After ten years she was probably used to it!

'Yes, Hawk?' she prompted softly; a beautiful woman, she usually knew what he wanted before he did.

It had been her complete efficiency at her job that had thrown him into a panic four years ago when her marriage began to flounder and she had considered the idea of leaving her job to see if that might stop her husband jumping into bed with every woman who so much as smiled at him. Knowing her husband as he had, Hawk hadn't believed anything would stop him playing around with other women, but he hadn't tried to interfere; he knew that if Sarah loved Paul she should stay with him. However, he had been very supportive when she decided to divorce the bastard after finding him in her own bed with a woman she had thought was her friend. He hadn't been averse to using a little of his charm to persuade her to stay on with him either, after she had voiced the possibility of perhaps making a completely new start; he knew that he would never be able to find a more efficient secretary, wining and dining her until she agreed to stay on.

But for once her cool control irritated him. 'Find out all that you can about a Leonie Spencer—*Mrs* Leonie Spencer,' he added grimly. 'Especially anything about *Mr* Spencer. She lives in the wilds of Buckinghamshire,' he supplied absently. 'I want to know everything there is to know about her, and I don't care who you have to disturb on this English Sunday afternoon to get it,' he warned harshly.

'Will that be all?' Sarah arched blonde brows.

'Yes!' Hawk glared at her. 'Damn woman,' he muttered once he was alone with Jake.

'Who, Sarah?' his assistant mocked disbelievingly.

Grey eyes raked over him mercilessly. 'Why do I keep you on the pay-roll?'

The other man grinned. He possessed the type of fair-haired good looks that had caused more than one female to bemoan the fact that he was determined to remain a bachelor since his divorce sixteen years ago. 'Probably because I'm a damned good assistant,' he drawled.

'Oh yeah,' Hawk acknowledged dryly. 'I knew there had to be some reason why I put up with you!'

Jake's grin widened. 'You're just put out because

the woman on the plane last night offered me a date instead of you.'

Hawk gave the other man a scathing look. 'So that's why your bed wasn't slept in last night! I should watch it, my friend,' he drawled, remembering the over-familiarity of the beautiful brunette on the plane; it was far from the first time she had picked up a man in that way! 'You expose yourself to—all sorts of dangers that way,' he added derisively.

'Ouch!' Jake grimaced, putting the contracts to one side. 'So your meeting with the author didn't work out,' he remarked thoughtfully. 'Don't you think, in this day and age, especially with two old reprobates like us as an example, that perhaps you should be grateful Hal just wants to marry a woman you don't approve of?'

'I think that if Stephen came home and told you he intended marrying a woman he's only known three weeks, a woman who's older than him, you'd react the same way I did,' Hawk grated.

Jake shrugged. 'I can think of plenty of worse things he could come home and tell me.'

'Maybe,' Hawk accepted grudgingly. 'Maybe I should have made Hal go to college with Stephen instead of giving in to him when he said he wanted to learn the business by experience. They always got on well together, and Stephen might have been good for Hal, stopped him growing up quite so quickly.'

When Jake had come to work for him fifteen years ago he had just been awarded custody of his five-year-old son after his divorce, and with Hal being a similar age the two boys had gravitated to each other from the first. Their friendship was probably as deep as his and Jake's was. The two young men were opposites, Stephen always getting into mischief, and usually taking Hal along with him. Yes, maybe he should have insisted Hal attend college rather than going straight to work. But it was too late for that now.

'He seems to be doing all right,' observed Jake.

'Too well,' Hawk scowled. 'Why the hell he wants to tie himself down with a wife I have no idea.'

'Because he loves her,' Jake suggested softly.

Hawk gave a disbelieving snort. 'He *thinks* he loves her,' he corrected firmly. 'And I object to being called an *old* reprobate,' he added suddenly, and Jake grinned at his ability not to forget anything that was said to him. 'The reprobate was fine, but I've already had enough aspersions cast on my age today without you starting too. How could anyone feel anything else but old after being in Leonie Spencer's company for half an hour?' he added disgustedly. 'Her mind leaps from subject to subject without giving any indication that you're now talking about something completely different! And even when she's sitting still you get the impression she'd rather be on her feet and moving. She is definitely not a relaxing person to be around!'

'Sounds familiar.' Jake looked at him pointedly.

'Very funny,' snapped Hawk.

'Who *is* Leonie Spencer?' Jake asked slowly. 'I thought you went to see a Laura Brandon?'

'Leonie Spencer is an infuriating, provoking, *kooky*——'

Jake whistled through his teeth. 'Whoever she

is, she made quite an impression!'

'About as much as a puppy-dog chewing at my pants leg,' Hawk replied. 'She has six cats. *Six*!' he repeated disbelievingly.

'Shocking,' Jake taunted.

'Stop being so damned——Sarah,' Hawk pounced as she came quietly back into the room, 'what did you find out?'

'Mrs Leonora Spencer lives at——'

'I know her address, damn it!' He glared at her.

Blonde brows rose over reproving blue eyes. 'She's twenty-five years old,' Sarah continued undaunted. 'Her parents were killed years ago in a car accident. She has one sister, her twin, Laura Brandon——'

'Ah,' Jake nodded comprehendingly, shrugging as Hawk gave him a quelling glance.

'Laura Brandon,' Sarah continued determinedly. 'Leonie was married at twenty to Michael Spencer. The marriage doesn't appear to have been a success——'

'Was he rich?' Hawk cut in suspiciously.

Sarah glanced at the notes she had made. 'It says here he was a clerk in a——'

'Not rich,' drawled Jake.

Hawk scowled as the theory of Leonie having married for money too was taken away from him. If only he could find *something* to dislike about the woman!

'Shall I go on?' Sarah enquired coolly.

'Sure,' he instructed tersely, ignoring Jake's smile of amusement.

'The marriage lasted only a short time——'

'They're divorced?' Hawk interrupted sharply.

'It would appear so,' Sarah nodded.

'Any children?'

'None were mentioned,' said Sarah in her usual precise way that was somehow managing to annoy him deeply today. 'Leonie co-authors books with——'

'Thanks, Sarah,' he cut in dismissively. 'I know the rest.'

She shrugged, sharing a puzzled glance with Jake before returning to her bedroom to continue working.

'Divorced,' murmured Hawk triumphantly, suddenly realising he no longer *needed* a reason to dislike Leonie Spencer, none that need matter to them. Hal and Laura were completely separate from this. 'Jake, my friend, I'm going out again,' he announced determinedly.

'Am I allowed to enquire where?' the other man drawled.

He grinned. 'I'm going to show a woman, who believes a man of my age must be suffering from a mid-life crisis, just how wrong she is.'

'*What?*' Jake was astounded by his explanation.

'You heard me,' said Hawk with satisfaction. 'And, Jake——' he paused at the door.

'Hm?' The other man still looked dazed.

'Don't wait up,' he advised softly.

CHAPTER ONE

'THREE more months of this torture!' Laura bemoaned with a heavy sigh.

Leonie gave a grimace of sympathy from her position on the adjoining lounger, knowing Laura had just finished reading a letter from Hal. 'Try not to think of it as a life sentence,' she encouraged gently.

Her sister frowned at her. 'How can it be any other way when I love Hal so much?'

'Darling, you were the one who agreed to the year's wait,' Leonie reminded her softly. 'Said you wanted to give Hal time to be sure too.'

'I know,' Laura gave a choked sigh. 'But how could I know Hawk Sinclair was going to make sure Hal was out of the country most of the time!'

Leonie gave a pained frown. A year, Hawk Sinclair had asked Hal and Laura to wait, assuring them that if they really did love each other it would pass quickly. As she had known he would, Hal had raised strong objections to the idea, wanting to marry Laura right away, but Laura had told him that perhaps it would be better if they waited, so that *they* could be sure of their feelings for each other too.

Leonie had always known Laura wouldn't object to anything Hawk Sinclair asked of them, but Hal had been hurt by what seemed to be Laura's indecision about their love, storming out on all of them after accusing Laura of believing he was still a child too!

He had come back, of course, as soon as he calmed down enough to realise Laura wouldn't change her mind and marry him straight away as he wanted, and with both Laura and his father against the idea of an instant marriage he had finally agreed to wait the year.

It hadn't been too bad at first. Laura and Hal had seen a lot of each other, but then his father had begun to send him to other hotels that they owned for weeks at a time, straining their relationship as he and Laura had to rely on telephone calls and letters to tell each other of their love.

Hal had been in Acapulco for over six weeks now, and those weeks had been difficult ones for her sister, Leonie realised. Laura was thinner than she used to be, fine lines of strain around her eyes that hadn't been there before.

All this pain and suffering because Hawk Sinclair had decided to play God with their lives!

Leonie didn't doubt that Laura would still want to marry Hal at the end of the year's wait, or that Hal would feel the same way, in fact the two of them had already started discussing wedding plans.

Leonie's illness hadn't helped Laura's peace of mind; the emergency operation she had gone through had been frightening for them both, and the weeks she had spent in hospital had left her still feeling weak and far from well. Laura had taken complete control during the crisis, and was still doing so several weeks later. Today she was having to go alone to their publisher to explain why the book he was waiting for from them still wasn't finished.

'Are you sure you're going to be able to handle this meeting with Desmond on your own?' Leonie frowned her concern.

Laura grinned. 'I know you usually walk in and totally disarm the poor man, but I'm afraid that today he's going to have to make do with me!'

Leonie's mouth quirked. 'You could always pretend you're me!'

'Darling, much as I love your idiosyncrasies, there *is* no one else like you!' her sister teased. 'Are you going to be all right here on your own?' She frowned her concern.

'But I'm not alone,' Leonie shrugged dismissively. 'We have June to take care of us now.' She mentioned the woman in her mid-forties they had employed to take care of the cooking and housework now that she felt too weak to do it and Laura was too busy taking care of her.

'Call her if you need anything,' Laura directed firmly. 'You're still far from strong. The doctor said you were to take things very easy.'

Leonie looked down ruefully at the cat curled up on the bottom of her lounger, Pop stretched out on her legs from knee to thigh. 'I think I'm about as relaxed as I can be,' she drawled. 'The sun's out, there's a gentle breeze, the jug of fresh lemonade's within easy reach.' She looked pointedly at the table beside her on the lawn. 'I certainly don't envy you your trip into London.'

Laura grimaced. 'Someone has to go and placate poor Desmond. The television series is going wonderfully in America, and the book they want to be published parallel with it hasn't even been completed yet!'

'That's because you won't let me near my typewriter——'

'I nearly lost you, Leonie,' her sister cut in emotionally. 'I'm not taking any chances with your health now.'

Being rushed to the hospital in the middle of the night, hearing the ambulance bell ringing and knowing it was for her, the examination before the stinging prick of the needle that rendered her unconscious for the operation, had frightened Leonie as well. She still felt far from well, but as much as possible she tried to hide that from Laura, knowing how illness worried her twin.

Several months ago they had been approached by a television company in America who wanted to serialise their books, and after establishing that they would have some say in the scripts that were used they had signed the contract. They were now richer than they had ever dreamt of being, but Laura was still unhappy without Hal, and *she* had never felt so terrible in her life. That adage 'money can't buy happiness' certainly seemed true for them. And Hawk Sinclair's wealth didn't seem to have made him happy either!

Leonie's mouth tightened as she thought of him, the fascination she had initially felt for his strength now completely dispersed after what he had asked of Laura and Hal.

Laura stood up determinedly. 'Oh well, sitting here complaining isn't going to get this meeting with Desmond over with. I think I'll pop into the hotel for a chat before coming back,' she added lightly.

Her sister had become friendly with quite a lot of the staff at the Sinclair London hotel the last few months, and Leonie knew that chatting to the girls who worked on the reception desk made her sister feel a little closer to Hal.

She smiled encouragingly. 'You do that. And don't worry about Holly and me, we'll be fine,' she assured her.

A frown marred Laura's brow. 'Hal's going to be so angry when he finds out I didn't tell him the baby came early,' she sighed. 'But if I'd let him know he would only have wanted to have come back, and then his father would have said I wasn't keeping to the agreement, and——'

'Darling, Hal will understand,' Leonie cut in firmly. 'And we both agreed it would be best not to worry him.'

Laura nodded abruptly. 'Are you sure you're going to be able to cope with Holly on your own this afternoon? I'd take her with me, but——'

'That would totally confuse Desmond,' drawled Leonie. 'Holly and I will be just fine together,' she assured her twin.

'She's been fed and changed, and she's sleeping now, so——'

'I can manage, Laura,' Leonie cut in softly. 'You just worry about placating Desmond.'

She kept the bright smile on her face for as long as it took Laura to go around to the front of the house, only relaxing back against the lounger when she heard the car leave the driveway.

Could she cope with the baby? Until Holly's arrival into their lives she had never had anything to do with babies, small or otherwise. And Holly was very small, only six pounds at birth. And she was so very beautiful too, with her cap of golden hair and blue-grey eyes that Laura was sure would eventually turn a deep grey. Her sister had read every baby book she could find before Holly's birth, so Leonie was sure she knew what she was talking about. What was Hawk Sinclair going to say when he found out about the baby's existence? She shuddered to think!

She *would* cope with the baby, even though it was the first time she had been left on her own with her. She and Laura had shared Holly's care from the day she came home, there was nothing different about it just because she was on her own. There was always June to call if she got into difficulties, their housekeeper having had a child of her own years ago. She *could* do it!

She must have fallen asleep in the warm sunshine, because the next thing she knew June was gently shaking her shoulder to wake her.

'What is it?' She immediately shot into a sitting position. 'Is it the baby? What——'

'Calm down,' June chuckled softly; she was a gently rounded woman with laughing brown eyes and peppered brown hair that refused to be anything but flyaway; Leonie and Laura had liked her immediately when she came for her interview, and she had moved into the house with them within a few days. It was a move none of them seemed to have regretted. 'I only came to tell you that there's a visitor.'

Leonie blinked to clear her brain of the fogging she so detested about the daytime naps she couldn't seem to get out of since coming home from hospital.

She took a sip of the lemonade to rinse out her mouth and moisten her lips. 'Who is it?'

'Mr Sinclair,' June told her. 'He asked for Laura, but I——'

'Hal!' Leonie cried excitedly, feeling a sudden surge of energy. He had come home from Acapulco to pay Laura a surprise visit! Or perhaps he had even decided to end this nonsense and come to tell Laura she was marrying him right away; she doubted Laura would still insist they wait after the agony of the last six weeks' loneliness.

'I'm sorry to disappoint you,' drawled a familiarly mocking voice. 'But as far as I'm aware Hal is still in Acapulco!'

Leonie looked up to meet Hawk Sinclair's derisive gaze with a feeling of dread, the energy of moments ago draining just as suddenly as it had arrived.

She looked so delicate lying there, her skin almost translucent against the shimmering brightness of her hair. All the laughter had gone from her eyes, her cheeks were drawn and hollow, the impish tilt to her chin completely gone too. What the hell had happened to her in the last nine months?

What was he doing here? thought Hawk. He had seen Hal only two days ago, and although his son was resentful he was still determined; he was going to claim Laura Brandon at the end of the year. And so Hawk had come here today to admit defeat, to admit, if Laura still felt the same way, that he had been wrong!

His life had been shot to pieces over the last nine months. Hal was barely civil to him, the business no longer held the appeal for him that it always had, and just yesterday Jake had given him the three months' notice his contract required. After almost sixteen years Jake was walking out on him; he hadn't been able to believe it. Jake claimed he wanted to do other things with his life when Hawk pushed him for a reason. What other things? The hotel business was of more interest to Jake than it was to Hawk, and the shares he possessed in HS Hotels had meant he always looked after that interest. Yesterday Jake had offered him those shares with his resignation!

And through the whole of the last nine months he hadn't been able to get this sprite out of his mind! It was stupid, insane, and he had told himself so a million times, but the memory of her persisted.

And now he found her looking like a shadow of her former self, as if a strong breeze might knock her off her feet and on to that tight little bottom he found it so dangerous to think about—and which had never been far from his thoughts all these months!

The cats were still the same, though, Pop stretched out on her legs, next to the ginger tabby and black cat, the two he hadn't seen on his last visit, and so the cat lying at her feet, the ginger tabby, had to be either Pansy or Daffodil. Hawk found it totally out of character that he had remembered the cats' names, but then when had he acted *in* character since meeting Leonie Spencer!

She didn't look very welcoming, but after what he had done, who could blame her? Maybe if he told her he had come to make peace and not war—!

'Thanks, June,' she dismissed the housekeeper who was a new acquisition. 'Mr Sinclair and I can manage now.'

Manage? She looked as if lifting that glass of lemonade to her lips might snap her slender wrist in two!

She wasn't exactly beautiful, nothing at all like the sophisticates he was usually attracted to, but she had possessed an impish charm that had made it impossible for him to put her from his mind. Something had happened to her during the last nine months to rob her of even that.

Despite what she had told him about Laura that day he had believed Leonie to be the stronger of the two, the way she had jumped so ably to her sister's defence reminding him of a cat with its kitten. Laura had come as something of a surprise to him, not just because she *was* an exact copy of Leonie but because her strength had been of a different kind; the certainty of knowing her own mind, her own feelings, and of instilling confidence in those around her to believe she did. If he hadn't been so damned mad by the time he did meet her he would probably have respected that strength and entrusted Hal's future happiness to her more than capable hands!

As it had turned out he had been unreasonable, his anger out of all proportion to the situation, asking more from them than he had the right to. Only Laura's calm acceptance of waiting a year, her determination that they should, had prevented him from losing Hal right then and there.

Hal had argued, though, and he hadn't stopped arguing, only his love for Laura keeping him to the promise they had both made. Hawk knew damn well it had nothing to do with respecting *his* wishes!

He had behaved like a damned fool, and in the end it had had little to do with Hal and Laura—and *everything* to do with this woman who was barely recognisable as the fighting bantam hen she had appeared then.

What had happened to her? Was she ill? Dying . . .?

Why didn't he say something? thought Leonie. What was he doing here? There were still three months to go before Laura would finally agree to marry Hal. Oh God, nothing had happened to Hal, had it?

The colour drained from her hollowed cheeks. 'Is it Hal——'

'I told you, he's in Acapulco,' rasped Hawk. 'What's happened to *you*?'

She sat back self-consciously, aware of her scarecrow thinness. 'I've been ill——'

'You still are, by the look of you!' He looked her over critically.

The same couldn't be said for him; he looked as healthy as ever, his skin tanned darkly brown. He was lithe and virile in the light blue shirt that somehow managed to make his eyes appear the same colour, and fitted denims that moulded the firm contours of his legs and thighs. He exuded leashed vitality, making a mockery of the reference she had once made to his age; he was fitter than many men half his age.

'You should have seen me when I first came out of hospital,' she dismissed lightly. 'Then you would see how improved I am.'

His eyes were narrowed. 'What was wrong with you?'

She gave him a cool look. 'I don't believe that's any of your business—you aren't a member of this family yet!'

'If you were that ill Laura should have told us,' he bit out harshly.

'Why?'

His expression darkened. 'Are you really getting better?'

'Really,' Leonie confirmed dryly, wondering what all the fuss was about. The last time they had seen him he had given the impression that he didn't care if both she and Laura disappeared off the face of the earth!

The inclination of his head seemed to say he was satisfied with her explanation—for now. 'I see there's a series of Winnie Cooper stories by Leonaura Brandon planned to be shown on television in the States in the winter.'

Good manners, and the fact that he seemed determined to engage in conversation even though Laura wasn't here, dictated that she invite him to sit down on the adjoining lounger. But where this man was concerned she was all out of good manners. 'Surprised they'd bother with such fourth-rate stories?' she challenged.

He shrugged. 'Only time will tell. You and Laura must be financially secure by now?'

'We've always been financially secure,' Leonie

snapped resentfully. 'All we've ever needed was a roof over our heads and enough money to feed ourselves——'

'And the cats,' Hawk drawled dryly as sharp claws dug into Leonie's leg as Pop stretched on her lap.

'And the cats,' she conceded, unhooking the claws from her flesh. 'Is that why you're here?' Green eyes flashed as she looked up at him. 'To see if all that money has made Laura change her mind about loving Hal?'

'Has it?'

She drew in a ragged breath. 'It's a pity men like you can't see past the end of their chequebooks, otherwise you would have seen last year that Laura doesn't have the least interest in money, our own or anyone else's. In fact, she would probably have been happier if you'd just disinherited Hal so that they could have married straight away. But she knew Hal wouldn't have been happy then, not without you or the money; you've both been in his life for so long he couldn't do without either one of you!'

'Men like me?' Hawk echoed softly.

Leonie made a weary gesture as her head dropped back against the lounger. 'I really don't feel in the mood to argue with you just now, Hawk.' Her voice was faint with fatigue.

He came down on his haunches beside her. 'What the hell is wrong with you, that you tire this easily?' He frowned darkly. 'Are you sure your doctor knows what he's doing?' he scowled.

She gave a slight smile. 'Very sure; I'm already so much stronger than I was. And I think you should know that Laura still loves Hal, and would if he had nothing at all!'

'Good.'

'Good?' Her eyes widened. 'You weren't of that opinion the last time you were here.'

He shrugged, so close Leonie could see the dark shadow of the beard on his jaw where he was already in need of his second shave of the day. 'Things change,' he grated.

Leonie gave him a frown of suspicion. 'What things?'

He gave an impatient sigh and straightened, thrusting his hands into his denims pockets, pulling the material tighter than ever across his thighs. 'Are you pleased about the television series?'

Why did he keep changing the subject? Why couldn't he just say what he wanted here—and it certainly wasn't to discuss the television series!—and then go! 'Yes, I——' A sudden thought made her frown. 'Do you have any shares in Westley Productions?' she asked in a hushed voice, the sudden suspicion that had taken hold of her making her feel nauseous.

His gaze didn't falter. 'I *own* Westley Productions.'

'For how long?'

'Since it was created.'

Leonie swallowed hard. 'My God, you couldn't resist trying to buy us off, could you?' she suddenly attacked. 'And what is it now that you know that's failed—a touch of blackmail? The series is dropped if Laura doesn't agree to stop seeing Hal?'

'Leonie——'

'I can tell you now that the answer will still be

no,' she sat forward tensely. 'Laura wasn't even interested in the series, *I* was the one who persuaded her to take a look at it. I thought it would take her mind off her unhappiness because of Hal. You can keep your television series, Mr Sinclair, and shove it——'

'Leonie!' he rasped harshly. 'That isn't why I'm here at all. Why do you persist in casting me as the Black Knight?'

She gave a choked laugh. 'I have no reason to see you in any other way. In fact a knight of any kind might be too much of a compliment—even the bad ones were possessed of a certain strength, a code that they followed. *You're* just out to destroy lives!'

He had gone very pale, a nerve pulsing in his cheek. 'Leonie, I know you and I got off to a bad start, but I'm here to try and make amends——'

'Not to me, I hope,' she scorned. 'Laura might accept your apology—after all, you're going to be her father-in-law soon. But I want as little to do with you as Laura's and Hal's marriage will allow the only other two members of their family. Which won't be a great deal, I hope!'

Hawk's mouth tightened. 'I want——' He broke off as he saw her stricken gaze move towards the house, turning to follow the direction of that gaze, his eyes widening incredulously as he saw the tiny bundle in the housekeeper's arms.

Holly lay contentedly in June's arms, showing she wasn't yet desperate for her next feed, but at almost four weeks old she was starting to need less and less sleep between feeds, considering the rest of the time playtime. Leonie wished this hadn't been one of those times!

She looked up reluctantly at Hawk Sinclair and could see by the ruddy hue of his cheeks that the baby's existence angered him. She bristled defensively and sat up to take the baby, smiling her thanks at June.

'I'll bring the bottle out in a few minutes,' the other woman told her, smiling brightly at the stunned Hawk before going back into the house.

Leonie kept her head down as she looked at the baby, the silence above her testament to the fact that Hawk had been rendered speechless for the second time since she had met him. It was when he regained his voice that she dreaded!

Holly gazed up at her with trusting blue-grey eyes, content just to be held, having put on weight since her birth, but still very tiny in the white Baby-Gro. Her hair gleamed golden in the sunlight, and Leonie shifted slightly so that the baby was under the shade of the bright-coloured umbrella above them. Holly began to blow bubbles to amuse herself.

'No wonder Laura accepted my suggestion last year that they wait!' Hawk suddenly exploded, his wrath as chilling as a north wind. 'She'd already taken out insurance that guaranteed Hal would marry her!'

Leonie's head snapped back. 'That's a lie!'

'She knew *I* wouldn't turn away Henry Hawker Sinclair the Fourth either!' His eyes glittered with fury as he glowered over her.

The baby began to wave her arms about at the sound of the angry voices above her; until now she had never heard a voice raised in anger near her.

'Her name is Holly,' Leonie bit out precisely. 'Holly Laura.'

'What the hell does it matter what her first names are?' he attacked viciously. 'She's a Sinclair!'

'Holly is *my* baby——'

'Don't take protecting your sister too far,' he scorned harshly. 'That baby has to be at least three weeks old——'

'Almost four,' she confirmed.

He nodded impatiently. 'Which means Laura must have conceived her almost the first night she and Hal met,' he accused. 'She was taking no chances on him changing his mind, was she?' he added with contempt.

Whatever 'amends' he had come here to make it was obvious that knowing about Holly negated all of them; he was now more angry than ever about Laura and Hal. And Leonie just didn't have the strength to fight for them right now.

'Does Hal know about his child? Hell, of course he must do,' he furiously answered his own question. 'Damn it, I know he's still mad as hell at me, but he should have told me about the child!' He glared at Leonie. 'Your sister certainly had me fooled with her sweetness and understanding routine!'

'Hawk——'

'They have to get married now, and soon,' he accepted harshly. 'But believe me, if I've lost this battle I've far from lost the war!'

Leonie felt a shiver of apprehension run down her spine; she knew he could still make things very unpleasant for Laura and Hal.

'Holly *is* my baby, Hawk,' she told him again,

wishing she could sound more forceful.

'She's a Sinclair, damn it!' He gazed down at Holly with dislike. 'She looks exactly as Hal did when he was a baby.'

Leonie looked down at the fair-haired, pale-complexioned baby. She could see no resemblance to Hal at all, except perhaps that Holly's eyes would soon turn completely grey. But Hawk seemed convinced he knew who Holly's father was.

'Where's Laura now?' he demanded aggressively.

'With our publisher——You can't go there and confront her with this, Hawk!' she cried as he looked ready to do just that.

'I assure you I can do exactly that,' he bit out coldly. 'By the time I've finished with her she'll know exactly what I think of her method of trapping my son into marriage. She'll also realise what a formidable enemy I can be; I haven't even started yet!'

Leonie felt a sinking feeling in her chest; she wished she felt stronger. Before her illness she wouldn't have hesitated to tell him exactly what she and Laura thought of his threats. Now she was shaking so badly with fatigue it was all she could do not to burst into frustrated tears.

'Can't you realise—and accept,' she said weakly, 'that Hal *wants* to marry Laura?'

'He hasn't got any choice now, has he?' Hawk attacked. 'Your devious sister took care of that!'

Laura didn't have a devious bone in her body. But she did have the strength that Leonie lacked at the moment to stand up to this man.

'You're right, Hawk,' she sighed. 'I think it would be best if you spoke to Laura——'

'Oh, I intend to,' he warned, dangerously soft.

Leonie watched as he strode angrily across the lawn to the driveway, some of the tension leaving her as she heard his car accelerate away from the house with a screech of tyres.

Holly had tired of blowing bubbles now, her arms waving about in earnest as she decided that it was time for her afternoon tea. Leonie gave a smile of gratitude as June seemed to anticipate the need and came out of the house with the promised bottle. Holly latched on to it eagerly.

June looked Leonie over critically. 'Mr Sinclair didn't upset you, did he?'

She gave a wan smile. 'Mr Sinclair *never fails* to upset me!'

The housekeeper lingered concernedly. 'He seemed very—agitated when he left just now.'

Leonie gave a choked laugh. 'Let's not be polite; he was furious!'

'At you?' June frowned.

Leonie shrugged. 'He doesn't seem to approve of unmarried mothers,' she evaded.

'Hmph,' June gave a disgusted snort. 'In that case I hope he never comes back here.'

Oh, Hawk would be back, Leonie had no doubts about that!

CHAPTER TWO

MY GOD, thought Hawk, he had been about to
apologise, to admit he had been wrong about
Laura Brandon's mercenary intentions! She had
taken out the most effective insurance to guarantee
that he had no choice but to accept her marriage
to Hal: she had had his grandchild.

He had been about to tell Leonie exactly how
often he had thought of her the last nine months,
admit how much he desired her. If the housekeeper
hadn't appeared with the child at that moment he
would have told Leonie Spencer just how obsessed
he had become with her!

That baby—Holly, Leonie had said her name
was—was Hal's daughter, there was no doubt
about that. Hal had looked exactly like that when
Amy had brought him home from the hospital; it
had only been when he reached six or seven that
his hair had darkened to the almost-black it was
now. Hal was a father when he was nothing but a
child still himself!

He could forgive Laura Brandon anything but
that! Hal was too young to be a father, he had
plenty of years before him to take on that responsibility. But Laura Brandon was older than him
and had obviously decided that motherhood would
assure her of a place in his life.

And it would. He didn't doubt that Hal was
overjoyed at the child's existence. Holly was

certainly a beautiful baby; she would probably have those cute little freckles on her nose just like her aunt's in later years——

Hell, he wasn't going to allow himself to think about Leonie Spencer again. She had to have known what Laura was doing, and all these months she had condoned it. She was as morally guilty as her sister.

Laura had already left her appointment with her publisher when he arrived at the office, and rather than backtrack all the way to the house and find she still wasn't there either he put a call through to the house.

The housekeeper greeted him politely enough until he identified himself, and then her warm manner froze over. My God, thought Hawk, you'd think it was *his* fault Laura Brandon had used such trickery to gain a rich husband!

The woman informed him that Laura wasn't home yet, and that Leonie was resting in her bedroom. He only just stopped himself from asking if she was feeling ill again! The welfare of the Brandon sisters was none of his concern.

He had the shock of his life to see Laura Brandon walking across the reception area of the hotel when he arrived back there after deciding there was nothing else to do but wait.

Her cheeks flushed guiltily, and his mouth tightened when he thought of exactly what she was guilty of!

'Mr Sinclair,' she greeted him breathlessly, her hands moving nervously.

'I want to talk to you,' he declared, clasping a firm hold of her arm. 'Upstairs in my suite.'

She gave him a puzzled look as he dragged her along beside him. 'Is there something wrong?' she frowned.

His mouth tightened. Something wrong? Dear God, she and Hal had kept his grandchild's birth from him, and she asked if there was *anything* *wrong*!

'I went to the house to see you, Laura,' he bit out coldly. 'I saw Leonie instead. And Holly,' he added pointedly.

Laura's blush became one of anger. 'So?' she faced him defiantly.

His eyes flashed with fury. 'So I think we need to—talk about her, don't you?' he grated softly.

'No, I——'

'Upstairs,' he muttered, pulling her into the lift with him, retaining his hold on her arm as she struggled to free herself.

Strange, although the two sisters were mirror images of each other, from their fiery red hair to their tiny feet, he had felt nothing for Laura Brandon except detached interest from the first. Her sister had been something else completely!

His fingers tightened in anger—with himself, and with the circumstances that had ever introduced him to the sisters.

'You're hurting me!' Laura complained with a pained frown.

His fingers slackened slightly, but he didn't release her. 'I'd like to break your devious little neck,' he ground out as they stepped straight into the penthouse suite. 'Leave us,' he ordered Jake and Sarah as they worked together in the lounge, watching them arrogantly as they packed up the papers they had been working on and left the room without complaint. He felt a moment's regret that such a good friend and assistant as Jake should want to leave his employment, and then he turned his full attention to the woman at his side. 'Now let's talk about Holly.' His voice was silky-soft.

Laura rubbed the red marks his fingers had left on her arm. 'I can't imagine what you want to know about her,' she shook her head.

His mouth twisted. 'Why do both you and your sister persist in thinking I wouldn't be interested in her?'

She frowned. 'You didn't say anything to Leonie to upset her, did you?' she asked sharply. 'Because if you did——'

'Believe it or not, I do not, physically or verbally, abuse women who already look like hell!'

Her cheeks flushed defensively. 'Leonie has been ill——'

'I'm well aware of that,' he stated. 'But it's Holly I want to talk about!'

Laura shrugged. 'There's nothing to say.'

'Like hell there isn't!' he flared furiously. 'Don't you think you and Hal should have told me about her birth instead of just letting me go to the house and finding out about her the way that I did?' he scorned.

'She's completely innocent in all this,' Laura bristled. 'And so is Leonie. You can't be telling me that Holly's existence makes a difference to your approval of the marriage?' She looked disbelieving.

Both Leonie and Laura had the ability to wring your emotions to the fullest, and then still make you bleed! He didn't want to dislike this woman, he had wanted things to work out for Hal, but there was no way he could condone this use of trickery.

'All the difference in the world,' he grated, giving a cold inclination of his head.

'But why?' she cried. 'I can't believe an unmarried mother in the family would bother you that much,' she added disgustedly. 'If it does then I'm not sure I want to marry Hal after all!' Her voice trembled with emotion.

'There's no way any of us could stop Hal legalising Holly's birth,' Hawk rasped coldly.

'What?' Laura looked at him as if he had gone insane.

'I can't stop him going through with the marriage now,' he conceded scornfully. 'But if you think I'm going to make things easy for you by approving of the marriage then you're going to be disappointed. I can't accept your——'

'Wait a minute.' Laura had the look of a person who had completely lost track of the conversation. 'Hal isn't Holly's father——'

'Believe me, Laura, you'd be much better telling me he is,' Hawk told her warningly.

'But of course he isn't,' she said irritably.

'I saw Holly, damn it!' Now he was beginning to wonder if he hadn't lost *his* grip on the conversation too!

'Beautiful, isn't she!' Laura gave an indulgent smile. 'Although why on earth you should think Hal had anything to do with her birth, I don't know. Michael is her father, of course,' she dismissed impatiently.

'Michael *who*?' Didn't she realise she was only

making the situation worse by disclaiming Hal as the father of her child? What on earth did she hope to achieve by doing that? Hal certainly wouldn't accept another man's child in those circumstances!

'Michael Spencer,' Laura supplied abruptly. 'Leonie's ex-husband.'

The Brandon sisters certainly had the ability to render him speechless! After years of always being in control, Hawk found these two women completely took his breath away, for one reason or another.

'*You*, and this man Spencer——'

'No, of course not Michael and I,' Laura denied indignantly. 'Holly is *Leonie's* and Michael's child,' she explained impatiently. 'I can't believe Leonie didn't tell you she was Holly's mother,' she frowned.

She had, of course. But he had chosen to disbelieve her. Because Holly looked like Hal!

'She did. I just——Are you sure this guy Spencer is the father?' he groaned. 'They're divorced, aren't they?'

'Most definitely,' said Laura with some relief. 'But Michael was round asking for money about the time Holly was conceived, and although I know Leonie can't stand him, Michael isn't the sort of man to take no for an answer!' she added grimly.

'You mean——he'd force her?' challenged Hawk, fury coursing through him at the thought of any man using force on that silken body.

Laura shrugged. 'I'm really not at liberty to discuss my sister's marriage. But I couldn't stand him. And Leonie quickly learnt what a brute he was.'

Hawk swallowed hard. 'He—hurt her?' His hands clenched into tight fists.

'If he felt like it.' Laura's cold anger was directed towards the memories. 'Michael *has* to be Holly's father, because Leonie hasn't been out with anyone since their marriage and divorce.'

He frowned. 'No one at all?'

Laura gave a hard laugh. 'If you'd been married to a man who threatened you, stole from you, humiliated you, you might feel more than a little apprehensive about becoming involved again!'

'She should have left him earlier than she did,' Hawk declared harshly, hating the thought of anyone hurting Leonie in that way.

Laura shrugged. 'She believed in the vows they'd taken, and tried to be true to them.'

'While that bastard broke every one of them!' His eyes glittered furiously. 'Why the hell would Spencer go to Leonie for money—or anything else?' he grated hardly.

Laura sighed. 'Michael refused to recognise the divorce, and as he's out of work and Leonie earns money from our books . . .' She shook her head. 'She was doing so well, regaining some of the confidence and self-respect being married to Michael had taken from her, and then she found out she was pregnant! God, I don't know why I'm telling you all this.' She looked at Hawk with pained eyes. 'Leonie's life is her own affair. And so is the father of her baby,' she added defensively.

Michael Spencer had abused his wife, taken advantage of her giving nature—— Hawk couldn't believe that Leonie would let the other man possess her body any more after that.

'She's been through so much lately,' Laura continued brokenly. 'The premature birth, her own illness——'

Hawk became suddenly still. 'Holly was born early?'

Laura nodded. 'At least four weeks, the doctors estimated. They had to do a Caesarian operation in the end. I nearly lost both of them,' she remembered with a shudder.

Holly was premature . . .! Hawk began to shake.

'Leonie was so ill after the operation,' Laura was saying now. 'She had no idea what was happening around her for days, even Holly's birth. I didn't think she was going to come through it,' she added emotionally.

'Did Leonie tell you Spencer was the baby's father?' Hawk watched Laura with narrowed eyes.

She shook her head. 'She refuses to talk about Holly's father at all.'

Because Michael Spencer wasn't Holly's father— *he* was!

Leonie had nearly died giving birth to *his* baby. Nine months ago he had taken her to bed, made love to her—and he hadn't been able to get her off his mind since. He had given her a reminder of him that meant she would never forget him either!

Why hadn't she contacted him as soon as she had learnt she was pregnant? She had to know that she carried his child, and that he would want to know about it.

He had a daughter! That tiny bundle of blonde-haired, blue-eyed beauty was *his daughter*.

He knew. Leonie could see the knowledge in his eyes as he faced her across the lounge after arriving with Laura a few minutes ago. Her sister seemed her normal chatty self when she came in, so he obviously hadn't told her he was Holly's father.

As she had known he would, he had come back here as soon as he discovered the truth, and she had guarded against it. Nothing he said or did could hurt her.

Just as nothing he had said or done nine months ago had hurt her.

She had been surprised when he returned to the house that evening, even more dismayed when he had told her he had decided to wait for Laura and Hal to get back; she had known the other couple weren't coming back that night.

Rather than tell him the truth she had decided to brave it out and hope it became so late he would eventually leave and come back tomorrow.

Trying to entertain a man like Hawk Sinclair wasn't an easy thing to do. She had noticed a little self-consciously that he seemed to be entertained just watching her! And those glinting eyes through narrowed lids unnerved her.

'Do you play Monopoly?' she encouraged.

He shook his head.

'No.' Perhaps he didn't need pretend games. He succeeded only too well at the games he played for real! 'I'm really not into games. I never take unfair advantage of a woman,' he drawled softly.

Why did she have the feeling that statement had a double meaning? Probably because it had! This man wanted her, she could see that by the intensity of his gaze and the way he never took his eyes off her.

She didn't want him. She found him fascinating to watch, like seeing a sleek animal in action, but she didn't *want* him.

What if she repulsed him? Would it affect his decision concerning Laura and Hal? She hoped it wouldn't actually come to a point where she had to make a choice.

'Let's go for a walk,' she said impulsively, standing up.

His brows rose. 'A walk?' he echoed reluctantly.

She grinned. 'Well, I realise that being rich you're probably driven everywhere you want to go, but you surely haven't forgotten that if you put one foot in front of the other you actually move forward? If you put one foot behind the other you can even——'

'Okay, Leonie,' he said dryly, 'I get the picture. It is the end of September,' he reminded her hopefully.

'Yes?'

'The nights are getting colder——'

'Not that cold.' She pulled him to his feet, moving away instantly as she sensed he was about to put his arms around her. She wasn't afraid of him, she just didn't want him in that way!

'All right,' he shrugged into the leather jacket he had draped over the chair when he arrived. 'If the lady wants to walk, we'll walk,' he said wearily.

She doubted if Hawk Sinclair's idea of a walk was to have six cats accompany him!

The *cats'* idea of a walk round the garden was

to ambush them every couple of steps, leaping out at them from behind bushes and tree-trunks, wrapping paws around their ankles until they were gently shaken off. Leonie and Hawk's progress was severely handicapped by their mischievous antics.

Leonie's mouth twitched with amusement as Hawk tried his best to hide his annoyance; he was obviously not used to having animals about him.

'How did you ever end up with six cats?' he finally burst out impatiently.

'Strays,' she supplied. 'Every one of them. If a cat's found wandering in the village and no one claims it then it's brought here. We never turn them away.'

'No dogs?' he quirked dark brows.

She shook her head, her hair fiery-red in the last of the sun's rays. 'No dogs.'

'Why not?' He pointedly removed Rose, her pure white cat, from around his ankle.

She shrugged. 'It wouldn't be fair on them, neither Laura nor I have the time to walk them.'

His mouth tightened. 'I'm sure your sister's time is fully occupied with bedazzling Hal!'

She gave him a reproving look. 'Laura is my image,' she drawled. 'And neither of us has the assets to dazzle anyone!'

He came to an abrupt halt at her side, looking down at her with dark grey eyes. 'You don't think so?' he murmured softly.

She stiffened warily. 'No.'

'I'm dazzled,' he stated quietly. 'By you.'

Leonie gave a dismissive laugh. 'Now look, Hawk——'

'I have,' he said abruptly. 'And I want it. Want

you. Are you going to let me have you?'

Or what? Would he demand that Laura never see Hal again, would he smash the delicacy of their love because *he* had been denied what he wanted? She knew he was capable of doing exactly that, because although Hal might disregard his disapproval, Laura never would.

Could she make love with this man, with any man for such a reason? She would do anything to ensure Laura the happiness she hadn't been able to find herself, even make love with a man who merely 'wanted' her for his own gratification. He would never be able to touch her emotionally, no man had been able to do that since her marriage to Michael. And the taking of her body couldn't hurt her; it had been done too many times by Michael for one more time to matter!

He was going to be very disappointed if he thought making love to her would be more than that. Her only lover had been her husband, and his idea of lovemaking was to take his pleasure as quickly as possible, taking what he wanted like a thief in the night. If there were any other way to make love—and she was sure there had to be when so many people found the act addictive!—then she had never experienced it. And Hawk Sinclair looked as if *he* had experienced every pleasure that was available to him.

She drew in a nervous breath, her decision made. 'We'd better go back to the house, the cats have no respect for privacy.' She gave a nervous laugh. 'Tulip once jumped on Michael's back when——' She broke off abruptly. 'Michael was my husband,' she added awkwardly as Hawk began to chuckle at the image she had created.

'So I gathered,' he drawled. 'Better make sure we close the bedroom door—the only scratch marks I want on *my* back tonight are yours!'

Leonie swallowed hard, wondering if she could go through with this after all. Hawk was making it obvious he expected some sort of grand performance from her in bed, and she knew she couldn't give him that. But as they reached her bedroom she knew she had no choice, that it was too late to change her mind now. She was committed, she would see it through.

She trembled slightly as he slowly unbuttoned her blouse, revealing her bared breasts; Michael had never undressed her in this way, and he had never ever left the light burning beside the bed so that they could look at each other as they made love. Hawk was more than looking, he was touching too now!

Red-hot pleasure coursed through her, to remain a throbbing ache between her thighs. Hawk's mouth was against her breast, his tongue lightly stroking the hardened nipple.

She whimpered low in her throat, that whimper turning to a groan as his hard mouth claimed hers, tasting her, his fingers wreaking havoc against her aroused breasts, cupping their firm weight as he lightly brushed the aching tip.

She didn't *want* this man. Then why was she trembling with uncontrolled passion, knowing the first heady-sweet sensations of desire?

She gasped as his flesh seared hers, his shirt unbuttoned too now, her breasts crushed against the damp hardness of his chest. He wanted her so much a fine sheen of perspiration glistened on his body!

Her eyes widened apprehensively as he dropped to his knees in front of her, his gaze holding hers as he unfastened her denims and slowly slid the zip down, several inches of her flesh bare above the lace of her briefs. Air was sucked into her lungs as, breaking her gaze, he bent and his mouth moved surely over that exposed flesh. Tiny pinpricks of explosions spun through her body as he kissed her through the material of her denims, sliding them down her thighs to cast them aside, the barrier between her and his caressing lips even thinner now. The explosions grew almost out of control as she felt the probe of his tongue against her.

'No!' she cried protestingly.

He firmly removed her hand from his hair as she would have pulled him away. 'But you like it,' he said gruffly. 'And God knows so do I!'

The dampness of lace clung to her, that sheer barrier no defence against his marauding tongue, and as his fingers probed beneath the lace Leonie felt her knees buckle as she fell to the floor beside him.

'Lean back,' he instructed huskily, bending his head as she obeyed, his mouth closing hotly on the nipple that had escaped his attention earlier, sucking strongly at the aching bud, easing some of her tension, but evoking another one between her thighs. As if he was aware of her discomfort his hand trailed to the valley between her thighs, discarding the briefs that hid her from him, covering that fiery mound with his palm as he explored the moist vulnerability between her legs, feeling her readiness for him, entering her to ease some of the aching desire.

She was out of control, trembling all over, too weak to even support her weight on her knees as she fell to the floor, taking Hawk with her, sure she would die if he didn't go on.

She groaned her dismay as he suddenly left her, watching him through narrowed lids as he threw off his shirt before slowly taking off his denims, standing between her parted legs as he revealed the throbbing shaft that promised so much pleasure Leonie was mesmerised by the glistening velvet.

'Tell me if I hurt you,' he groaned as he moved between her thighs, drawing her apart and up to him, entering her slowly, sinking deeper and deeper into her flesh as she surged up towards him. 'God, that's good!' His head was flung back, his eyes closed as she sheathed the full length of him, closing around him, moving against him.

His mouth claimed hers, one hand against her breast, as he slowly began to move inside her, almost withdrawing completely before thrusting back to his fullest, his tongue entering her mouth in the same rhythm, the dual invasion leaving her mindless and begging for release.

Her whimpers of ever-increasing pleasure seemed to drive him beyond control, surging into her with fierce power, pulling her legs wider apart so that he could enter her more deeply with each thrust, the fire in her loins burning out of control as quake after quake of pleasure washed her higher and higher, knowing she had taken Hawk with her as he became rigid inside her before spilling himself, hot and powerful, into her waiting warmth. She took his gift greedily, moving against him until she was sure he was completely pleasured, her arms about him as he collapsed weakly against her breasts.

Neither of them spoke, as if they knew something rare would be destroyed if they did. And soon they had no need for words anyway; Hawk was hardening inside her as his mouth moved against her in slow drugging kisses.

This time their lovemaking was hot and quick, Hawk rolling over to pull Leonie above him, holding her hips as she rode them both to shuddering release, his teeth biting hungrily on her offered nipples.

Exhaustion quickly claimed her; she was unaccustomed to even one of those earth-shattering explosions that had taken her to the heavens, having reached that pinnacle twice, her body racked by only slighter, smaller rockets of emotions in the interim. She fell asleep with her head resting on Hawk's chest and their bodies still joined, feeling complete for the first time in her life.

Morning brought with it a rude awakening!

'Your little diversion didn't work!' Hawk rasped furiously.

Leonie woke slowly at the sound of his anger, knowing instantly that she was alone in her bed, that the body she had nestled up to in the night after Hawk had carried her here some time before dawn had been removed. She opened heavy lids to look up at a fully dressed Hawk, fury glittering in accusing grey eyes.

She sat up, pushing the hair from her face,

pulling the sheet up over her breasts as she realised her movement had bared them to his gaze. Not that he looked as if he could be aroused just now. Except to anger, of course!

'What's wrong?' She blinked to clear the exhaustion from her mind, her body aching from the fierceness of the lovemaking she and this man had shared the night before. Maybe she should feel uncomfortable about having made love with a man who had been a stranger to her until yesterday afternoon, but the pleasure they had shared precluded her feeling anything but gratitude. She now knew what it was like to feel completely a woman, a desirable woman.

'What's wrong?' he repeated scornfully, the forceful lover of the night before replaced by a man held in the grip of burning anger. 'You knew damn well that Hal and Laura weren't coming back here last night, and you used your body to distract me from that fact.'

'What?' Her eyes were wide with disbelief.

His eyes glittered coldly. 'Don't play the innocent with me!' he stormed, the heavy stubble of a beard darkening his jaw, giving him a piratical look. 'You went to bed with me last night purely as a way of diverting my attention from the fact that Hal and Laura weren't returning—a fact that you were well aware of when you brought me here!'

The tiny bubble of hope that had begun to emerge from their closeness last night was firmly burst, the small bud of trust withering and dying, and Leonie assumed her air of detached recklessness like an old, well-worn glove. 'I believe it was *your* idea that we make love, Hawk,' she mocked lightly. 'But you're right, I did know Laura and Hal were away for the whole weekend. You're completely wrong about my motives, however.'

'Oh yes?' he prompted contemptuously.

'Hm,' she nodded. 'I had it more in mind that you might look a bit more favourably on their relationship if *you* had what you seemed to want—me.' She met his gaze challengingly, knowing that none of her inner disillusionment showed; she had learnt long ago to hide her true feelings. 'Obviously I misjudged the situation,' she added derisively.

'Damn right you did!' growled Hawk. 'Care to try a little blackmail of your own?' he prompted softly.

Her eyes widened, then she gave a slow smile. 'It wouldn't look too good to Hal if he were to find out you'd taken me to bed, the sister of the woman he loves, only hours after meeting me,' she taunted. 'But I wouldn't do that to Hal, Hawk,' her eyes flashed. 'He doesn't deserve to be hurt by knowing what a bastard his father is!'

His mouth thinned. 'Maybe *I* ought to tell him, just to show him how far you and your devious sister are prepared to go!'

Her trembling hands gripped the sheet in front of her. 'Maybe you should,' she agreed flatly.

'But I won't,' he declared. 'It's bad enough that *I* know what sort of a fool I was last night. But if you think what happened made me look with favour on Hal's and Laura's relationship you couldn't be more wrong; God knows what your sister is capable of if you're capable of going to bed with a man to give her what she wants!'

Leonie sat forward in the bed. 'What are you

going to do?' she asked.

His mouth twisted, his eyes mocking her. 'Whatever it is you can depend upon it being a direct result of what *you* did with your sexy little body last night!'

And he had left her then.

If Laura had been any other than what she was Hawk would never have got away with asking them to wait a year before marrying; he would have lost his son. He hadn't realised, still didn't seem to realise, that it was because of Laura that he still had a son who loved him.

Hawk's daughter had been conceived that night in his arms when Leonie had briefly begun to hope again, even her veneer of cheerful recklessness stripped from her when she learned that she carried his child.

Looking at Hawk now, as he faced her so steadily across the lounge, waiting for her to deny that Holly *was* his child, Leonie knew he was the last man she should have gambled even the tiniest piece of love on, that it was just as well he had killed the emotion before it had even begun to possess her. She would have been destroyed utterly by caring for this man. Or his child.

'If you've come for Holly I'm sure June could have her things packed in about half an hour or so,' she told him calmly. 'Do you have someone you can get to take care of her for you?'

CHAPTER THREE

WHAT the hell did she mean, he could just pick up the baby and walk out of here! She had almost died giving birth to Holly; didn't she care for her at all? He couldn't accept that. Leonie loved Laura with a fierceness that bordered on over-protectiveness; she couldn't possibly care any less for her own child!

And yet she *had* just told him he could take Holly with him when he left.

He drew in a ragged breath. 'Laura has gone to call Hal,' he told her abruptly. 'I've withdrawn all my objections to their getting married.'

If he had hoped that news at least would please her he was disappointed; she remained as unmoving as ever. What was wrong with her, damn it! Could she have post-natal depression? He had heard it could totally devastate a woman after she had had a baby, especially if she had been through a rough birth.

'Leonie, did you hear what I said——'

'Did *you* hear what I said?' she interrupted calmly. 'I told you Holly can be ready to go when you are.'

Hawk rose forcefully to his feet. 'You can't mean that!' he exploded.

'If you would rather wait until you've made arrangements for someone professional to take care of her she can stay on here for a while,'

Leonie offered. 'She's quite comfortable here. We have a nursery——'

'Quite com——!' Hawk echoed thunderously. 'That's *your child* you're calmly discussing giving away!'

She looked at him with emotionless green eyes. 'I'm not giving her away—she's your daughter.'

Even though he had already been certain of that it still left him breathless to hear Holly called his daughter. He and Amy had always wanted other children besides Hal, but she had been killed before it became possible. At his age he had given up any idea of having other children, deciding he would bounce Hal's children on his knee instead when the time came. Holly was an unexpected—and delightful!—gift to him; he couldn't accept that Leonie didn't feel the same way about her.

'I have no intention of taking Holly away from you,' he bit out between gritted teeth.

The uncertainty in her eyes was quickly masked. 'You don't?' she enquired coolly.

'Leonie, you almost *died* giving birth to her!' He frustratedly tried to elicit some show of emotion from her, aching inside at the thought that he might have lost her for ever and not known about it until now.

She gave a vague smile. 'I told you, I'm much better now.'

If anything she looked more ethereal this evening than she had earlier, the daylight hours seeming to have drained her of the small store of energy she had.

He had done this to her, had wanted her to the point of madness that night, and then tried to blame it all on her the next morning.

Because all those months ago she had got to him in a way that no other woman had, not even Amy. She had touched him with her humour, with her spirit, and lastly with the overwhelming capacity she had for passion. He could have stayed buried in her all night long, on one long continual high, never wanting to reach the point of release. God, he *had* stayed in her most of the night; it was only when morning came, the cold light of dawn revealing her duplicity to him, that he had forced himself to remember exactly who she was. He couldn't allow himself to care for her!

When she had admitted to going to bed with him only as a means of placating him for Hal's and Laura's sake he had struck out in the only way he was able without actually exerting physical violence, and had watched as the softness drained out of her, as she too forgot the beauty of their lovemaking.

But his respite from the torture of reliving her softness in his arms had been only brief, never a day passing during the following months when he hadn't imagined he could smell her, taste her on his lips, feel the very essence of her as her body melted into his. It had been a frustrating nine months, when no other woman had felt right in his arms, until eventually he had stopped even looking at other women, knowing it was this sprite he wanted. He had taken Sarah with him to any social functions he just couldn't get out of, knowing he didn't have to put on an act with her, that she just ignored his bad temper. Neither did she expect him to make love to her at the end of the evening, and get upset when he didn't want to!

He had been hell to live with, making Sarah's and Jake's lives hell too. No wonder Jake was walking out on him! He should really be grateful that Sarah wasn't considering leaving too!

But it was reaching Leonie that concerned him right now! 'I was wrong that day nine months ago,' he came down on his haunches beside her armchair. 'I was angry with myself——'

'And me,' she put in dryly.

'Yes,' he admitted with a sigh. 'It never even occurred to me that you might feel you *had* to go to bed with me because it was what I wanted. Leonie, I don't use women in that way,' he shook his head.

'I know,' she nodded. 'I think I knew that as soon as you began to make love to me.'

He took one of her hands in his, surprised at how cold it was considering the temperature inside and out. 'Then why *did* you do it?' he prompted softly.

She shrugged, releasing her hand with the minimum of fuss. 'I thought it would anger you if I said no.'

He drew in a ragged breath. 'That really was the only reason?' He looked at her searchingly, hoping for some sign that she had felt even one tenth of the attraction that he had—that he still did! She had lost all her vitality, and the sparkle had gone from her eyes, but she was still Leonie, the woman he wanted to the point of obsession.

'I enjoyed our lovemaking——'

'That's something!' He sighed his relief.

Her mouth twisted with dry humour. 'Don't

worry, Hawk, you didn't rape me that night.'

He had known that; her response had been complete and uninhibited.

'But,' she continued—and he felt a sinking sensation in his chest, 'being shown the delights of the flesh rather than the abuses—because that's what my marriage consisted of,' she added hardly, 'would make any woman feel pleasure,' she finished dismissively.

Hawk rose slowly to his feet. Perhaps he should feel grateful that he was at least able to give her that. But he had come here earlier today knowing he wanted much more than a physical relationship from her. After months of fighting himself he had finally come here to admit he had been wrong, to ask Laura to please make Hal happy by marrying him, and to claim Leonie for his own. Instead he had jumped to a wrong assumption about Holly's parentage, alienating himself from this woman yet again.

He didn't know how to handle this situation any more, he was too close to it all. One thing he was sure of, Leonie cared nothing for him.

But once they were married——*Yes*, that was the answer! She would be his wife, and Holly would be his daughter. And then he would be able to show her just how much he cared. He might even stop making a damned fool of himself every time they were together!

'We can be married as soon as Hal arrives——' he began.

'I'm not marrying you!' Leonie cut in incredulously, staring at him with wide eyes. 'I'm not going to marry anyone!'

His mouth tightened. 'I'm not "anyone", damn it, I'm the father of your child!'

She gave a weary sigh. 'I've told you you can take Holly.'

Hawk's hands clenched at his sides as he fought down the need he felt to pick her up and shake her; she looked as if she might disintegrate in front of his eyes if he so much as touched her. 'I don't just want Holly, I want you too——'

'Hawk,' she cut in quietly, rising slowly to her feet, 'I don't want to marry you. I don't ever want to be married again.'

He longed to put his arms about her, to take away the vulnerability that she couldn't hide, no matter how valiantly she tried to do so. 'It wouldn't be like last time, Leonie,' he assured her gently. 'I'm nothing like Michael Spencer,' he added hardly, wanting to crush the other man—*slowly*—for the pain he had inflicted on this woman.

'I don't want to marry you,' she told him again harshly. 'And there's no way you can force me to do so. I'm sure that if you tried to stop Laura and Hal marrying now they'd *both* defy you!' She looked at him challengingly.

He shook his head. 'I'm not going to try and interfere in their lives any more. I certainly wouldn't use that as leverage against you. Didn't I convince you of anything just now?' he added gruffly.

Leonie shrugged. 'I'm willing to accept that you had no idea of the obligation I would feel because you wanted me and you had complete control over my sister's happiness——'

'You don't accept it at all,' he groaned, his eyes closed. 'But it's the truth, I swear it!' He had

believed his desire for her to be completely recip-
rocated that night, totally separate from Laura and
Hal. He had never had to use coercion as a way
of getting a woman into bed with him, and he
certainly hadn't done so, knowingly, with Leonie.

'I accept it,' she said wearily. 'Now if you'll
excuse me, I'm very tired, I'd like to go to bed.'

'I want to marry you!' he called after her as she
reached the door.

She turned slowly. 'Just tell me when you want
Holly and I'll see that she's ready.' The door closed
softly behind her.

She couldn't mean that, she couldn't mean to
give her child up without a fight! There had to be
more to it than that.

Hawk was sitting in an armchair absently
stroking the silky fur of a long-haired tortoiseshell
cat as it sat on his lap when Laura came into the
lounge. The cat was either Daisy or Tulip, and he
was giving it the benefit of the doubt and assuming
it was Tulip, the cat which had jumped on the
back of Leonie's ex-husband, Michael Spencer, the
man Hawk had already decided would find his fist
in his face if he ever met him.

'Tulip, stop that!' Laura shooed the cat off
Hawk's knees, confirming her identity. 'I'm sorry
about that,' she gave him a bright smile. 'Leonie
lets them do just as they want.'

Hawk studied the young woman with a more
discerning gaze than he had so far used today,
noting how the last months had left their mark on
her too. He had caused unhappiness in four people's
lives, and then been too damned obstinate to admit
he had been wrong. He had even continued to play

his stupid game by trying to tempt Laura away from Hal with the offer of the television series for Leonaura Brandon. As far as he could see neither of the sisters had used any of the considerable payment they had received from the television rights to change their life in any way. Only the housekeeper was an addition to the household. The furnishings were as old and comfortable as before, and he was sure that the sisters could have paid for June's services out of their royalty payments on their books. Neither Laura nor Leonie had a mercenary bone in their bodies, and he had just put pressure on all of them for nothing.

Laura and Hal might be able to forgive him for that—at least he hoped they could!—but he doubted if they were going to be quite so understanding when he admitted to being Holly's father! He wasn't quite sure he forgave himself for that, knowing it had endangered Leonie.

'Hal's getting the first plane here,' Laura told him glowingly. 'He should arrive some time tomorrow.'

Time enough then for him to admit to being Holly's father. He might as well make his confession a sweeping one!

'Laura,' he began slowly, 'what's wrong with Leonie?' He studied her with narrowed eyes.

'I told you she's been ill——'

'It's more than that,' he interrupted harshly. Steady, he cautioned himself impatiently, you're letting your emotions take over again! 'She doesn't seem as—attached to the baby as she could be.' Again he watched Laura closely for her reaction, this time noticing a shadowing of her eyes.

Something *was* wrong.

'She cares for Holly very much——'

'But?' he prompted impatiently.

Laura gave a pained frown. 'There's a barrier there,' she admitted. 'As if she daren't care. I suppose it's only natural after last time, but——'

'Last time?' Hawk echoed sharply, his heart beating an erratic tattoo against his chest.

'Mr Sinclair, I really don't think——'

'Hawk, damn it,' he rasped. 'And I want to know why your sister daren't let herself love her own baby!'

Laura glared at him. 'Because her son died only hours after he was born!'

He couldn't have felt the blow any more if someone had taken a fist and slammed it into his stomach. Leonie had had a son?

'Michael didn't want the child,' Laura continued with a hard glitter in her eyes for the man who had caused her sister so much unhappiness. 'He refused to accept the doctor's advice that Leonie should be treated with extreme caution during her pregnancy, continuing to *exercise his conjugal rights*, as he put it,' she said harshly. 'Leonie went into labour too early again, even earlier than she did with Holly. They did everything they could to save little Daniel, but he died three hours after he was born. Leonie never left his side.'

Hawk felt the prick of tears behind his lids. Leonie—oh God, his poor Leonie! She had suffered so much for one so young.

'Thank you for telling me,' he said gruffly. 'I had no idea.'

Laura shook her head, sighing deeply. 'Why

should you have? But I'm sure Leonie does love Holly, she's just afraid that she'll be taken from her too.'

By him. Leonie had known that he would one day come back into their lives, her faith in Laura's and Hal's love for each other was complete, and she had also known that he would recognise Holly as his daughter. And after her experience with Spencer she was prepared to give Holly up rather than marry again.

Then he wouldn't demand marriage of her. Not yet anyway. And he wouldn't take Holly away from her either. Holly was perhaps the only one who could break through the barriers Leonie had built about her heart. He accepted that Leonie wouldn't allow herself to love Holly because of the son she had already lost. But finally, eventually, Holly would break through all those barriers, and when she did *he* intended going through them with her, both of them nestling in Leonie's heart, where they belonged.

Marriage had been the last thing on his mind when he arrived here earlier today, just knowing, once the problem of Hal's and Laura's future together was out of the way, that he wanted to spend time with Leonie, make love with her again, as often as she would let him, until this obsession he had for her had burnt itself out. One look at her as she lay so still and fragile on that lounger and he had realised he wanted much more than that!

He had come here to claim Leonie, now he found she wouldn't be claimed—for any price. She had his daughter, but he refused to take Holly from her. Which only left him with one course open, as far as he could see.

'Laura, would you mind if I moved in here for a few days?' he requested bluntly.

His father had always told him that if you asked a question you had to expect a negative answer as well as a positive one; at that moment he had the feeling Laura would very much like to turn him down!

'Of course,' she accepted stiffly. 'I'm sure you and Hal will have a—lot of catching up to do.' She gave a tremulous smile.

She thought he was staying on to spend time with Hal! His son had wished him many places in the last nine months, and none of them had been in the same residence as himself!

'I have no intention of intruding on you and Hal,' he drawled. 'I'd just—welcome the break here.' Tomorrow was soon enough for this young woman to learn why it *had* to be here. Also for her to realise, when he brought Jake and Sarah down to join him, that this would have to be a working vacation!

'Of course,' Laura's smile brightened. 'It is very restful here. I'll just go and ask June to make up a room for you.'

He was going to want more than a room. He intended moving into this house, and Leonie's life, completely, taking over, if necessary!

Leonie had come to love—and dread!—this time of night.

The house was all quiet; Laura and June were asleep in their rooms, the cats likewise in the room downstairs that they occupied at night, even the birds that sang outside so merrily in the daytime were silenced by the darkness.

The only sound was the sucking enjoyment of Holly's lips against the bottle her rosebud mouth pulled on so avidly.

When she had first come home from the hospital with the baby Leonie hadn't been strong enough to wake for these night-time feeds, but already Holly was down to one bottle between ten o'clock at night and eight o'clock the next morning, and so she had taken over from Laura a week ago, allowing her sister her much-needed rest.

Three o'clock in the morning was a strange time to be awake, she had discovered; all her defences were down. Not the perfect time to be holding this sweet-smelling bundle. Holly's hair was golden in the soft lamplight, her skin taking on a peachy tone. One of the tiny hands clutched at Leonie's finger, the other moving spasmodically against her own chest as she drew sustenance from the bottle.

Leonie hadn't deliberately planned not to feed Holly herself; she had just been too ill to do so at first, and by the time she was strong enough her milk had all but disappeared. Now she thanked God she *had* been too ill to feed Holly herself. She was sure the pain of giving her up would be all the stronger if she had established such a bond.

As it was, her heart was breaking into a thousand pieces of crystal at the thought of saying goodbye to her daughter. But she had already said goodbye to so much that mattered in her life, so much she loved, that she knew it was better to give up that love before it destroyed you. And she had no doubt that Hawk would love Holly, that she would know the same caring and protection from her father that Hal had always had. It wasn't even as if she would never see Holly again, she told herself at times like this. Hawk would be a part of her family once Laura and Hal were married.

She should have known Hawk would offer marriage. He might live in a different world from her, a world where sex—and anything else he desired—was readily available to him, but even so he had developed a moral code of his own, a code that said he couldn't give a woman his child without marrying her.

He had been stunned when she offered to give Holly up, she had seen that clearly. But she had known from the first, during the difficult months of her pregnancy, the trauma of Holly's birth, the month of physical weakness since, that she was only caring for Holly until her father came to claim her. Of course she loved Holly, but in a distant way that allowed all women to care for a tiny defenceless human being. To allow herself to feel any more than that would be to open herself up to all sorts of pain, like the pain she had known from Holly's father when she realised that night that she *did* want him, that she could more than love him if he were patient with her. Men like Hawk didn't want a woman's love.

It was only during these night-time hours, with Holly snuggled so trustingly against her, that her defences crumbled a little.

'I thought I heard her cry a little while ago.'

Leonie's head snapped back as she looked up at Hawk with wary eyes. Laura had told her of his request to stay on at the house, and the way he looked he had obviously just left his own bed, his hair tousled over his brow, grey eyes lacking some of their usual alertness, a knee-length robe he had borrowed from Laura—and which would have been ankle-length on her!—covering his nakedness.

'I'm sorry if we woke you,' she bit out abruptly.

'I'm not.' He closed the door behind him, part of the intimacy of the room now. 'It's a long time since I watched a woman feeding my child at her breast,' he added softly.

Leonie's mouth twisted at his effort to disconcert her. 'I'm only giving her a bottle, Hawk,' she drawled. 'Even you could do it!'

He crossed the room to stand looking down at her with darkened eyes, reaching out a hand to gently touch Holly's downy temple.

'Shall I help you?'

She turned away. 'If you doubt my ability to care for Holly——'

'I don't,' he reproved lightly. 'I don't want to help in that way. Come with me,' he invited huskily, pulling her gently to her feet so that the movement wouldn't disturb Holly as she remained rapt on her bottle.

'What are you doing?' Leonie asked as Hawk took her through to her bedroom next door.

'Trust me,' he encouraged softly as he deftly removed her robe and threw it across the foot of the bed.

'Trust you? But—Hawk——!'

'Relax,' he soothed, placing the pillows up against the headboard of her bed before propping her back against them. 'Now we can get comfortable.'

With Holly held firmly in her right arm she was completely defenceless as Hawk manoeuvred himself, lying across her body, resting the baby's padded bottom against his chest.

It was the oddest, most intimate sensation she had ever experienced. Hawk wasn't trying to arouse her, he was intent only on holding her, while their child fed.

But the intimacy was so much more than that, binding not just her and Holly but the three of them. And there lay danger.

She shifted uncomfortably. 'Hawk, that's enough——'

He released her slowly, looking up at her between sensually narrowed lids. He seemed to know a great deal about caring for a baby. Because he had been through all this with his wife!

No doubt he and his wife had shared every detail of Hal's life; Hawk was the sort of man who would want to know everything about his child and the way it was being brought up. No doubt he had shared moments just like these with his wife!

'Holly has fallen asleep,' she told him harshly, her sharp movement dislodging him. 'I'm sure you and your wife enjoyed these little games,' she scorned, 'but I find it distasteful!' She tried to move, but his weight held her down.

He looked up at her consideringly. 'Would you like to hear about my life with Amy?'

Hear how he had been one of the lucky ones, how for six years he and Amy had lived in heaven! 'I'm not interested,' she muttered, pulling the folds of her nightgown together as a compromise to getting up completely as his weight across her prevented her doing. 'Holly has to go back into her cot.'

Hawk straightened, looking down at his daughter with softened eyes. 'Let me.' He gently lifted the baby into his arms, holding his daughter to gaze down at her. 'She's beautiful, Leonie,' he breathed softly.

She didn't even glance at the baby. 'Perhaps you'd like to take her back to her room on your way to your own?'

'Look at us, Leonie.'

She gave a startled jump at the harshness of Hawk's voice, but did as he instructed, paling slightly as she saw how small Holly looked in his arms, so small and beautiful. A part of him.

'I sat in her room just watching her most of the evening,' he began to talk softly. 'I wanted to hold her so much, ached with wanting to hold her when Laura fed her at ten o'clock——'

'Did you tell her?' she sighed, knowing—and accepting—how shocked her sister was going to be when she learnt the truth of Holly's conception. She had allowed Laura to go on believing Michael was Holly's father because she just hadn't known how to tell her the truth, and couldn't begin to guess how her sister and Hal were going to react to the news that Hawk was the father!

'Once Hal has arrived I'll tell them both,' Hawk bit out. 'Their reaction to the news is up to the two of them. I'm proud to have Holly as my daughter, and I'm not going to apologise for her birth. To anyone,' he added firmly.

Not even to her, she read the unspoken message.

'I apologise for hurting you,' he continued gruffly. 'But not for creating this beautiful baby I'm holding in my arms for the first time. Oh yes, Leonie, I waited,' he confirmed at her stunned look. 'I wanted us to be together when I held our daughter for the first time, so that you could see how right we all look together.'

She recoiled from the tentacles of closeness he persisted in trying to wrap about her. 'I've told you to take Holly with you when you go,' she snapped.

'When we leave here—if we leave here; this seems a pretty good place to bring up a child,' he shrugged. 'Then we'll all go together, all three of us,' he added firmly.

'No——'

'We're your family now, Leonie,' he told her determinedly. 'Holly and I.'

She swallowed hard. 'Once Laura is married to Hal I won't have a family,' she stated flatly. 'There'll just be the cats and me.'

His mouth twisted. 'I finally figured out this attraction you have for cats,' he rasped.

Her head went back in challenge. 'Oh yes?' she scorned.

'They don't demand anything from you, not love or attention. They need food, somewhere dry and warm to sleep, but ultimately they're independent creatures, needing no one but themselves.' He shook his head. 'No matter how hard you try, Leonie, you can't be like them. I'm going to make sure you never are!' he added grimly.

She couldn't seem to stop trembling once he had gone to take Holly back to her room.

CHAPTER FOUR

HAWK HADN'T meant to push so hard that Leonie kept to her bedroom the next day.

He had heard the baby cry in the night, and had known Leonie wouldn't welcome his presence when he heard her talking softly to the baby in the nursery. But in the end the temptation to be with them both had been too much.

She had looked like a Madonna as she sat with Holly in the nursery-chair. She had never been more beautiful to him, her hair a red cloud about her shoulders, green eyes almost luminous in the lamp's glow, a small dusting of freckles across her nose and the paleness of her cheeks. The neckline of her nightgown gaped open slightly, and he could see the tender curve of her breasts, breasts that had no doubt ached to feed her child and she had been too ill to do anything about it. His wife had claimed that feeding Hal herself was the most satisfying experience she had ever known. And even though Leonie held herself distanced from Holly he didn't doubt, especially after she had lost her son so tragically, that she would have fed the baby herself too if she had been able.

'What are we doing here, Hawk?' sighed Jake, interrupting his thoughts.

His assistant and secretary had arrived shortly after lunch, and if Sarah thought there was anything strange about the three of them moving down here she gave no sign, but was her usual efficient self in organising the study Laura had told them they could take over as she and Leonie weren't using it at the moment. He should have known Jake wouldn't be so easily satisfied.

Hawk shrugged. 'My son is getting married, why shouldn't I want to spend time at his fiancée's home?' he evaded with an arrogant lift of his brows.

'His *fiancée's* home?' Jake echoed softly. 'I know we haven't seen her yet, but doesn't Mrs Leonie Spencer live here too?'

'Drop it, Jake,' scowled Hawk. 'She's been ill—she's vulnerable.'

Blond brows rose. 'She must be special.'

'Not that it's any of your business,' he rasped. 'But yes, she is.'

'You haven't seen her for months,' the other man derided. 'And I'm damn sure you weren't thinking of her last month when Maggie Soames propositioned you——What the hell——?' He frowned his surprise as Hawk grabbed hold of him by his shirt-front. 'Hawk?' he queried uncertainly.

Hawk's eyes glittered angrily at the other man, all his frustration centred in the anger he let control him. 'For your information, Maggie was a very disappointed lady at the end of that conversation. Not that that's any of your damned business, anyway,' he added harshly. 'And in future when you talk about Leonie I'd like to hear a little respect in your voice. Understand?' He shook the other man slightly.

Jake shook his head, completely undaunted. 'Are you in love with her?'

Jake had asked the very same question that had been plaguing Hawk since he had seen Leonie again. He wanted to take care of her, she was the mother of his child, he desired her to the point of madness, but was all that love?

He had loved Amy, had loved her as a boy and then as a man. But it was nothing like the emotions Leonie raised in him. Amy was totally self-reliant, had been brought up to believe in her own worth, never accepting second-best in anything. They had shared love; she certainly hadn't needed his protection the way Leonie did. He and Amy had been two people who happened to love each other who had shared life; Leonie made him feel protective, jealous of any life she had known before him, violent towards her marriage and the man she had loved. And he couldn't even claim he felt that way because of Holly, because he had felt all those emotions before he knew their one night together *had* produced a child. But was it love?

How the hell did he know, he hadn't been in love for fifteen years! Loving Amy had been a warm flowing of emotion, not this almost violent need to possess, and go on possessing. He had no idea if he loved Leonie, but he wanted her, and he wasn't going to take their child without her.

'If it takes you this long to think about it maybe you'd better not answer,' drawled Jake.

Hawk gave an impatient sigh. 'If I knew the answer don't you think I would have given you one?' he replied. 'We've never had secrets from each other.'

The other man looked away. 'No,' he acknowledged. 'Are we going to go through the figures for the Alton Hotels takeover, or would you rather we gave work a miss for today?'

'Jake——'

'Hawk, I'm going to the airport to pick up Hal,' Laura interrupted them excitedly. 'Do you think I look all right?' She chewed uncertainly on her bottom lip.

She looked as young and vulnerable as her sister at that moment, a shadow in her eyes that he had never seen before, as if she too doubted that someone could actually love her. But that was ridiculous; Laura had never gone through an experience like Leonie's. He had to be imagining these things because Leonie had hidden herself away from him today.

He moved forward impulsively to kiss her lightly on her forehead. 'You look beautiful. Just don't let Hal become so enthralled that the two of you forget to come home,' he added teasingly.

She blushed prettily. 'Maybe *I'll* become too enthralled!'

'In that case,' he drawled, 'we'll see you both tomorrow some time.'

Her blush deepened. 'Thank you.'

She knew, as he did, that he had just made her a gift of his son. He knew Laura well enough now not to doubt her ability to love Hal for the rest of their lives.

'You're welcome,' he returned just as softly.

'Holly is with June at the moment,' she explained with a frown. 'Leonie seems to be having one of her bad days,' she apologised.

Leonie intended having as little to do with him as possible. Probably she hoped he would have left before she had to leave her bedroom again. She could spend the rest of her life in there waiting for him to do that!

He nodded. 'Don't worry about a thing, I'll take care of everything here.'

Laura gave him a considering look, once again looking very like her sister. 'Why do I have the feeling I can trust you to do just that?' she mused.

'Probably because you can,' he drawled.

She came up on tiptoe to kiss his cheek. 'Thank you for Hal,' she smiled.

His expression softened. 'Don't mention it.' He watched her as she hurried from the room to go and meet the man she loved. His son. He had been worse than a fool not to have accepted that from the first.

If he hadn't been so bloody-minded all these months he could have been with Leonie through her pregnancy, could have watched her grow big with his child. He would have liked to have seen that. Now he knew, even if he could persuade her to marry him, that he never would see her pregnant with his child, that after two difficult births he would never put her at risk in that way again. He would make very sure of that if he had to.

'Are they identical?'

He turned sharply at the sound of Jake's voice, having forgotten his friend was still in the room. 'Sorry?' he frowned darkly.

'Are the sisters identical twins?' Jake repeated softly.

'Yes,' he confirmed challengingly.

'Laura is very lovely,' Jake said consideringly.

'Then obviously so is Leonie,' snapped Hawk.

'I know June is the housekeeper, but who's Holly?' Jake quirked light brows. 'Another sister?'

'Something like that,' Hawk evaded, not intending to broadcast Holly's parentage; he owed Leonie more than that, telling Hal and Laura only because they had a right to know.

And a right to judge him for the bastard he was! He had set out to make love to Leonie that night, and although he hadn't known it, he had succeeded only because of who he was and the destruction Leonie had known he could cause in her sister's life. He really hadn't known she felt that way, had never had difficulty attracting women to his bed on his own merits, and she hadn't given the impression earlier that she found him repulsive. She had touched him so naturally he had believed she wanted him too. He should have looked beneath the kookiness that had so unnerved him and which he had discovered now, to his cost, had all been a sham, a barrier to her real vulnerability. She was too weak now to erect that barrier, and he and everyone else could see just how badly she was bleeding.

Damn, he shouldn't have gone to the nursery last night. Today Leonie had retreated from him completely. It had been too soon for her; he *had* to go more slowly.

'Let's go through the Alton Hotels proposal,' he said needing something to occupy his mind other than Leonie; he would go insane if he didn't stop thinking about her for at least a brief respite.

Leonie couldn't stay in her bedroom for ever. There was nothing wrong with her, her strength was returning daily, and although she had been happy to spend days at a time in her room when she first came home she felt restless and penned in now.

But outside this door was Hawk Sinclair. He could still reach her, despite all the pains she had taken not to be vulnerable where he was concerned, last night he had touched her in an emotional way, not just a physical one. And he had done it quite unselfishly.

She would have to make him take Holly and go, before it was too late!

'Oh!' She had bumped into a complete stranger walking along her own hallway!

The woman was tall, very elegant, possessed of a classical beauty that would only increase as she got older, her hair an ash-blonde swirl about her shoulders, the smooth lines of her face pure perfection, her figure very slender in a midnight-blue dress that made her eyes appear almost as dark a blue.

And Leonie was sure she had never seen the woman before!

The woman smiled, the warmth filling her eyes. 'You must be Mrs Spencer,' she greeted softly.

'Yes.' Leonie still looked puzzled.

The woman gave a husky laugh. 'But who am I, right?' she acknowledged self-derisively. 'My name is Sarah Ames. I'm Mr Sinclair's private secretary.'

Hawk's *secretary*. Was that all this woman was? Somehow Leonie doubted Hawk would omit to take full advantage of having such a lovely woman working for and with him. But even if this woman were just Hawk's secretary, what was she doing *here*?

'I was just on my way to Hawk's bedroom to collect some papers,' Sarah Ames explained lightly. 'If you'll excuse me?'

Leonie absently acknowledged her assent. Papers? Surely Hawk didn't intend actually working here? And if he did, did he intend moving Sarah Ames into their house too?

As she strode into the study unannounced she saw that Hawk had another employee with him besides Sarah Ames, a tall fair man who stood beside him as they bent over some blueprints on the desk. She spared little time to notice that the other man was about Hawk's age, with a reckless attraction that rivalled even Hawk's. She was too angry to care if he were Robert Redford's double with the lethal charm to match; her home was full of strangers, and it was all Hawk's doing!

'Hawk, I want to talk to you alone,' she snapped. 'Now,' she added forcefully.

His eyes widened as he slowly straightened. 'Has something upset you?' he frowned.

'Not something, *someone*,' she corrected angrily, her eyes flashing. 'Now do we discuss this alone or in front of your associate here?' She faced him challengingly, twin spots of angry colour in her cheeks.

'Jake,' he instructed, his gaze never leaving hers.

The other man gave a mocking inclination of his head. 'Sure,' he drawled, strolling across to the open door. '*This* is the vulnerable one?' he taunted Hawk before closing the door softly behind him.

Leonie's eyes flashed again as she turned to face

Hawk. 'What did he mean by that?' she demanded.

'It isn't important,' he dismissed with a shrug of his shoulders. 'Why don't you sit down?' He indicated the chair opposite the desk.

'So kind of you to offer me a seat in my own study!' she flared, ignoring the chair. 'But then with the number of your employees walking about the place you probably think this is *your* house!'

His mouth quirked. 'You met Sarah,' he guessed dryly.

'On her way to your bedroom,' she confirmed agitatedly. 'Are there any more besides this Jake and her?'

He leant back against the desk, sitting on its edge, the long fingers of his right hand absently playing with the pen he still held. 'No more,' he drawled. 'Just my assistant and my secretary.'

'*Just?*' Leonie echoed disgustedly. 'Hawk, you can't just move in here!' she protested.

He shrugged. 'I already have. Sarah and Jake brought everything down from the hotel with them when they came this morning.'

'Then they can just take it all back again,' she told him heatedly. 'This is my *home*, not your damned office!'

'It's Laura's home too, and she invited me to stay,' he said quietly.

'And now I'm uninviting you!' she snapped. 'I won't let you take over my home.'

Hawk shook his head. 'I'm not leaving here unless you do. Besides,' he added firmly as he could see she was about to protest, 'are you denying me the right to be involved in my son's wedding arrangements?'

'You don't have to *live* here to be involved in them,' she flared impatiently.

He shrugged. 'For the moment I'm sick of living in hotels—even my own.'

'Then go home to New York!' Her voice rose frustratedly.

'I'm perfectly comfortable here, thank you,' he taunted. 'And don't worry about Jake and Sarah, they're staying at a hotel in Claymont.'

The town of Claymont was about eight miles away from the village, and boasted three hotels, none of which was anywhere near the standard of Hawk Sinclair's hotels. 'Why don't you just move in with them?' she urged irritably. 'Better yet, why don't you all go back to London?'

He shrugged. 'I've already told you why. We'll try not to get in your way,' he added mockingly.

'Having the three of you underfoot for eight hours a day——'

'Sometimes more than that,' drawled Hawk. 'I'm in the middle of negotiating a take-over for another chain of hotels,' he explained at her outraged look. 'Jake and I are burning the midnight oil, I'm afraid.'

'Trying to wipe out the competition?' she scorned.

He grinned. 'I don't *have* any competition,' he murmured softly.

As head of the leading hotel group in the world he was probably pretty sure of that, nevertheless his arrogance rankled. 'What does this hotel chain have that you want?' Leonie asked dryly.

His smiled deepened. 'Most of the hotels are second-rate, but they have three prime locations . . .'

'And those three locations are worth all the others put together,' she guessed in a bored voice.

'Right,' he nodded, appreciation for her quick grasp of the deal in his eyes. 'I'll sell off the other hotels to recoup my losses, and the other three will become new HS Hotels.'

'All very neat and tidy,' she jeered. 'What about the poor man you're buying them from?'

'Company,' he corrected. 'If it were a single man they would probably never have got into the financial difficulties they're in. Too many chiefs . . .'

'Obviously that will never happen to HS Hotels,' she said disgustedly.

'Not while I'm still in control,' Hawk conceded seriously. 'But my two children might have differing views on how things should be run.'

'Two children? Oh,' she stiffened, 'you mean Holly,' she realised. 'Surely HS Hotels should all go to Hal? After all——'

'My daughter is entitled to her share,' Hawk cut in harshly. 'Fifty per cent when the time comes.'

'Oh, but——'

'We have years to argue about this, Leonie,' he put in wearily. 'Holly isn't going to be old enough to care one way or the other for a long time to come.'

'But Hal is,' she protested. 'He isn't going to like——'

'Hal will adore his sister.' Hawk stood up forcefully. 'Who could help but love Holly?'

Leonie flinched at the taunt, knowing he had meant to wound, that this man never did anything by chance. 'It's your decision, of course,' she dismissed coldly.

'As my wife you'll be left everything else in my will,' he added arrogantly. 'Just in case I die before you do.'

'I will *never* be your wife,' she snapped. 'And you're likely to meet your end very prematurely if you don't leave me alone!'

'Leonaura Brandon never kills off her characters,' he drawled mockingly. 'Laura was a little annoyed about the television series, by the way,' he recalled with amusement. 'Accused me of trying to buy her off in another way.'

Leonie's mouth twisted. 'She was perfectly right, of course!'

'Of course,' he acknowledged unabashedly. 'But I can admit defeat gracefully when I have to.'

Again she had the feeling the remark was directed at her. And she would never admit defeat by marrying this man!

'Perhaps that's as well,' she bit out coldly. 'Because I have a feeling it's going to become a habit!'

Hawk's mouth quirked. 'I don't think so,' he drawled.

'No, you wouldn't,' she snapped. 'You know, you were wrong last night about my reason for preferring cats. I like them because unlike most humans they aren't arrogantly sure they're always right, nor do they act with a total disregard for the feelings of others!' She turned on her heel and walked out of the room, completely missing the triumphant grin that lit up Hawk's harsh features.

She could hear Holly's cry for attention even as she approached the kitchen, halting uncertainly in the doorway as she walked in to find the man named Jake sitting at the kitchen table drinking coffee while June tried to calm the baby as her bottle was warmed through.

Leonie's attention zeroed in on her indignant daughter as her tiny fists struck at nothing but air, vaguely aware that Jake had risen to his feet at her entrance, watching her now as she took the baby from June.

She turned at his sharply indrawn breath. 'Is there something wrong, Mr . . .?'

'Colter. Jake Colter,' he supplied, his gaze fastened on Holly. 'And this is . . .?'

Her arms tightened instinctively. 'My daughter,' she replied defensively. 'Holly.'

'Holly,' he nodded slowly. 'Well, I'd better get back to Hawk,' he added abruptly. 'Thanks for the coffee, June.'

'What's wrong with him?' The housekeeper raised her brows as he hurried out of the room. 'Unless he's as in awe of Mr Sinclair as everyone else appears to be!' she added dryly.

'I doubt it,' Leonie derided; Jake Colter had looked as if he was perfectly capable of taking care of himself—and anyone else he chose to. She had a feeling the two men worked well together, Jake a little less arrogant then Hawk, but obviously just as capable. 'Maybe he doesn't approve of single parents either,' she dismissed.

'I doubt if that was it.' June shook her head. 'He was telling me before you came in that he brought his son up on his own after his divorce.'

Leonie shrugged. 'Then I have no idea what's wrong with Mr Colter.' She gratefully took the warmed bottle from June, sitting down in the rocking-chair beside the unlit fireplace in this huge country kitchen to begin feeding Holly.

'Well, you certainly "showed her", didn't you?'

Hawk looked up with a frown as Jake rejoined him in the study. 'I wondered where the hell you'd got to,' he scowled, having been going through the figures on his own for over half an hour since Sarah had brought them in to him.

Jake strode angrily into the room. 'I went for a walk,' he snapped.

'A walk?' Hawk leant back in his chair. 'You may have handed your notice in, Jake, but I don't pay you to go off for *walks* in the middle of the damned day!'

'It was either that or come in here and punch you out,' the other man growled.

Hawk put up his hands soothingly; he had never seen Jake this angry before, in fact he couldn't ever remember seeing the other man angry at all; Jake was easygoing to the point of laziness sometimes. Except when it came to work, he had always given over the hundred per cent of his attention to that. What the hell was wrong with him lately, giving in his notice and refusing to tell him why, and now coming in here attacking him like some crazy man?

His eyes narrowed. 'Maybe you would care to explain that remark?' he encouraged, silky-soft.

'I went to the kitchen while you were in conversation with Mrs Spencer,' Jake bit out. 'I made the acquaintance of a rather lovely young lady.'

'June . . .?' The housekeeper was attractive enough, but he would hardly have called her young.

Still, if Jake thought of her that way . . . But why was Jake so angry with him after meeting the housekeeper? June certainly made no effort to disguise her disapproval of *him*, and had treated him with only cool politeness since he had arrived yesterday.

'No, this young lady's name was Holly.' Jake watched him with narrowed eyes. 'Your daughter, I believe?'

Hawk's eyes narrowed. 'Did Leonie——'

'Tell me?' Jake finished scornfully. 'Of course she didn't,' he snapped. 'But I remember how Hal looked as a kid; the resemblance between the two of them is incredible. I repeat, you certainly "showed" Leonie Spencer nine months ago, didn't you?' he scorned with distaste.

Hawk gave a weary sigh. 'I never meant for that to happen——'

'I'm sure you didn't plan Leonie Spencer's pregnancy,' Jake jeered. 'But you certainly planned her seduction!'

'What the hell does it have to do with you anyway?' Hawk demanded impatiently. 'I made a mistake——'

'And those two are going to pay for it,' Jake attacked. 'Isn't it time you grew up, Hawk?' he challenged. 'Took time out from the life you've led and realised just what a selfish bastard you've been all these years!'

Hawk's eyes narrowed on his friend as he realised the remark—and the anger—was directed at Jake as much as at him. God, how he wished the other man would confide what was worrying him! But Jake was adamant that nothing *was* bothering him, he just wanted to do different things with his life than he was doing now, he said.

'Jake——'

'Are you going to marry her?'

Hawk shrugged. 'I've asked her. She doesn't *want* to marry me, Jake,' he confided as he saw his friend's anger rising again. 'She says I can take Holly, though,' he added huskily.

Jake blinked his uncertainty. 'You aren't going to?' he finally asked softly.

Hawk drew in a ragged breath. 'No. I told you, she's—special. She was even before I know about Holly,' he admitted gruffly. 'Now how about telling me what's been bothering you all these weeks?' he prompted softly.

He could visibly see the way Jake suddenly distanced himself, as if he deeply regretted becoming involved in the conversation.

Jake gave him a derisive look. 'Can't you believe I would want any other sort of life than the one we've been leading the last sixteen years?' he taunted.

Hawk gave an inward sigh of regret. He and this man were too close, had been through too much together, for them to lose their friendship now. But it seemed to be slipping away from them.

'It hasn't been that bad, Jake,' he chided huskily.

'No?' his friend scorned. 'We're both over forty—just, in your case,' he acknowledged derisively. 'And what do either of us have to show for our lives, *really* have to show?'

'Now this *is* a mid-life crisis——'

'I'm serious, damn it!' Jake rasped impatiently. 'I'm forty-three years old, my son's lived away from me for so long he's almost a stranger, and I go home to an empty flat and an empty bed every night. I may not deserve more from my life, but I *want* it!'

Now wasn't the time to point out that until quite recently Jake hadn't gone home to an empty bed very often, because in the last few weeks that *had* been the case. Why hadn't he realised that Jake hadn't dated anyone recently either? Because, he admitted heavily, his own mind had been too full of wanting to see Leonie again.

But whether Jake accepted it or not, it did sound as if he had reached a point in his life, and at forty-three he had definitely reached mid-life, where he wanted the normality of a family life, like other men had. Knowing how badly he wanted that with Leonie now, he could sympathise with his friend.

'It isn't too late, Jake——'

'You don't know a damn thing about it,' the other man bit out harshly. 'I lived my life the way I wanted to, and now I've got to pay for it.'

'What——'

'Does Hal know about Holly?' Jake cut in abruptly.

End of subject? It would appear so, from his friend's expression. Damn it, just when he had been so close to breaking through the barriers Jake had built up around himself lately! But if Jake wanted to change the direction of his life what right did he have to stop him? There were several things in his own life, especially recently, that he would have done differently if he could have done them over.

He frowned. 'I'm going to tell him and Laura

when they arrive later. I don't need to tell you that what you know about Leonie and me—and Holly—is to go no further than the two of us?' He studied his friend with narrowed eyes.

'Doubting the confidentiality of your personal assistant?' derided Jake.

'Trying to protect Leonie—and I don't need you to tell me I'm a little late!' Hawk added harshly. 'I'm doing the best that I can to make amends.'

Jake nodded. 'I can see that. I only hope Hal can too.'

He gave the other man a considering look. 'What do you mean?'

Jake shrugged. 'You seduced the sister of the woman he loves; I doubt if he's going to take that sitting down!'

'Neither do I,' Hawk admitted ruefully.

CHAPTER FIVE

HER SISTER was ecstatic, Leonie thought; there could be no doubting her happiness at being reunited with Hal. The misery of the last months had been completely erased in her now glowing eyes and happily curving lips.

Hal couldn't stop touching Laura, as if he needed that physical assurance that they were finally going to be married. He was as handsome as ever, a young version of his father, although only in looks, possessing none of the cynicism so prevalent in his father's nature. Leonie was sure that with his marriage to Laura he never would learn that cynicism!

With them they had brought a young man by the name of Stephen Colter, and from his looks—and the obvious help of his surname—Leonie realised this had to be Jake Colter's son. He was perhaps a year older than Hal, and the two young men were obviously good friends. In fact, Hal had brought the other man with him so that he could be a witness at the wedding.

'Hal didn't tell me Laura had a double, otherwise I would have asked for an introduction sooner,' Stephen leant slightly across the dinner-table to confide.

Leonie smiled slightly at his obvious flirting, relieved that she was seated between him and Hal at the table.

She hadn't wanted to see Hawk any more today, that one encounter had been enough to have seriously damaged her defences, but she had realised it would only upset Laura if she hadn't joined in the family dinner to celebrate her engagement to Hal. The emerald ring he had presented to her sister as soon as they met at the airport flashed brilliantly on Laura's left hand; the wedding itself was planned for several days' time.

Hal had greeted his father a little distantly, and it appeared the last months had put a severe strain on their relationship too. Leonie had little sympathy for Hawk, as knowing how much Hal had always admired his father she knew how deeply he must have been hurt to treat Hawk the way he was doing.

Hawk. It was a round dining-table, so no one could sit at its head, and yet Hawk seemed to dominate the proceedings. Leonie ignored his presence as much as she was able.

Which wasn't all that easy when there were just the five of them seated for the meal, Stephen and Laura sitting either side of Hawk. Looking at him now, as his narrowed gaze watched the close attention Stephen was paying her, she thought he definitely had the look of that bird of prey his name implied!

Why shouldn't she enjoy Stephen's company! He was a very pleasant young man, and had his father's recklessly handsome good looks. And most important of all, he was uncomplicated. After the battering her emotions had taken lately that came as a welcome change!

Stephen's father and Sarah Ames had already

returned to their hotel for the night by the time the threesome arrived from London, and with Laura and Hal's preoccupation with each other Stephen seemed to want her company too.

'I think Hal must have also forgotten to mention that if we'd been introduced any sooner, before a month ago anyway, you wouldn't have given me a second look!' she returned teasingly.

'How do you know pregnant women don't turn me on?' he returned with a devilish twinkle in his eyes.

Leonie laughed. She couldn't help it. After the tension of the last couple of days Stephen's sense of humour appealed to her.

'Hey, don't laugh!' He looked affronted, although the twinkle remained in his eyes. 'A lot of men are, you know.'

'Are what?'

Leonie sobered as Hawk picked up their conversation. And if the steely glitter in his eyes was anything to go by he didn't care for the fact that she and Stephen were conversing at all.

'Leonie and I were just discussing the merits of pregnant women,' Stephen supplied in all innocence. 'I think they must be very sexy.'

Grey eyes narrowed dangerously. 'And what does Leonie think?' rasped Hawk.

Her smile was directed at Stephen. 'I think you men ought to try being pregnant for a while and see how sexy it makes *you* feel!'

Stephen looked disappointed. 'And I thought a woman's hormones went wild at times like that!'

'Maybe they do,' she consoled. 'I was just feeling too ill most of the time to notice.'

'That bastard Spencer has a lot to answer for,' Hal grated, his face flushed with anger.

Leonie shot Hawk an uncertain glance. Hal and Laura had only arrived with Stephen a short time ago, so there had been no opportunity to talk to the engaged couple alone.

'Can't you see you're embarrassing Leonie?' declared Hawk. 'We can discuss this some other time,' he reproved his son.

'Sorry, Leonie.' Hal looked abashed, a tall self-confident young man who lacked none of his father's arrogance. 'I just get so angry when I think of what you've gone through the last nine months!'

Which didn't augur well for when he was told the truth about that painful time. But she knew the truth couldn't be kept from him or Laura, that it was too important for that.

Stephen put down his fork even though he had only eaten half of his meal. 'I'd better drive into town and say hello to Dad,' he grimaced.

'You don't have to hurry off on our account,' Leonie protested, aware of their rudeness in discussing something he could have no knowledge of. 'Please stay and finish your dinner,' she encouraged.

He smiled, shaking his head. 'I really had better go and let Dad know I'm here. He's been acting a little strange about things like that lately,' he added ruefully.

'I think he just feels,' Hawk answered softly, 'that he's missed out on a lot of things in his life by working at the pace we have.' He looked at Hal before focusing all his attention on Leonie. 'I think we both have,' he added gruffly.

'He's not old,' Stephen dismissed. 'Women certainly find him attractive enough,' he mocked lightly. 'You too, Hawk.' He looked admiringly at the older man.

Leonie found nothing admirable about the way Hawk had used and discarded women most of his life, although she accepted that a lot of women would accept the challenge of attracting such a man. She would give anything not to have him attracted to *her*!

'It isn't enough, Stephen,' grated Hawk. 'And your father realises that too.'

Stephen shrugged. 'Dad can do anything he wants with his life, it's the way he's been trying to take over mine that I object to,' he gave a rueful grimace. 'A fine time to think he can step in and start running things his way!'

Hawk gave a rueful laugh. 'It seems to be something all fathers try to do at some time in their lives. It often takes us a while to realise it, but in the end we have to admit we were wrong and butt out.' He looked apologetically at Hal and Laura. 'If we're lucky we're forgiven for our arrogance,' he said huskily.

'I hope Dad realises he's wrong pretty soon,' Stephen sighed. 'At twenty-one I'm a little old to start being treated like a child again!'

There was complete silence in the room once Stephen had left, and Leonie could see from her sister's pained expression that she was waiting as tensely for what happened next. Hawk had given a public apology to Hal just now, but how was Hal going to react to it?

He drew in a ragged breath, his hand resting

over Laura's as it lay on her thigh. 'I know what you were trying to say just now,' he bit out. 'And I even understand why you did what you did. Just don't expect me to thank you for it!'

Hawk nodded acceptance of his son's anger. 'Maybe once you're a father yourself you'll realise just how difficult it is to always make the right decision where your children are concerned. There isn't any formal training for this job, you know, it's all a question of trial and error.' He gave a weary shrug. 'I've made my share of mistakes with you, and I'm sorry for it. I can only hope to try and do a better job with——'

'Your grandchildren,' Leonie put in quickly, flashing Hawk a warning look as he turned to her frowningly.

She hadn't realised the resentment Hal felt towards his father was still so strong; she knew that if Hal were to learn now that Holly was his sister it could strain the relationship to breaking point. Much as she disliked Hawk, and wished him far away from here, and her, she didn't want to achieve it that way, sure the implication of Holly's birth, when she had been conceived, was something Hal wouldn't be able to accept at this moment in his life.

'Leonie——'

'I think I'd better take your father away and give the two of you some privacy before he starts telling you just *when* you should start providing him with these grandchildren,' she told Hal lightly, and was rewarded with his grin of amusement and Laura's coy blush as she stood up to look pointedly at Hawk.

He got slowly to his feet, obviously not happy with the situation, and followed her out into the garden with angry strides.

'Why the hell——'

'Because Hal still resents what you asked of them too much to understand what happened nine months ago,' she groaned. 'And feeling the way that he does he's going to think you deliberately used me, set out to hurt me, because of his involvement with Laura.'

'I did hurt you,' he rasped.

She sighed. 'Not deliberately. But I very much doubt Hal will believe that, and he'll blame himself for it. And how do you think he's going to feel about marrying Laura when he believes you did that to her sister? And it's no good saying it shouldn't affect them.' She shook her head as he went to speak. 'Hal just may be honourable enough to feel he shouldn't marry Laura at all after what you did to me.'

Hawk came to an abrupt halt, fighting an inner battle with himself, finally sighing heavily, a pained frown on his brow. 'God, I've made a mess of things!' he groaned, running a hand through his hair, leaving the trail of his long fingers in the ebony softness.

'You only made love to a woman you desired, *I* was the one who chose to bring Holly into the world. If I hadn't that night nine months ago could have been forgotten by everyone,' said Leonie dully.

He shook his head. 'You couldn't have done anything else, not after——Daniel.'

Pain like a knife being thrust into her chest

coursed through her at the mention of her son's name. He had been so tiny, so perfect, and she had sat holding his hand as he lay in the incubator he had been placed in straight after birth, watching the shuddering of his tiny chest as he drew air into his lungs, until that tiny shudder came no more, and she knew her son was dead.

She could guess exactly why Laura had told Hawk about Daniel. With Daniel had died all her hopes and dreams for the future. They had to remain dead.

'No,' she acknowledged gruffly. 'But I don't think we should tell Hal you're Holly's father until after the wedding next week.'

Hawk gave a deep sigh. 'I'm not happy with leaving things the way they are——'

'You think I am?' Her eyes flashed. 'Go ahead, Hawk,' she challenged. 'Tell Hal and Laura you took me to bed one night and fathered Holly, but don't blame me if you gain a daughter only to lose your son!' She was breathing hard in her agitation, swaying slightly as the strength seemed to drain from her. 'Don't touch me!' she ordered Hawk as he would have reached out for her. 'Haven't you touched me enough?'

Never enough. He wanted to touch again the silken satin of her body, to kiss every freckle she had. And every delicious inch of her was covered in those adorable freckles.

Maybe he shouldn't desire her now, she hadn't long had his baby, and was still unfit, if her lack of strength was anything to go by. But he couldn't stop wanting her, and now he wanted to protect her as well. It was a dangerous combination.

'Yes, you bastard!' Hal was suddenly upon him without warning. 'Haven't you *hurt* her enough!' His powerful right hand landed angrily against Hawk's jaw.

The force of the blow, the unexpectedness of it, knocked him off his feet. 'What the hell——' he began.

'Holly woke up while the two of you were out walking,' Hal's eyes glittered as he towered over Hawk, his hands still clenched into fists at his sides. 'Laura introduced me to *my sister*!'

Hawk drew in a steadying breath as he got slowly to his feet, studiously brushing the dirt from his palms. He was very much aware that what he said in the next few minutes could affect his relationship with Hal for the rest of their lives. But what could he say to vindicate himself? The fact that he hadn't known of Leonie's emotional scars didn't excuse what he had put her through.

'Hal, stop this!' Surprisingly Leonie was the one to answer him. 'I realise meeting Holly that way, recognising her, has been a shock to you——'.

'Shock!' echoed Hal scornfully. 'It was like looking at pictures of myself as a baby! I should have known you wouldn't let Spencer near you again, that *he* had something to do with your pregnancy!' He glared at Hawk with dislike.

'I——'

'He had *everything* to do with Holly's existence,' again Leonie was the one to answer Hal. 'But I wanted him too, Hal,' she added quietly.

Hawk looked at her with sharp eyes. Was she just saying that for Hal's sake or did she really mean it? My God, he thought, she meant it! He could see the truth of it in her eyes. He could also see that it wasn't an admission she enjoyed making, to herself as much as anyone else. But she had admitted it! Did she still want him? The emphatic answer to that had to be no; he was another emotion she had cut out of her life.

'I don't believe you,' Hal dismissed, reminding Hawk that it was his son he should be concerned with right now. 'He isn't your type at all.' He looked at Hawk with disgust.

Years of taking what, and who, he wanted came back to haunt him at that moment. Hal was right, he doubted if the way he had lived his life appealed to Leonie at all. But she had admitted to wanting him. It was all the hope he had.

'No,' Leonie confirmed. 'But for that one night I did want him,' she insisted huskily.

Uncertainty flickered in Hal's eyes, then they hardened again as he turned to Hawk. 'And what did you want, Dad?' he demanded hardly. 'Another woman to warm your bed, no matter that she was the sister of the woman I love? Or was that it?' he grated. 'Were you trying to prove your point about Laura being mercenary by making Leonie look the same way?'

Hawk reacted instinctively, his own fist making contact with Hal's mouth, and his son's head recoiled from the blow, blood trickling down on to his chin as he straightened. Hawk drew back in shock at what he had done. 'Oh God, I——'

'Stay away from me,' Hal warned softly, the threat all the more effective because of that. 'I admired you,' he rasped. 'Always thought I wanted to be like you.' He shook his head. 'Maybe there was a softness to you once; my mother must have found something in you to love. But now you're hard and selfish, you don't give a damn who you hurt to achieve what you want.'

'Hal——'

'Don't try and defend him, Leonie,' Hal said sadly. His eyes glittered as they returned to Hawk. 'And don't *you* ever try to tell me how to run my life again!' He turned on his heel.

'Where are you going?' Hawk demanded tensely.

Hal stiffened but didn't turn. 'To explain to the woman I love what a bastard my father is. And hope that after I've done so she'll still marry me,' he added raggedly.

'Let me——'

'I warned you!' Hal turned and hit him with all the anger he had in him.

This time Hawk stood his ground, but he could taste blood in his mouth, could feel the ragged cut to his inner lip. But none of that mattered, not when Hal was dismissing him from his life. The angry pain in his son's eyes was almost too much to bear. But there was nothing he could say to stop Hal as he slowly walked away.

'Go after him,' Leonie told him sharply. 'You can't let him go to Laura like that! He'll just blurt out the truth to her, ruin everything. Laura would understand if the situation were handled properly,' she said desperately.

Remembering the way her twin defended her, the way they defended each other, he wasn't so sure of that. He had the feeling Laura Brandon would probably want to black his eye once she learnt he was Holly's father.

But he did agree with Leonie that just blurting out the truth, embellished with Hal's own bitterness, was not the way to do this.

He also doubted that Hal would ever forgive him. But what could he do, what could he say, to make his son understand what had happened between him and Leonie nine months ago?

He suddenly had the answer to that, an answer he had even been denying to himself.

He looked down at the tiny woman at his side who clutched so frantically at his arm. He knew she wasn't ready for the truth yet, but it was something he had to give to his son.

His hand briefly covered Leonie's, but he removed it before he could feel her stiffen and move away from him. 'I'll go and talk to him,' he nodded.

'You can't let him talk to Laura when he's so angry,' she urged worriedly.

'I won't,' he assured her gruffly.

'Well, go on, then,' she ordered impatiently as he continued to look at her. 'Things could have become so out of proportion in his mind by now that he could have told Laura you raped me that night!'

His little bantam hen was returning. Leonie might not have realised it yet, but first this afternoon, and again just now, her fighting spirit had been back in full force. The day it came back and stayed was when he would make his claim.

'And take a couple of ice-packs with you,' she called out as he walked off in the direction of the house. 'By the looks of you you'll both have

swollen mouths pretty soon,' she added disgustedly.

His jaw ached quite badly already, and he gave
June a rueful grimace as she provided him with the
two ice-packs without comment, grinning a little
as she shook her head impatiently, then sobering
as he reached Hal's room and heard him moving
impatiently about inside. He opened the door
without knocking, sure that if Hal knew who his
visitor was he either wouldn't open the door at all
or would come at him with fists flying again.

Hal straightened abruptly, his eyes narrowing
warningly. 'What do you want?' he demanded
aggressively.

'Have you spoken to Laura yet?' Hawk prompted
softly.

His son shook his head. 'She's still busy with—
Holly,' he ground out tightly.

'None of this is the baby's fault,' Hawk reminded
him gently. 'She's very beautiful. I hope you'll
come to love her as much as I do.'

'Why, you——'

'I do love her, Hal,' his father continued firmly.
'Not as much as I love her mother, but Holly is
very special to me.'

Hal looked thunderstruck. 'You—love——'

'Leonie,' Hawk finished softly.

And he did. He had told himself he wanted her,
that he wanted to look after her and Holly, but it
was so much more than that.

He loved everything about her, and it was a love
so unlike the undemanding love he had felt for
Amy that at first he had just thought it was a need
to possess. Outside in the garden with her just now

he had known it was love, a wild, stormy love that completely controlled him.

'Would you like to talk about it?' he compelled Hal.

CHAPTER SIX

HOLLY was again engrossed in her bottle.

Again it was a time for thinking. Why did the mind suddenly decide that three o'clock in the morning was the perfect time to start functioning?

Ever since Leonie had awakened to Holly's impatient cry, quickly changing the baby while waiting for her bottle to warm through, she had listened out for Hawk, but so far he hadn't put in an appearance. She hoped he wouldn't do so, but that didn't stop the warm ache of her body as she remembered what had happened last night at this time.

She had no idea what Hawk had said to Hal, but whatever it was Hal's attitude had undergone a drastic change and he was very supportive when they had all told Laura the truth about Holly's father. Poor Laura had been so stunned, but Hal had smoothed things over with his admiration for his baby sister. Both men looked as if they had been through a battle—and lost—so there had been no delaying revealing the truth to Laura.

'Your poor daddy,' she murmured softly to Holly. 'He almost lost your brother's love today.'

Holly didn't even falter in her gulping down of the milk, and Leonie gave a rueful smile at her daughter's complete lack of interest in anything but her food.

'It's all just nonsense to you, isn't it?' she said

softly, gently smoothing the golden hair on Holly's forehead. 'You're going to love Hal when you're older,' she smiled. 'He's already talking to Laura about having a daughter just like you.' She felt strangely proud that her daughter was so beautiful everyone seemed to fall in love with her. 'But you mustn't get conceited,' she reproved softly. 'You may be a Sinclair, but——'

'Is she?'

She gave a start of surprise; once again Hawk had entered the room without her being aware of it. 'I wish you wouldn't do that,' she whispered waspishly.

He wore a black silk robe that fitted him much better than the one he had worn the previous night, and which was obviously his own. But again he seemed to wear nothing beneath the robe. Did he always sleep naked? He had that night he had stayed with her, but she had thought that was just because he was with a woman. It made her nervous to know that silk material was all that covered the bronze strength of his body.

'Is Holly a Sinclair?' he frowned, moving stealthily across the room.

'You know she's your daughter——'

'But is her name Sinclair or Spencer?'

Leonie had thought long and hard about the naming of her baby, and had given her the name Holly because it was pretty and because it followed the tradition the Sinclairs had of giving their children names with the initial H. The surname had been a little more difficult to decide upon, but as she had known Holly would ultimately go to her father . . .

'Her name is Holly Laura Sinclair,' she told him with slow precision.

The tension slowly left him, making her aware of just how taut he had been as he waited for her answer.

'Thank you.'

She felt the warm colour in her cheeks, irritated with herself for caring that the name had pleased him. 'I had to think of the fact that you might not have *wanted* to acknowledge her as your daughter,' she bit out.

His mouth twisted. 'You knew that I would.'

'I made sure of it,' she snapped.

Hawk smiled. 'I also want to acknowledge *you*.'

'As what?' she derided.

A strange emotion flickered in his eyes before it was quickly masked. 'I've asked you to marry me,' he reminded her gruffly.

'Let's not go through that again——'

'Why not!' He came down on his haunches beside her chair. 'I'm going to keep on asking——'

'And I'm going to keep saying no!' Leonie cut in vehemently.

'You wanted me, Leonie,' he reminded her huskily.

She drew in a harsh breath. 'I told Hal that——'

'Because it was the truth,' he finished softly.

She shrugged. 'Perhaps.'

'It was,' he insisted.

'What difference does it make?' Leonie dismissed, her face devoid of expression. 'It's now that matters.'

All the challenge seemed to go out of him, the

gleam in his eyes dulling, making the bruising about the side of his mouth more noticeable.

'Does that still hurt?' She frowned at him.

He pressed his fingertips gingerly against the swelling. 'Like hell,' he acknowledged. 'That's why I didn't come in earlier.' He nodded in the direction of the baby. Holly was fast asleep again, her mouth lax where she had finished feeding. 'Put Holly back to bed, Leonie,' he said gruffly.

And then what? She didn't even want to think about it.

'Have you held her today?' she prompted distantly.

'With so many people in the house all eager to be near her I haven't had the chance,' he admitted ruefully.

'Take her now.' Leonie didn't give him the chance to agree or disagree, thrusting the baby into his arms. 'You may as well get used to each other if you're going to be together all the time.' She busied herself clearing away the debris from Holly's meal.

'Do you think she'll have freckles like you?'

She straightened sharply. 'What?' she frowned.

'We're going to have our hands full fighting off the boys if Holly gets even one freckle on this adorable nose,' he teased indulgently. 'Once I've kissed one of her mother's freckles I just have to kiss all of them.'

'Holly has fair skin like Laura and me, so I would say it's quite probable she will have freckles later on,' Leonie answered him dismissively, refusing to be drawn by his verbal seduction.

'How can you even think of giving her up,

Leonie?' He gazed down at his daughter with proud eyes.

She remained distant. 'How do you think other women give up their children for adoption?'

'Usually by breaking their hearts,' he said challengingly. 'Will your heart break when you hand Holly over to me for the last time?'

Tears flooded her eyes. She couldn't stop them. She had tried not to love Holly in a way that would ultimately leave her devastated, but she was very much afraid she was failing as each night like this Holly wound herself closer and closer about her heart.

And then she remembered Daniel, the last in a long line of people she had loved who she had also lost. Holly would be better off with Hawk.

'Hearts don't break, Hawk,' she bit out. 'They're much more resilient than you give them credit for.'

He drew in a ragged breath. 'You worry me——'

'Leonie, are you all righ——Oh!' A surprised-looking Laura came to an abrupt halt in the nursery doorway, taking in Hawk's presence there with Leonie with wide eyes.

'We were just feeding the baby,' Hawk drawled in the awkward silence.

Leonie shot him a censorious glance before turning to her sister. 'We were—well, we were——'

'Just feeding the baby,' Laura finished uncertainly.

She gave a pained frown. 'Yes.'

'I heard noises and I thought something was wrong,' Laura explained uncomfortably. 'I had no idea the two of you were—together.'

'We weren't,' Leonie snapped. 'At least, only because of Holly,' she amended awkwardly.

Hawk chuckled softly. 'I'm sure Laura understands how much I enjoy these moments alone with you and Holly now that we don't have to pretend I feel nothing more than a cursory interest in the baby.'

Leonie was sure her sister didn't understand anything of the kind. Poor Laura still looked dazed that she could have gone to bed with Hawk in the first place! So was she. But she would never admit to Hawk that, although she *had* worried about his reaction to Laura and Hal that night if she had refused him, she had forgotten all about them when he began to make love to her! He would take that as too much of a victory.

'Don't look so worried, Leonie,' he drawled. 'Laura will have to get used to seeing the two of us together once we're married.'

'Married?' Laura echoed dazedly. 'You didn't say anything earlier about getting married.'

'That's because I've turned down Hawk's proposal,' Leonie told her abruptly. 'Several times,' she added hardly.

'I believe I once told you I never take no for an answer,' Hawk reminded her softly.

The very first time they had met when she hadn't realised exactly what a dangerous adversary he could be. How could she forget anything about that day? Or night.

'This time you'll have to,' she stated dismissively.

'Leonie, surely marriage would be the best thing——'

'Best for whom?' she challenged her sister.

'Holly,' Laura said flatly.

She drew in a ragged breath. Holly's future was something else she hadn't got around to telling her sister. 'Hawk is quite capable of taking care of Holly,' she said softly.

Laura gasped. 'You can't mean to——'

'No, she doesn't,' Hawk cut in harshly. 'Don't worry, Laura, Leonie *will* marry me.'

'I'd feel much more comfortable about travelling with Hal once we're married if she did,' Laura nodded. 'But of course, it's your decision,' she added hastily as Leonie's mouth set mutinously. 'It would keep Michael away from here once and for all,' she persisted firmly.

Michael. Michael of the charm, the humour, until things didn't go the way he wanted them to. Then he became violent, a man to be feared. And she had seen none of that until they were married and it was too late. Another of her dreams shattered. Until she was afraid to dream.

She could see Hawk was none too thrilled at the mention of the man who had been her husband either!

'Just what——What the hell——?' Hawk frowned as a loud crash could be heard down the stairs, and he handed the baby to Leonie before moving to the stairs to investigate.

Leonie looked worriedly at her sister. Surely Michael hadn't . . . Even he wouldn't . . . He would.

The noise seemed to be coming from the lounge, and Hawk moved stealthily to gently push the door open. A loud curse filled the air as another loud crash resounded around the room.

'If you're a burglar you're a damned inept one,' Hawk drawled dryly, flicking the switch by the door at the same time.

A heavy frown settled over his brow as he saw it was Stephen weaving about the room trying to keep his balance. The reason he couldn't was obvious, he was too drunk to stand up straight!

'Stephen, what the hell . . .!' Hawk moved forward quickly as the young man looked ready to fall flat on his face. 'Steady,' he soothed quietly, bracing Stephen's weight against him.

Stephen looked up at him with dazed eyes. 'I's all right,' he slurred. 'I wash jusht goin'—goin' to bed,' and with the last he keeled over completely.

Trying to support a drunk was never easy, especially when the man was almost as big as you were and his legs had suddenly turned to jelly!

Hawk placed him in a chair, straightening to look down at the unconscious man. What on earth had happened tonight to make him get into this state? Jake had been in a strange mood lately, but surely he hadn't driven his son to this?

'What happened?' Leonie hurried into the room, quickly followed by Laura.

Hawk's mouth twisted. 'I didn't knock him out, he passed out!'

Leonie shot him a reproving glare as she went down on her knees beside Stephen. Hawk instantly remembered another time when she had got down on her knees beside him in that way. Thank God Stephen was in no condition to be affected by her the way he had been; the younger man had already shown a decided preference for her company, he thought grimly.

'He's drunk,' he bit out harshly, instantly ashamed of his jealousy concerning Leonie and her worry over Stephen. But damn it all, she hadn't been this worried over him earlier when Hal had tried his best to beat his brains in!

She gave him a scathing glance. 'I can see—and smell—that,' she wrinkled her freckle-covered nose with distaste. 'I think we should get him upstairs so that he can sleep it off.'

Hawk's thoughts were better kept to himself. But he found it difficult, increasingly so, to share any of Leonie's time with anyone else. His mouth still hurt, damn it, why didn't she show some concern for that!

On one plane he recognised that her concern for Stephen was of a polite level for a guest staying in her house, that she was able to show this interest only because Stephen *was* a stranger to her. But on another level he would have welcomed having her soothe his aching mouth earlier instead of calmly recommending an ice-pack!

He nodded abruptly. 'I'll carry him up,' he grated impatiently.

Laura watched frowningly as he slung Stephen over his shoulders and strode out of the room with him. 'Does he do this sort of thing often?' she asked uncertainly.

Hawk gave a grim smile. 'Only when he's had an argument with his father. I would say he and Jake had a full-scale battle, judging by his condition tonight!'

'Parents certainly seem to put their children through it,' Leonie put in censoriously.

Now was not the time to remind him of the idiot he had made of himself concerning Hal's relationship with Laura! 'You should know,' he rasped, instantly regretting the taunt as her freckles were suddenly very livid against the paleness of her cheeks.

He was trying to go slow with her, and considering that he hadn't cared this much about a woman's feelings since he had been with Amy it wasn't coming easily to him. But that had been a low blow when he knew exactly why she held herself aloof from Holly.

'I'm sorry,' he said gruffly, searching the wounded expression on her face as she moved to open the door of the bedroom Stephen was sharing with Hal. She looked as if he had beaten her! He didn't want to *hurt* her, he just wanted to *love* her. He was out of practice of loving any woman. Amy would have told him exactly what an idiot he had been making of himself, he acknowledged ruefully. Poor Leonie, in contrast, had taken so many knocks from life that she didn't even realise he was reacting instinctively, *jealously*.

He was forty years old, he knew when he wanted a woman, and he usually took one. It wasn't easy standing back and not pressing the advantage Leonie having admitted once wanting him gave him, knowing that if she had wanted him before then he could persuade her to want him again. But he was in love with Leonie, had made love to her without realising that, and now he had to go back to the beginning and start all over again. Although he needed a little of Leonie's lovemaking to sustain him, even if he admitted it was too soon for them to make love the way he longed to do.

The first thing he intended doing was making it clear to the young pup he had thrown over his shoulder that Leonie was off limits to him. As soon as Stephen sobered up, of course!

The light from the hallway gave him enough vision to be able to see where to put Stephen down. The figure in the bed opposite slept peacefully on.

'Get used to it,' he told Laura in a hushed voice as she looked down on Hal indulgently. 'He's been this way since he was a kid,' he added ruefully. 'He even slept through an earthquake once!'

She smiled, her eyes full of love. 'I have my own way of waking him,' she admitted a little shyly.

'I'm sure you do,' he drawled ruefully; when was he going to realise that Hal was going to marry this woman! 'Maybe you would like to use it now,' he added dryly. 'I could use a little help getting Stephen undressed.'

Laura blushed. 'I——'

'I'll help you,' Leonie cut in briskly, already unbuttoning Stephen's shirt.

'Stop that!' Hawk bit out harshly, clasping her hand tightly in his. God, seeing her touch another man like that made him feel violent! 'I can do it,' he told her gruffly, slowly releasing her hand, sorry for the livid marks he had made there. But it had driven him wild to see her touching Stephen.

'But——'

'I said I can do it,' he insisted roughly. Anyone would think she actually *wanted* to take Stephen's clothes off! 'Maybe I won't bother,' he added grimly. 'It isn't going to hurt him to sleep in his clothes for once. It will remind him in the morning that he has something to apologise for!' He closed the door forcefully behind them, sure that both young men slept peacefully on. How was *he* supposed to go back to sleep after this! He needed to be alone with Leonie. But he didn't doubt that she wouldn't come back to his room with him, or that she wouldn't welcome him in her room either! The last months of celibacy were certainly taking their toll on him.

'I think I'll go and make a cup of coffee,' Laura said wearily. 'I don't think I can go back to sleep just yet.'

Coffee sounded good to him. Perhaps the caffeine would help calm his ragged nerves. Although he wouldn't count on it! 'I think I'll join you,' he nodded. 'Leonie?' he raised his brows.

She looked undecided, probably not relishing the thought of him being alone with Laura and so able to ask as many questions as he liked about her, but also not wanting to spend any more time with him tonight. He felt irritated when the latter won. Damn it, he wasn't some sort of ogre, a selfish bastard perhaps, but not some sort of monster!

And then he noticed the way she was trying to avoid looking at him, as if something about him greatly disturbed her. It was better than nothing, he supposed, but what —He gave her a considering look as, having glanced down at himself, he realised that carrying Stephen had messed up his robe, the belt at his waist having kept him decent, but his chest was almost completely bared. And it was bothering Leonie! Maybe she wasn't so indifferent to him after all.

The woman moving about the kitchen preparing the coffee looked like Leonie, even smelt a little like her, of fresh spring flowers, and if he shut his mind off to the fact that it wasn't her he could almost imagine what it was going to be like being married to Leonie. He daren't allow himself to even think of failure.

The coffee did little to soothe him, and he stared down at the black heavily sweetened brew with dissatisfaction.

'It's decaffeinated,' Laura told him as she saw his preoccupation.

'Oh.' He pushed it away uninterestedly. 'Laura, will you and Hal be free to babysit tomorrow night? I mean tonight,' he added, the kitchen clock showing it was almost three-thirty in the morning.

'Of course,' she nodded instantly, sitting across the table from him. 'But don't you think you should ask Leonie *if* she wants to go out with you before making any arrangements?' she added dryly.

He gave a rueful smile. 'If I asked she'd say no, so I'll present her with a fait accompli.'

Laura sobered. 'The way you did with Holly?'

He drew in a harsh breath, relaxing with a heavy sigh. 'Go ahead,' he invited softly. 'You're entitled.'

She shook her head. 'It's none of my business. Just don't hurt her.'

He gave a puzzled frown. 'Hal was more vocal than that,' he reproved.

Laura sighed. 'Leonie needs—someone. Someone who will care for her, love her as she deserves to be loved. If that someone is you then I'm not prepared to judge your methods of achieving that.'

They were a puzzling pair, these two sisters.

Hawk doubted if Hal realised just how little he really knew of the woman he intended marrying. There were things about Laura and Leonie that they didn't seem prepared to reveal to anyone, things that probably held the key to what had made them the women they were. Even love didn't seem to be able to unlock those doors.

But if Laura found his relationship with Leonie unexpected she didn't exactly disapprove, and that was much more acceptable than the opposition he had been expecting.

Now all he had to do was persuade Leonie into going out with him!

But first he had to talk to Jake about Stephen, and the mood the other man had been in of late, that didn't augur well for their friendship.

When he came downstairs the next morning he found Jake alone in the kitchen drinking coffee. And he didn't look any more pleased with the result than *he* had the night before!

'It's decaffeinated,' Hawk supplied dryly, taking a seat opposite the other man, ignoring the pot of coffee.

Jake pushed the cup away with a disgusted snort. 'Like sex without the climax!'

Hawk had heard it put more delicately than that, but that just about summed it up! Obviously Jake's mood hadn't improved any. 'Did you and Stephen argue last night?' Might as well get straight to the point; Jake didn't look as if the subtle approach would reach him this morning.

Jake's head went back sharply, his expression suddenly wary. 'What's it to you?' he challenged.

Hawk shrugged, holding his temper with difficulty; Jake might be feeling like hell at the moment, and from the look of him he probably had a hangover that would rival Stephen's when the younger man finally woke up, but in all the sixteen years of their friendship Jake had never spoken to him this way before.

'When the son of my friend comes back to his hostess's house at three o'clock in the morning stoned out of his mind I think I have reason to feel concerned.' He raised questioning brows at Jake.

The other man pushed his chair back noisily as he stood up. 'Stephen is my affair and I'll deal with it,' he bit out harshly. 'Where is he now?'

'Still in bed. Look, will you calm down, Jake?' Hawk attempted to soothe. 'He only got drunk. Neither Leonie nor Laura minded. But you looked a little hungover yourself this morning, and I just wondered——'

'Stay out of this, Hawk,' Jake cut in coldly, his eyes glacial. 'I'll deal with Stephen in my own way.'

Hawk shook his head, never having seen Jake anything like this before. 'Maybe you should deal with yourself first,' he suggested softly.

Jake turned to him sharply. 'What's that supposed to mean?'

He sighed, wishing he could talk to Jake as he used to. Maybe they really had come to the end of their friendship. He had hoped Jake would eventually reconsider his resignation, but the other man seemed to be getting worse, not better. And taking his frustration out on Stephen wasn't going to help the situation.

'I think Stephen's problem might be *you*——'

'Keep out of my life, Hawk,' Jake growled savagely. 'Just keep the hell out of my business!'

Hawk released his breath slowly as his friend stormed out, at a complete loss as to how to deal with that situation.

At a complete loss as to how to deal with *anything* at the moment!

CHAPTER SEVEN

'WHAT am I doing?' Leonie questioned Rose as the pure white cat sat on the dressing-table watching her enquiringly as she applied a light make-up. 'He tells me we're going out to dinner, that he needs the break. I told him I didn't want to go, and yet here I am getting ready,' she said self-disgustedly, shaking her head.

The cat just continued to look at her, her beautiful green eyes completely untroubled by this human dilemma.

'And where have you been when I needed you?' Leonie turned to Tulip as she lay on the bed washing her long fur with a wet rasp of her tongue. 'You used to terrorise Michael if he came anywhere near me!' She remembered the dislike had been mutual; Michael had put the cats out of the house every chance he got. But she had thought her husband was going to strangle Tulip the night she had leapt on his back as he made love to her. After that Tulip had spat at him every time their paths crossed. Today Leonie had actually seen the tortoiseshell cat lying on her back while *Hawk tickled her tummy*! 'You have no taste,' she reprimanded the unconcerned cat. 'Well, perhaps some,' she conceded, remembering how Michael had turned out. 'But it doesn't extend far enough!' She waggled her hairbrush at Tulip as the cat continued to wash, completely unaware of the faux pas she had committed today.

Everyone, even the creatures she had believed to be her friends, seemed to accept Hawk's presence in the house as if he had a perfect right to be there. Laura and Hal were even babysitting for Holly tonight while Hawk took her out to dinner. And if that wasn't turning traitor she didn't know what was!

She had protested that she didn't want to go, that she didn't feel strong enough yet, but Hawk had completely overridden all her objections, telling her the change would do her good.

So what was she doing getting ready to go out with him? She didn't know any more than Rose did!

'Neither of us has any taste!' she told Tulip vehemently. 'Because after months of being cooped up in the house I actually *want* to go out—even if it is with Hawk Sinclair!'

'I'm glad to hear it.'

She turned guiltily at the drawled comment, her cheeks fiery red. Although any retort she might have made to Hawk's intrusion got stuck in her throat as she took in his appearance; the black evening suit and snowy-white shirt fitted him perfectly, emphasising the bronze of his skin. She dispassionately acknowledged that he looked perfectly beautiful, better than she did, in fact! Her silver-red dress was one she had worn before she had Holly, and although she had lost weight her hips were slightly larger than they used to be; the dress clung a little too revealingly for comfort.

'I was on my way downstairs when I heard you arguing with someone,' he drawled dryly. 'I was a little concerned, and when you didn't answer my knock . . . I had no idea you were arguing with your cat.' He looked at her blandly.

Leonie put down her hairbrush. 'And I was losing too!'

Hawk chuckled softly. 'I think my witchchild is on the way back!'

'Your *what*?' She looked at him disbelievingly.

He shrugged, coming completely into the room to close the door behind him. 'That first day we met you bewitched me in some way,' he admitted huskily. 'And yet you still looked so much like a child. You became my witchchild.'

Leonie reminded herself that he was a master at the art of seduction. 'Well, my bewitching days are over,' she dismissed in a bored voice. 'And I'm certainly no longer a child,' she added.

His silver gaze watched her steadily. 'Part of you will always be a child,' he finally answered softly. 'The part of you that seeks love and approval in spite of yourself.'

Leonie stood up abruptly. 'Shall we go?' she prompted coolly. 'The dinner reservation was for eight-thirty, I believe you said.'

He didn't move out of her way as she approached the door, and her heart began to hammer against her chest. Then at the last moment he seemed to think better of it, opening the door for her with a flourish. Leonie's breath left her in a relieved sigh as she swept past him.

June had retired to her room for the night, Stephen had disappeared for the evening again, only Laura and Hal sat in the lounge. And the two of them looked as if they were just longing for the time they would be alone for a few hours.

Leonie felt a little guilty that it should be herself and Hawk who were going out and not the engaged couple; the two of them hadn't been alone since Hal arrived yesterday.

Hawk clasped hold of her arm before she could speak. 'We'll see you both later,' he informed them firmly, drawing Leonie out of the house.

'Why did you do that?' She released her arm as soon as they were outside. 'I was only going to——'

'Offer to let them go out instead of us,' he finished dryly, unlocking his car door. 'Couldn't you see they didn't want to go anywhere—except perhaps into Laura's bed?' He held her car door open for her.

By the time he slid in next to her behind the wheel she had the blush on her cheeks under control. Of course Laura and Hal wanted to be alone in the *house* and not surrounded by a roomful of strangers! And trust Hawk to point that out to her so bluntly.

She took undue interest in the surrounding countryside as he drove in to Claymont, all the time aware that he kept shooting her mocking glances. If he had said just *one word* . . . But he didn't, being more astute where she was concerned than she would have given him credit for. Or just more prudent.

'I hope this is all right,' he remarked as he held her elbow lightly on the walk into the hotel where they were to eat. 'Jake said the food isn't too bad,' he shrugged.

The leading hotel in Claymont, it was nowhere

near as luxuriously furbished as photographs Leonie had seen of the HS Hotels. But what it lacked in luxury it more than made up for in charm; the dining-room was run with that old-world courtesy that was usually lacking nowadays.

'It's very nice.' She laid the damask napkin lightly across her lap as they were served their soup.

'So this is what it's like to be seen with a famous authoress,' Hawk remarked suddenly.

Leonie followed his gaze as he looked pointedly around the room. Not all the twenty tables were full in the large dining-room, but at the ones that were several people kept shooting curious looks their way.

Humour lightened her eyes as she leant slightly across the table to whisper conspiratorially, 'I think it's probably more a case of them speculating what you did to me to merit my punching you in the mouth!'

He put his fingers up to his mouth to hide the bruising. 'Witch,' he murmured.

He made her feel beautiful and bewitching. And he also made her fear both feelings.

His hand suddenly covered hers as it rested on the table-top. 'Don't let the laughter die out of your eyes,' he pleaded huskily. 'I've waited a long time to see it back there.'

It had been a long time since Leonie had allowed herself the luxury of laughter, and Hawk's intensity made her tremble slightly. She couldn't let him past her defences.

She pointedly removed her hand from beneath his. 'The soup is delicious, isn't it?' she remarked casually, putting another spoonful in her mouth.

She smiled at the waiter as he whisked away their soup bowls before serving them their main course. 'Your assistant didn't look too happy today.' She looked up with a frown once the waiter had departed back to the kitchen.

Hawk's hand faltered slightly as he lifted his wine-glass to his lips, taking a sip of the golden liquid before answering her. 'Believe me,' he said with a sigh, 'it hasn't only been today.'

'*Did* he and Stephen argue last night?' she frowned, remembering how embarrassed Stephen had been this afternoon when he had apologised to her for his behaviour during the night. Never having had a brother she wasn't too sure how a man of Stephen's age would react to an argument with his father; Hal certainly wasn't a typical twenty-year-old, so his responses to Hawk were no example to go by!

Hawk's mouth twisted. 'Neither of them is talking. To me, at least,' he added ruefully. 'Did Stephen say anything to you today?'

Leonie shrugged. 'Well, he apologised, if that's what you mean. He also said he thought it might be better if he stayed in London until the wedding. I assured him it wasn't necessary.'

'And?' Hawk frowned.

'And I think he feels embarrassed about what happened last night,' she dismissed.

His mouth was grim. 'He damn well ought to feel embarrassed!'

Leonie gave him a chiding look. 'Haven't you ever had a little too much to drink and done something stupid?'

'I drink wine with a meal, and the occasional whisky socially, but if I intend getting drunk I drink alone,' he bit out.

She gave him a searching look. Yes, she could see him as a man who went off to be alone if he intended losing any of his self-control. 'Maybe Stephen didn't intend getting drunk,' she excused. 'It just worked out that way.'

'Because of Jake,' he nodded. 'Now *he* does seem to be a classic case for a mid-life crisis,' he drawled, his eyes mocking.

Had she ever arrogantly assumed that was this man's trouble concerning Hal's relationship with Laura? She had obviously known nothing about him at the time; nothing as trivial as reaching forty would disturb him!

'After sixteen years as my assistant and friend he's decided he wants a change,' Hawk continued hardly. 'That he needs something more in his life.'

Leonie shrugged. 'Maybe he does. And the way the two of you live at the moment isn't conducive to having a wife and family.'

He gave her a penetrating look. 'That's all going to change very soon. It's already changing,' he added as she went to protest. 'I'm going to settle here in England. And any travelling I do in future will be kept to a minimum, especially once Holly starts school and the two of you won't be able to accompany me; I missed out on too much of Hal's childhood to make the same mistakes with our daughter.'

Our daughter. Such a simple phrase, and yet it bound them together in a way she could never cope with. 'I'm sure Holly will appreciate that.

And it would be nice if the two of you settled in England so that I could see her occasionally.'

His mouth tightened. 'You'll be seeing her every day—whether you marry me or not we're all going to stay right here in the same house!'

Leonie shook her head. 'You can't just move in and stay for ever.'

'Let's not argue about this now,' he dismissed firmly. 'We're out on our first date together, the last thing I want to do is argue with you.'

And it could be the only way she could keep him at a distance! She knew what he was doing by talking about his problem over Jake, could feel the tentacles of involvement tightening about her. Hawk was an astute man; he would know all there was to know about Leonie Spencer if she weren't more careful.

'Do you often argue with your cats?' he added with amusement.

She shrugged. 'Why not? Usually they listen without arguing back. Although Pop can be a bit reproving at times, but that's probably because he's a male.'

'Ooh, low blow!' Hawk chided teasingly. 'I can't imagine conversing with a cat,' he added derisively.

'Didn't you ever have a pet as a child?' Leonie asked disbelievingly.

He shook his head. 'My dad said it wasn't fair when I was away at school most of the time. But my mother did buy me one of those little goldfish in a bowl that I had for sixteen years. Although I remember that wasn't much fun to talk to,' he dismissed dryly.

'You had one of those tiny goldfish for *sixteen*

years?' She had had some too as a small child, and they had never lived more than a couple of years.

He nodded. 'His name was Boris. Actually,' he smiled, 'it was about six different goldfish. When they died my mother used to replace them without telling me, so that I wouldn't be upset. She finally stopped replacing them when I went to college.'

It felt strange to imagine Hawk as a child, to think of his mother loving him enough to want to protect him from the death of the only pet he was allowed to have. It sounded as if, for all his parents were wealthy, Hawk had had a lonely childhood, and his mother had done her best to change that. She felt strangely like crying.

'I didn't get wise until the second replacement,' Hawk grinned. 'Then I noticed it seemed to have shrunk slightly. For days I stared at it expecting it to get even smaller, but it just started getting bigger,' he revealed disappointedly. 'After that I was wise to my mother's tricks. Although I kept hoping she'd make a mistake and get me something more interesting, like a piranha!'

His childhood might have been lonely, but he had been a typical ghoulish little boy! 'You never told your mother you knew about the changed goldfish?'

'I couldn't.' His grin deepened. 'You see, my dad thought this goldfish was amazing—he told everyone who came to the house about this little goldfish that I'd had for years. If either my mother or I had ever acknowledged to each other that we knew it wasn't the same goldfish we would have had to tell my father too! He was very upset when the last one finally died, said he'd never have another one in the house as it could never replace Boris!' Hawk chuckled, suddenly looking very boyish.

Leonie smiled too. 'I think it's very sweet.'

'Parents are like that, aren't they?' he shrugged. 'I'm sure your parents were just as wonderful. They would have had to have been to have produced two such lovely daughters,' he added seriously.

Leonie's humour died too. 'They were—very special,' she acknowledged abruptly. 'They were killed in a car crash.'

'That's tough,' he sympathised. 'My own parents were killed in a freak light-plane crash.'

'I'm sorry,' she murmured, looking down at her plate.

He shrugged. 'I was twenty-six at the time. How old were you and Laura?' His eyes were narrowed.

'Ten,' she bit out, pushing her plate away uninterestedly.

Hawk frowned. 'What happened to you after that?'

'We were brought up by—an aunt,' she dismissed, avoiding his eyes.

'Was she nice?' he probed softly.

'Very,' Leonie nodded abruptly. 'I don't think I want any dessert, do you?' she added briskly.

Hawk shrugged. 'I can't say I have a sweet tooth, no. Leonie, I haven't upset you, have I?' he sighed regretfully. 'You have to know that's the last thing I wanted to do. The subject of parents just came up, and I——'

'You haven't upset me,' she assured him lightly. 'But it is getting late——'

'I *have* upset you,' he said heavily. 'Hell, you

have to know that's the last thing I wanted to happen tonight!'

Her mouth quirked. 'What was the first thing?' she taunted.

His eyes darkened appreciatively. 'If I told you the thoughts that ran through my mind when I walked into your room earlier you'd probably consider having me locked away!'

Leonie had been able to guess at most of his thoughts, and for the briefest of moments, as she gazed at the caged savagery of him in the formal evening suit, she had felt the same way!

As she raised her head to answer him her attention was caught, and held, by someone watching them from the bar outside the dining-room.

She was doing her best to smooth over the awkwardness he had introduced into the conversation, but the paleness of her cheeks told him she wasn't really succeeding.

He hadn't realised that the subject of her parents was such a sensitive one. Even if he had he might still have brought it up, he needed to know everything there was about Leonie if he were to stand a chance of persuading her to love him in return.

The evening hadn't been a complete failure at least. They had learnt a little more about each other, had even laughed together. It was more than he had hoped for after bulldozing her into coming out with him in the first place.

'Not going to ask, hmm?' Hawk teased lightly. 'Probably a wise decision!' He stood up to pull back her chair for her, bending forward slightly more than he needed to as the softness of her perfume enticed him closer, only just resisting the impulse to taste her creamy throat, straightening with effort.

She didn't resist as he put his arm about her waist to guide her out of the restaurant, and he took full advantage of her closeness as his hand curved possessively about her hip.

'Would you like to have coffee out here?' His gaze flickered over the almost deserted bar. Several of the people from the dining-room had taken advantage of the more relaxed atmosphere out here to have their coffee, and half a dozen men were standing at the bar. And one of those men was Jake!

'I'd rather leave,' Leonie refused stiltedly.

Hawk turned back to her frowningly, having forgotten his own question as he watched Jake drink whisky as if it were water; Jake didn't normally drink at all! 'Do you mind if we say hello to Jake?' he prompted gruffly.

Her startled gaze flew to the bar before she nodded abruptly. 'Of course. Would you rather I waited outside for you in the car?'

There was more of a chance that Jake wouldn't make a scene in front of Leonie. 'I'll just say a quick hello,' he assured her, steering her towards the other man. 'Jake,' he greeted abruptly.

His friend turned sharply, almost knocking over the fresh glass of whisky that had been placed in front of him. 'Hawk,' he greeted unwelcomingly. 'Mrs Spencer,' he added more politely.

Jake wasn't too drunk to know Hawk wouldn't stand for any rudeness to Leonie! Although Leonie seemed very tense about the whole meeting; he could feel the tautness of her body against his. Maybe this hadn't been such a good idea after all.

'I just wanted to tell you we agreed with your opinion about the food here,' he dismissed. 'We'll see you in the morning,' he added lightly.

Jake nodded abruptly, turning back to his contemplation of the bottom of his whisky glass. Damn it, he didn't care whether Jake wanted to talk or not, he wasn't going to let the other man destroy himself in this way! There had to be something he could do to ease whatever was bothering Jake, some way he could help him through this crisis. God, it was what friends were for!

'I'm sorry about that,' he sighed as he drove them both back to the house. 'He's usually a really friendly guy, a good friend.'

'We all have our off days,' Leonie dismissed abruptly.

Hell, here he was worrying about Jake, when there was nothing he could do to help the other man until tomorrow, when right now Leonie was slipping away from him again. He could feel it as suddenly as if she had closed a door in his face!

'I enjoyed tonight, Leonie,' he told her huskily, giving her a sideways glance, sure he could see a slight blush on her cheeks.

What he would give for them to be married, for them to be going home together to look in on Holly as she slept before slowly making their way to the bedroom they shared so that they could make love. There was only one thing wrong with that fantasy; he could never *slowly* make his way anywhere if there was the promise of making love to Leonie at the end of it!

'It was—very nice,' she returned politely.

She was slipping further and further away from him! 'Can we do it again tomorrow?' he prompted harshly.

Her mouth twisted. 'June will think you don't like her cooking if we keep going out for dinner.'

He wanted to say 'damn June' *and* what she thought, but he knew Leonie wouldn't appreciate his sentiments. 'Maybe we could go out for a drive after dinner?' he suggested lightly.

'Hawk, I know what you're doing, but——'

'Then why won't you try and meet me even halfway?' he demanded impatiently. 'I'm trying my best with you, Leonie, taking things slowly, letting you get to know me. But you have to give me a chance!' He knew he sounded like a little boy being denied something he badly wanted, but that was how Leonie made him feel, as vulnerable and uncertain as a child! Could he be blamed for occasionally rebelling against that unfamiliar feeling?

'Hawk, if I were to ask you to just hold me I don't want you to expect any more than that.' Her voice broke emotionally. 'I just need to be held. Is that a crime?' she cried out. 'Sometimes I just need someone to hold me, Hawk,' she choked.

He could see by the moonlight that her cheeks were wet with tears, swearing under his breath as he pulled the car over to the side of the road, switching the engine off abruptly to pull Leonie hard against him. He just wanted to hold this witchchild in his arms for ever, to drive out the pain that could make her shake against him the way that she was. Her hands clutched at him, moving spasmodically against his back, her face buried against his chest. He could feel her tears wetting the fabric of his shirt.

Had he done this to her? When he had meant never to hurt her again, had he done *this* to her? Self-disgust made his arms tighten about her protectively. He would protect her from himself if necessary!

She shuddered against him as she fought to regain control. 'I'm sorry,' she sniffed. 'I—I think the outing tonight must have tired me more than I realised,' she excused as she moved firmly out of his arms.

He wanted to continue to hold her, but he could tell by the vulnerability in her pained eyes that she needed to be apart from him for the moment, that she regretted her moment of weakness. But she had turned to him for comfort, and surely if he had been the one to make her unhappy she wouldn't have done that? Maybe he was clutching at straws during a flood, but if ever there was a time he wanted to believe in miracles it was right now!

'Probably,' he accepted, giving her a meaningless smile of reassurance. 'I'll get you home so that you can get to bed.'

She nodded, turning away from him.

'Rest tomorrow, hm?' he encouraged after they had entered the house and he had locked up for the night.

Leonie shook her head. 'I thought I might start work on the last chapters of .our latest book tomorrow.'

He had more sense than to forbid her to go anywhere near work until she was feeling stronger! 'If you're feeling that much better maybe we could go out for our drive in the afternoon?' A morning's work was enough for her to start with!

She gave a slight smile. 'Shouldn't *you* be working in the afternoon?'

Hawk grinned. 'One of the perks of being the boss; I get to take time off when I want it.'

'My boss at the moment is a terrible tyrant,' she taunted. 'His demands for the finished manuscript are getting pretty desperate.'

'Why don't you tell him——You mean me,' he realised with a groan, having forgotten all about the Winnie Cooper television series and the book that should come out while it was still being televised during the winter. 'Are you going to get mad if I say I'll have a word with your publisher about being so pushy?' he grimaced.

Leonie's mouth quirked. 'Probably,' she acknowledged dryly.

He shrugged. 'That's what I thought you would say. Just don't work too hard, okay?' he prompted gently.

'I'm not sure I'll do any at all,' she sighed. 'I seem to have lost my enthusiasm for writing since Holly's birth.'

'Talking of our daughter, shall we go and say goodnight to her?' he encouraged huskily.

For a moment she looked undecided, then she nodded slow agreement, her eyes widely pleading as she looked up at him. 'I don't want you to come to my room tonight,' she told him firmly, her breathing ragged.

He enjoyed those times with her during the silence of the night, feeling as if they shared a unique experience during that time. But they had come quite a long way tonight, and he didn't want to spoil it now with his selfishness. And it was selfish to want to lie in her arms again.

He had never shared anything like this feeling with another woman, never felt that she was all things to him, lover, friend, mother, the woman he loved. But there would be other times when he would share that with Leonie, he was sure of it; he just had to back off now and give her a little room to breathe.

'Okay,' he agreed lightly, taking hold of her hand. 'Let's go and say goodnight to our daughter.'

A soft lamp glowed in the nursery as they stood beside the cot and looked down at Holly as she slept. Tonight she wore a pink sleeping-suit, and it gave her cheeks a peachy tint, making her hair look more golden than ever. As she lay on her tummy her hands were splayed out beside her head, golden lashes fanning her cheeks, her tiny mouth slightly open as she breathed. The way she was lying, her little bottom slightly elevated, Hawk had the feeling she would eventually sleep with her bottom high in the air, the way that her brother had when he was a baby.

How close he had come to losing both this adorable baby and the woman who was her mother! When he had telephoned the doctor and spoken to him about the birth the other man had been quite open with him about the fact that Holly had nearly suffocated before she was even born, and that Leonie had been so ill afterwards they had given up hope of her coming out of it. He had claimed that only a very strong lady could have survived that, and it was that strength that Hawk was relying on to eventually bring her into his arms where she belonged.

For the moment they were sharing this closeness with Holly, and their pride in their daughter was reflected in their eyes as they watched her sleep, sharing a smile of intimacy as Holly gave a windy smile in her sleep.

The pity of it was that once they left the warmth of this bedroom they were going to go to their separate rooms, and not together as he would have wished.

But half a fantasy had to be better than no fantasy at all!

CHAPTER EIGHT

LEONIE sighed as she put the portable typewriter down on the grass beside her, only having typed half a page the whole morning. Getting Winnie into one scrape after another didn't seem very important when her own life was in such a turmoil.

She shouldn't have let Hawk kiss her goodnight; she should have calmly parted from him at her bedroom door. Instead he had pulled her gently into his arms, and her defences had once again crumpled. It had only been his word that he wouldn't enter her room that had saved her.

She hadn't slept well after that, had already been awake when she heard Holly's call to be fed, lingering over holding her daughter, even though the baby had long fallen back to sleep. If she hadn't continued to hold Holly she was sure she would have gone to Hawk's room!

She deeply regretted breaking down in front of him the night before; she hadn't cried like that in a very long time. To his credit he hadn't pressed for an explanation. Even if he had she couldn't have given him one.

'Who is he, Leonie?'

She stiffened at the sound of that voice, taking her time about turning to face him, having been expecting him after last night.

'Doesn't he mind about your little bastard?'

Leonie's head went back sharply at the taunt,

her angry gaze narrowing on the man who had once been her husband. He was as handsome as ever, over-long blond hair swept back in a deliberately casual style, warm brown eyes hiding a multitude of sins, tall and lithe in fitted denims and an open-necked blue shirt.

'Holly is not a bastard, Michael,' she snapped.

'Oh, forgive me,' he sneered, moving away from his leaning position against the oak tree that stood in the middle of the big garden. 'Your love-child!' he amended derisively.

That description hardly fitted Holly either, but Holly *was* loved. 'What do you want?' she demanded harshly.

'You didn't answer my question.' He went down on his haunches beside Holly as she lay awake on a blanket beneath the sun-umbrella. 'Who——'

'Don't touch her!' she ordered as he would have put out a finger for Holly to touch. 'Don't ever touch her,' she repeated through gritted teeth, sitting on the edge of her lounger.

Michael was slow to remove his hand, his gaze challenging. 'Do you let him touch her?' he taunted.

Oh, how she would love to wipe the sneer from his lips by telling him that Hawk had a perfect right to touch *his own daughter*! But she wouldn't put a weapon like that into Michael's hands; she knew he was perfectly capable of using it, in any way that he thought would benefit himself.

'I asked what you wanted, Michael?' she prompted stiffly.

He straightened, strolling over to sit down beside her on the lounger. 'You don't sound pleased to see me,' he drawled in a hurt voice.

Her eyes flashed deeply green. 'I'm not!'

He shrugged. 'You knew I'd come after I saw you with him last night.'

Yes, she had known as soon as she saw Michael at the bar of the hotel last night that she could expect a visit from him very soon.

She had felt ill when she looked up and saw him standing there watching her; she had wondered just how long he had been doing so, feeling sick at the thought of him spying on her. *Michael* had been the reason she broke down in Hawk's arms the way she did. Just when she thought he had finally left her life he would appear again and totally destroy her peace of mind. Like now.

'What are you doing in Claymont?' she demanded.

'Visiting,' he drawled. 'You,' he added mockingly.

Her eyes widened. 'You're the last person I'd want to visit me!' she scorned, standing up just so that she could move away from him, hating to be anywhere near him after what he had done to her.

'The money was late last month, Leonie.' His eyes were narrowed. 'I came to warn you not to let it happen again.'

'I'm very sorry,' she snapped. 'I was giving birth to my daughter at the time!'

His gaze flickered coldly over Holly as she gurgled to herself. 'Were you so desperate for a kid that you finally went to bed with some man who won't even marry you to get one!'

'Oh, he would marry me, Michael,' she scorned. 'Tomorrow probably, if I were agreeable. But after having you for my husband I've found little about marriage to endear it to me!' She held her breath, knowing she shouldn't have let her temper get the better of her; with Michael that was never a wise thing to do.

His face twisted with anger. 'Why, you little——'

'Leonie, is this guy bothering you?' cut in a smoothly *dangerous* voice.

She turned sharply to face Jake, wondering just how much of her conversation with Michael he had overheard; enough to consider she needed rescuing, obviously! 'He's just——'

'Another one, Leonie?' jeered Michael, recovering well from the surprise of having someone interrupt him when he had been about to launch on one of his insulting tirades. 'Considering you're the original Ice Maiden I'm not sure how you're managing to keep them interested!' He looked at her contemptuously.

Leonie could sense Jake's burning anger, could feel the tension emanating from him. And remembering his aggression towards Hawk last night when he had merely said hello, she didn't want any more fights in her presence! 'I——' she began.

Jake answered him softly. 'Speaking from personal experience, I think there's nothing in the least icy about Leonie,' he drawled challengingly.

She closed her eyes, hoping this was all just a nightmare, but knowing, as she heard Holly gurgle from the comfort of her blanket, that it was all very real.

She had told Michael never to come here again; not even Laura knew of the arrangement she had with him. It was nice, very nice of Jake to defend her in this way, but——

'I know you, don't I?' Michael looked frowningly at the other man. 'My God, you were at the hotel last night!' he suddenly realised with a knowing smile.

The fact that Michael had been there too obviously came as a surprise to Jake, but considering his morose mood the evening before it wasn't surprising he hadn't been aware of the people around him!

'Yes,' he challenged slowly. 'And what were you doing there—spying on Leonie?'

Michael's mouth twisted. 'Hardly,' he sneered. 'Tell him, Leonie, I have no reason to spy on you, because I know everything about your life that I need to know.'

She could feel Jake's questioning gaze on her, and her head was high as she turned to meet that gaze. 'Michael is my ex-husband——'

'And as far as I'm concerned that gives him no right to come around here whenever he feels like it,' growled Jake, hands clenched at his sides. 'Get the hell out of here, Spencer, before I throw you out,' he warned Michael softly. 'And don't come upsetting Leonie again!'

Michael arched mocking brows. 'Is this one the father of your brat, Leonie?' he taunted.

'He——'

'Maybe you didn't hear me, Spencer,' Jake cut in softly. 'In the area of New York I come from we only issue a warning once!'

'But I haven't said hello to the baby yet.' Even as he spoke Michael moved to pick Holly up, looking down at her with distaste as she squirmed against his clumsy hold on her.

'Michael!' screamed Leonie, moving quickly towards him.

He turned with Holly held challengingly in his arms. 'Something wrong, Leonie?' he taunted.

'Put the baby down, Spencer,' Jake instructed quietly.

Michael arched questioning brows. 'Are you sure you aren't the father?' he mocked.

'Believe me,' grated Jake, tensed to leap at the other man, 'I'm a pussycat compared to Holly's father!'

Leonie's gaze was riveted on Holly, on her beloved daughter. It would only take Michael to calmly remove his hands, an act she knew he was more than capable of, and her beautiful baby would fall to the grass, doing heaven knew what injury to her tiny body.

'Really?' Michael looked down consideringly at the baby he held so casually. 'Then it must have been the tough-looking bastard she was with last night.'

'Hawk's been called milder names than that and men have lived to regret it,' Jake bit out icily. 'Now put the baby down, damn it!'

'Hawk,' Michael repeated consideringly. 'Unusual name,' he drawled.

Jake's eyes were narrowed to cold blue slits. 'He's an unusual man. And he's especially protective where Leonie and his daughter are concerned.'

'Hm,' murmured Michael unconcernedly, looking down at Holly again as she stared up at him with wide blue eyes. 'I suppose as babies go she isn't as ugly as most.'

Jake put out a restraining hand as Leonie took another step forward. 'You have precisely two seconds to put Holly down and then I'm going to deal with you in a way you'll find extremely painful. You understand?' he threatened.

'Of course,' the other man drawled. 'Here,' he dropped Holly into Jake's arms. 'I'll be in touch, Leonie,' he told her hardly, and disappeared through the hedge out on to the road.

Leonie didn't doubt that he meant exactly what he said, but for the moment she was too concerned with reassuring her daughter that she was safe, cuddling her protectively as she rained kisses over her soft cheeks. The baby let out a protesting yell at her exuberance.

She turned to give Jake a rueful smile, but he still stood as tensely as he had when she had taken the baby from him seconds ago, his narrowed gaze turned towards the road where Michael's car could be heard pulling away.

'Jake?' she prompted.

He drew in a ragged breath, relaxing with effort, his gaze softening as he moved to touch one of Holly's flailing hands.

And then Leonie remembered what he had said about the baby's father. He *knew* that man was Hawk. Close as the two men had been in the past, she couldn't believe Hawk had confided Holly's parentage to the other man.

'She's exactly like Hal was until he was about six or seven when his hair became darker and the baby plumpness left him altogether,' Jake supplied softly.

She sighed. 'Everyone seems to be able to guess that she's a Sinclair.'

'Not everyone,' he shook his head, his gaze warm. 'I only just remember Hal looking like this myself. Anyway, what difference does it make—you're going to let Hawk take her away with him when he goes, aren't you?' He shrugged dismissively.

Leonie's arms tightened about the baby. When Holly was first born she had been too ill to take care of her, and then even when she was well enough to bring the baby home she had shared Holly's care with Laura, knowing she couldn't become attached to the baby when Hawk would one day come to claim her. At the time she had welcomed that knowledge, holding herself aloof from Holly because she knew she couldn't keep her. But just now, when Michael had held Holly and threatened to harm her, she had known she couldn't give up her daughter, that she loved her too much.

Oh God, what did she do now!

'You know that he's dangerous, don't you?' Jake remarked at her silence.

She blinked. 'Hawk?'

'Spencer,' he corrected harshly.

Leonie gave a heavy sigh. 'I discovered that only a month after we were married and he lost his temper because a horse he'd bet on didn't win.'

Jake's eyes narrowed. 'What happened?'

She shuddered as she remembered Michael's temper, his violence. But they were memories that would remain locked inside her, with those other memories that she had buried so far back in her mind that to take them out and look at them would leave her an emotional wreck.

'He was—naturally upset,' she dismissed, straightening Holly's sun-suit unnecessarily.

'How upset?' Jake persisted harshly.

'Very.' She turned away. 'Thank you for— helping me just now,' she said lightly. 'Michael can be very overbearing.'

'I mean it, Leonie,' he told her firmly. 'Spencer is a dangerous man. Hawk isn't going to like him around his daughter again.'

She nodded. 'I'll make sure he doesn't come here again.'

'Can you do that?' He looked at her closely.

'Yes,' she nodded abruptly.

'How?'

She drew herself up to her full five feet in height, wishing she were taller and more imposing. She felt like a sparrow challenging an eagle; a hawk would be too reminiscent of the man who constantly disturbed her!

'Just accept that I can,' she snapped. 'And I would appreciate your not mentioning this to Hawk,' she added uncertainly.

Jake shook his head. 'I'm sorry, but I can't do that. Spencer *is* a dangerous man, and Hawk is likely to kill *me* if I keep my mouth shut and something happened to either you or Holly.'

'Nothing will happen,' she assured him, knowing exactly how to keep Michael happy—and away from her home!

'Nevertheless . . .' murmured Jake regretfully.

'Oh, all right,' she snapped. 'Tell your precious Hawk. But you're interfering in something that you don't understand.'

'I understand men like Spencer only too well,' he bit out grimly. 'I may have been travelling with Hawk for the last sixteen years, but I haven't forgotten my childhood in New York—or the scum that exist only to cause others pain. Spencer is a man like that.'

Leonie gave an unsteady laugh. 'I wish I'd had the benefit of your judgement five years ago!'

His expression softened. 'Let Hawk deal with it, Leonie,' he encouraged gently. 'He's more than capable, believe me.'

She was well aware of Hawk's capabilities; she knew that he would protect what he considered his own, no matter what the cost. For herself she didn't care about Michael, there was nothing else he could do to her that he hadn't already done, but today he had threatened Holly, and Hawk had a right to protect their daughter. God, she wanted him to keep Holly safe!

'I'll talk to him,' she nodded slowly. 'I will,' she promised Jake as he still looked uncertain. 'You're a very nice man, Jake Colter,' she smiled at him shyly.

'I wish,' he rasped, his eyes bleak.

'Join us for dinner tonight,' she invited impulsively, her eyes warm.

'I——'

'Please,' she encouraged softly.

His mouth twisted ruefully. 'No wonder Hawk's obsessed with you, if you wheedle around him this way!'

Obsessed? She couldn't imagine Hawk obsessed with anything, let alone a woman. He merely wanted her, as the mother of his child and as his wife.

'Then you will come to dinner?' she persisted lightly.

'I'll come,' Jake nodded wryly.

'Good,' she beamed her pleasure.

He shook his head. 'Poor Hawk, I bet he never knew what hit him!' he murmured.

'I thought you had "personal experience" of what had hit him,' she reminded him bitterly.

He frowned. 'I only said that for Spencer's benefit; Hawk has never discussed your relationship with me,' he confessed.

Some of the tension left her. 'It's time for Holly's next feed,' she excused. 'I'll see you at dinner. Perhaps you'd like to bring Miss Ames with you?' she suggested. 'Pleasant as the hotel is, the two of you must get bored alone there in the evenings. Unless . . .?' She gave him a sharp look, wondering if she had spoken out of turn. Perhaps Sarah Ames and Jake *liked* to be alone!

Jake smiled at her chagrin. 'Sarah is *Mrs* Ames, although she's been divorced for several years now. And after working together for almost eleven years I think we would have realised by now if we were attracted to each other,' he added dryly. 'We aren't,' he mocked.

'I'm sorry.' Leonie gave an uncomfortable grimace.

'I'm not,' Jake grinned. 'It would be hell working so closely with a woman I wanted in my bed at night. Hawk feels the same way,' he added softly. 'Not that we haven't both taken her out in the past, but purely for business reasons. And Hawk needed a platonic partner like that a lot the last nine months. In case you're interested,' he drawled.

Colour warmed Leonie's cheeks as she remembered the thoughts she had had about Hawk and his secretary when she had first met the other woman. But surely she could be forgiven for thinking something like that; Sarah Ames *was* a very beautiful woman.

Jake smiled. 'I always thought a woman with freckles must look damned unattractive when she blushed—you've just proved me completely wrong; you look cuter than ever!'

Hawk had been watching them together for the last five minutes; he had seen Jake bend gently over the baby as Leonie held her in her arms, had watched as they talked softly together, had seen Jake make Leonie laugh, had watched as she made him smile in return!

He hadn't meant to spy on them; he had only glanced casually out of the study window, but had been unable to look away when he saw Leonie and Jake together.

After weeks of Jake striding about the place looking grim Leonie had been able to make him smile! He didn't need to ask how, she only had to be herself to entice any man to fall in love with her.

But not Jake, damn it. Over the years he and Jake had often been attracted to the same woman, but neither of them had ever cared enough to actually argue about it, one of them always bowing out and leaving the way clear for the other. He couldn't do that with Leonie, and Jake *had* to be aware of that.

If he wasn't then it was time he was *made* aware!

'Don't look so worried, Hawk.' Sarah came to stand at his side, following his gaze out of the window. 'I'm sure Jake is just being polite to Mrs Spencer.'

He turned to her sharply. 'What the hell's that supposed to mean?' he rasped.

Sarah shrugged. 'Divorce is a difficult thing for a woman to get through. I know I would have fallen apart if it hadn't been for your support during mine.'

He relaxed slightly. 'You've never fallen apart in your life,' he joked.

'Perhaps not,' she conceded dryly. 'But I'm sure you needn't worry about Jake hurting Hal's future sister-in-law; she's bound to be very wary after the breakdown of her first marriage. I know I was,' she grimaced.

'She isn't interested in Jake, damn it!' he cried.

Sarah gave him a puzzled look for his vehemence. 'I know. I just said that.'

'Sorry,' he gave an impatient frown, shrugging. 'Maybe I need a break.'

Her expression brightened. 'How about lunch? There are some lovely country pubs in the area. We could just relax and talk.'

He glanced back out of the window as Leonie began to walk back towards the house. 'I'll take a raincheck on lunch, Sarah,' he told her absently. 'But I am taking the afternoon off,' he murmured softly, his gaze still on Leonie.

CHAPTER NINE

SHE SHOULD tell him about Michael now, should explain, before Jake did.

But it was a long time since Leonie had felt so at peace, sitting there on a blanket on the ground beneath the willow tree that hung over the side of the meandering river, the picnic basket open on the blanket and their lunch spread out upon it.

Hawk had invited her out on a picnic lunch, and although she had known it would be more sensible to refuse, she hadn't been able to resist the idea. And with Holly fast asleep in her cot after her own lunch just the two of them had set out.

June had surpassed herself with the food she had provided, even including a bottle of chilled wine for them to enjoy with the fried chicken.

Now only the debris from the meal was left, and the two of them lay back on the blanket, too full to move a muscle. She should tell Hawk about Michael now, Leonie knew, but somehow she didn't want to spoil the beauty of the afternoon.

She glanced at Hawk as he lay beside her, his eyes closed against the glare of the sun. He was the father of her child, a child she was finding it increasingly difficult to think about giving up. But her alternative was to marry this man. What sort of husband would he make?

'Tell me about Amy,' she encouraged before she could stop herself.

He stiffened, opening one eye to glance at her, then turning away again as he put his hands up behind his head to rest back against them.

Why had she asked him that? Even if his marriage to Amy had been a success, it didn't mean that any relationship *they* entered into would meet the same fate!

'She was tall and blonde, beautiful, with a wicked sense of humour.' He smiled at the memory.

Leonie waited, knowing there had to be more than that, wanting to know about their marriage.

'We were both a little spoilt.' He glanced at Leonie, as if expecting her to dispute the 'little'. She didn't. He smiled, closing his eyes again. 'We always had fun together, even when Hal put in an appearance exactly nine months after our honeymoon! When Amy's parents questioned the prudence of that she told them to be grateful it wasn't six, seven, or eight months,' he grinned. 'They never said another word about Hal being born too soon after we were married!'

'I can imagine,' Leonie said dryly.

He shrugged. 'It wouldn't have bothered us when he was born—we wanted him. I guess we were children playing at being parents. Whatever. It seemed to work out okay. When Hal started kindergarten Amy began working part-time—she'd always been interested in interior design. She'd only been at work for a week when some kid high on drugs decided it might be nice to drive on the wrong side of the road for a while, just for the hell of it, you understand,' he bit out harshly. 'He survived the crash, Amy didn't,' he supplied abruptly.

Leonie drew in a harsh breath. 'I'm sorry.'

'So am I; she was a beautiful woman.' Hawk shrugged. 'But I didn't really tell you about her, did I?' he realised. 'She was witty, vivacious—we were good friends as well as lovers.'

And he had loved the other woman very much, it was there in every word he spoke about her. How could he want to settle for less in a second marriage?

He suddenly rolled over, leaning on his elbows to look down at her. 'Now do you want to hear about Leonie?' he prompted huskily.

He was so close she daren't move, his arm pressed lightly against hers, the warmth of his breath lightly fanning her cheek.

She gave a nervous smile. 'I don't think——'

'I was in love with Amy at an age when I looked for idealism in everything, when I believed there was only one way to love.' Hawk spoke thoughtfully, but his gaze was fixed compellingly on hers. 'If Amy had lived I'm sure we would still be together,' he said without hesitation. 'That we would still have been happy together when we were both eighty. But it would have been a love that would have been changed by time, a mellow love, maybe even a love that we took for granted. Losing Amy the way that I did has taught me never to take anything for granted again. She isn't alive to share that love with me when we're both eighty, but I don't think—I'm sure of it!—that she would have begrudged my finding happiness with someone else.' His eyes were narrowed.

'Hawk —'

'We're here so fleetingly, Leonie,' he continued

with feeling. 'If there's more after this I don't know, so we have to accept the life we have now and make the most of it. I want to live the rest of my life with you and Holly.'

She was having difficulty breathing, emotionally moved by his impassioned speech, having difficulty concentrating as he began to speak again.

'I understand your first marriage was lousy,' he rasped. 'I realise that's bound to make you wary about trying again, but you have our child to consider. And I want to take care of Holly. And you,' he added huskily.

'No!' she denied harshly, shaking her head frantically, trying to get up.

Hawk held her down with his arm across her breasts. 'I love our daughter very much,' he grated. 'I love her, and she's going to have both her parents in her life!' he told her firmly. 'Whether you like it or not.'

She couldn't marry this man. He would demand too much from her, *take* too much.

His eyes suddenly darkened. 'Leonie . . .!' He gave a throaty groan.

If he kissed her——

She was lost. Like the very first time he had touched her all those months ago, she became his slave as he began to make love to her.

'Oh God, Leonie!' His mouth devoured hers with desperation, his arms about her as he pulled her up on top of him, one hand cradling the back of her head as he increased the pressure of her mouth against his.

A weak languor claimed her body as his hands impatiently caressed her from thigh to shoulder, groaning his satisfaction as he released the catch to her bra.

'No, Hawk,' she gasped as he would have removed her clothes. 'It's too soon! The baby——'

'Trust me, Leonie.' His big hands cradled either side of her face as he held her gaze with his. 'Trust me,' he repeated huskily.

She was a prisoner of the raw sensuality in his eyes, nodding slow agreement, knowing this man would never physically hurt her, that he had only ever given her pleasure.

He dispensed with her blouse and his shirt completely, the gentle breeze instantly cooling their skin before her nipples nestled against the blazing heat of his chest. The feel of the silken hair against the aching tips made her gasp raggedly.

'You like that?' Hawk lifted her slightly so that the sensitised nubs received the slightest of caresses—almost driving Leonie into a delirium of pleasure. And then he was above her once more, crushing her beneath him as his mouth ravaged hers with a sensual rhythm.

'Open your legs to me, Leonie,' he urged heatedly.

She did so instantly, feeling his weight shift as he settled himself between her thighs, the hardness of him there touching her through the thin barrier of her cotton skirt and lace briefs. And then he began to move, slowly, erotically, in a mime of lovemaking!

His fingers captured, then tugged, on her erect nipples, applying just enough pressure to cause her to cry out as he sensed her need.

Something inside her was building out of control,

a need, an ache, that his sensual movements against her just couldn't assuage. She gave a whimper of desperation.

'All right, love,' he kissed his way down her throat to her breasts. 'It's all right,' he soothed as his tongue traced a moist pattern across both breasts, taking his time drawing one of the painful peaks into the moist haven of his mouth.

It still wasn't enough. She was on fire for him, she needed——Oh God, she needed——

He knew, Hawk knew what she wanted, his mouth abandoning her breasts now as his tongue dipped erotically inside her navel, drawing the skirt and panties out of his way to throw them impatiently to one side. Leonie groaned her frustration as he became suddenly still. And then she knew what had halted him; she could feel his hand tenderly caressing the scar giving birth to Holly had left on her body.

'Tell me she was worth it, Leonie!' he groaned. 'Oh God, tell me you don't regret having borne my child!'

'I don't regret it, Hawk.' She gave a fevered shake of her head. 'Holly was worth it—all of it.'

'Aah!' He briefly closed his eyes in heartfelt satisfaction with her response.

Holly *had* been worth it, she was worth all the pain that was to follow too. Leonie felt she had been privileged to *be* Holly's mother. *Her* daughter. She was finally coming to realise that that was what Holly was, that her daughter was healthy and strong, that she had no reason to fear losing her except to this man. Oh God, the joy of knowing her daughter was healthy after the agony of losing

Daniel the way that she had.

'Marry me, Leonie,' urged Hawk determinedly. 'Marry me, and we can share our wonderful daughter for the rest of our lives.'

She wanted to keep Holly, *had* to keep the beautiful child that was part her and part this man beside her!

'Yes, Hawk,' she gasped, 'I—I'll marry you.'

Relief darkened his eyes, as he moved to cradle each side of her face with his strong hands. 'You won't regret it, Leonie,' he promised gruffly. 'I'm going to make sure you never know another day's unhappiness in your life!'

From any other man it would have been an impossible promise to keep, but she knew Hawk was quite capable of doing everything in his power to make sure that promise was fulfilled.

And then she couldn't think any more as he began to kiss her once again.

He had believed the taste of her breasts was the most erotic experience he had ever known, but as she opened to him completely he knew he was in paradise.

She was so beautiful here, the soft velvet of rose petals moistened with the gentleness of dew. He kissed each of those petals until she flowered beneath his penetration.

He could feel her tension rising now, cupping her tight little bottom to offer her up to him like a beautiful sacrifice, deeper and deeper as her breathing became a fevered rasp and her thighs tightened about him in pleading demand.

The flick of his tongue made her fingers clutch

into the blanket beneath them, and as he moistly laved her flowering bud he could hear the choked sobs in her throat.

She was so close, flowing against him, and although the taste of her was driving him wild, making him long to prolong her pleasure until she was insane with the need for him to give her fulfilment, he also wanted to feel her pulse against him as her desire reached its peak, to know he had given her pleasure and not pain.

She was so hot and moist against him, gasping each time he touched her now, her hips lifting off the blanket to him, pressing harder and harder against his mouth, driving him deeper and deeper, pushing her higher and higher.

And then she couldn't go any higher, as spasms of pleasure drove her against him again and again, convulsing as the heated ache became a molten flow that went on and on for ever.

She found it difficult to look at him, the warm ache that still heated her body reminding her of just how much she had 'trusted' Hawk beneath that willow tree beside the river.

She had never experienced anything like the pleasure he gave her so unselfishly, held against his chest afterwards as he soothed the convulsing of her body down to a tremble. Every time she remembered her abandonment beneath the intimacy of the willow the trembling began again.

Leonie had been completely shattered by the explosions inside her body, and she pressed her thighs together now as she ached there once again.

'Why don't you have a nap?' Hawk turned to

glance at her as he sat behind the wheel of the car driving them back to the house. 'You look tired,' he sympathised.

She was agitated! She felt as if she could sleep for a week, and then still wake up feeling lethargic!

And she had agreed to marry him. She suddenly felt panicked at the thought of being that close to anyone again.

His hand suddenly covered hers as it moved nervously against her thigh. 'We didn't do anything wrong just now, Leonie,' he told her gently. 'We didn't hurt anyone,' he added huskily.

This man hadn't done anything wrong; he had done everything oh, so right. But he was wrong about the pain; *he* must be suffering agonies of unfulfilment. She had wanted to ease his discomfort, but he had insisted he would be all right. He obviously was all right, but the strain hadn't left him.

'All right,' he finally gave a ragged sigh, 'I took unfair advantage of you. I shouldn't——'

'Don't be ridiculous, Hawk,' she cut in sharply. 'You made beautiful love to me.'

'I'm *never* going to apologise for making love to you,' he shook his head firmly. 'I *proposed* to you at a time when your defences were down. You're perfectly at liberty to tell me to go to hell now that—now that——'

'The madness has passed?' she finished dryly.

Hawk sighed. 'I want to marry you, Leonie,' he bit out. 'I want that any way I can get it. But you'll only end up hating me if you feel I've forced you into it,' he acknowledged heavily.

He hadn't forced her into anything, nothing at

all. She had wanted to marry him as surely as she had wanted him to make love to her. Oh yes, she was nervous about being anyone's wife again, she feared the closeness of such a relationship, but she didn't fear either of those things as much as she did being without Holly. She loved her daughter enough to want to give her the best, and that included having *both* her parents.

'I've accepted your proposal, Hawk, and I'll stick by my decision,' she told him firmly. 'Although I do think that perhaps we should wait until Hal and Laura are married before making any announcement ourselves,' she added with a frown.

His brows rose. 'Don't you think we have more reason to be married before them?' he drawled.

'I don't think another week or so is going to make any difference to Holly's legitimacy now, do you?' she said wryly.

'She's a Sinclair, damn it,' scowled Hawk. 'And anyone who casts aspersions on her birth had better remember that!'

She smiled at his protection of their daughter. 'I doubt if you'll let them forget it,' she teased.

He gave a rueful smile. 'I may be a bastard, but no one is going to call my daughter one,' he acknowledged dryly.

Michael had called Holly a bastard. But she didn't feel like talking about Michael just now, not when she had just agreed to marry Hawk.

He should never have agreed to waiting before announcing his claim on her, Hawk thought, although if Jake didn't already know that after the way he had warned the other man off Leonie this morning then he was being decidedly obtuse!

Leonie had been so determined they shouldn't detract from Hal's and Laura's big day by announcing that they were arranging one of their own, and because she had finally agreed to marry him—*some time*—he hadn't pushed the point, secure in the knowledge that she would keep to her word. He hadn't realised that agreeing to that condition would leave him standing impotently by in the background while every other man in the vicinity vied for her attention!

Stephen had taken his father's place at Leonie's side now, the father and son having been avoiding each other studiously since Jake and Sarah had arrived at the house for dinner as Leonie's guests.

He couldn't just stand here nursing this glass of whisky while those two clowns——

'Calm down, Dad,' Hal drawled quietly at his side. 'I can see the smoke starting to come out of your ears!'

Hawk gave his son an impatient scowl. 'Very funny,' he snapped. 'But if Stephen makes her laugh one more time I'll——'

'Come on, Dad,' Hal chided soothingly. 'I for one think it's great that Leonie *is* laughing—no matter who or what's the cause of it!'

Selfish bastard that he was, he wanted all her laughter to be for him. It was what had attracted him to her in the first place, and with its slow return he was falling more and more in love with her. But so was every other man in the room!

'I know you're right,' he told Hal with a sigh. 'I guess I'm just jealous,' he admitted heavily. 'You're in love with Laura; you must know how I feel.'

'Yes,' Hal acknowledged ruefully. 'How did your picnic go this afternoon?'

She agreed to marry me! She's mine! Hawk wanted to shout it from the rooftops, but knowing how angry his little witchchild would be if he did that he wisely kept silent.

He gave the grimace of a smile. 'I moved too fast—as usual.' And he intended 'moving that fast' again, as often as Leonie would let him. Damn the frustration it left him feeling, he just wanted to be close to Leonie. And that was as close as he *could* get for the moment.

Hal shook his head. 'I never thought I'd see the day *you* didn't know how to handle a situation,' he taunted.

'If Leonie were a situation I probably could handle it,' Hawk drawled. 'It's because she's a woman, a very special woman, that I'm in difficulty.'

Hal's expression softened as he watched Laura in conversation with Sarah. 'It's when they're so special you don't mind the occasional uncertainty that goes with loving them.'

Hawk looked sharply at his son. 'You and Laura——'

'Are fine,' Hal assured him firmly, but the smile didn't quite reach his eyes.

Hal was in love with Laura, he was sure of it. But something was obviously worrying his son. Could it have anything to do with that vulnerability he had seen in Laura before she went to meet Hal at the airport two days ago? The Brandon sisters seemed to have depths he and Hal couldn't even guess at.

'What is it, Hal?' he prompted softly. 'I know I was unreasonable about your relationship to start with,' he acknowledged ruefully. 'But I'm certain you and Laura love each other.'

His son smiled. 'Oh, there's no doubt about that.'

'But?' prompted Hawk.

Hal shook his head. 'I can't explain it. There's something——' he broke off.

'Yes?' Hawk demanded again sharply.

The younger man sighed, shrugging. 'It's going to sound stupid,' he grimaced.

'So sound stupid,' Hawk encouraged tensely.

Hal grimaced. 'Laura's wonderful, I love her very much, but——She doesn't argue with me! About anything.'

His father gave a disbelieving laugh. 'Most men would say that's a good thing!'

'Don't patronise me, Dad!' snapped Hal.

Hawk could see Hal was serious about this, that it really did bother him that Laura didn't argue with him. 'Not all women argue, you know, Hal,' he frowned. 'Especially when they're newly engaged. Give it six months or so and——'

'You don't understand,' Hal cut in impatiently.

'Then explain it to me!'

'I told you I can't,' he shook his head.

'You do still want to marry her?' Hawk probed softly. 'Because if you don't it would be kinder——'

'I told you I love her,' his son said harshly. 'She's the only woman I'll ever want to marry. Just forget I mentioned this, Dad,' he dismissed impatiently. 'It's probably nothing, as you said.'

He hadn't exactly said that. He was sure that if Hal thought there was a problem with Laura, enough to have mentioned it to *him*, then something was wrong. But he wasn't sure enough of Leonie yet to start asking her questions about her sister, he was sure *that* would only put her back on the defensive. He would just have to hope Hal could work this out for himself. It might be nothing at all, Hal could just be over-sensitive where the woman he loved was concerned.

He wasn't insensitive to Hal's problem, he just didn't know what the hell to do about it; he was having to tread so softly himself at the moment.

'I'd forgotten what it was like to eat as a family,' Sarah remarked wistfully at his side, Hal having crossed the room to be with Laura now. 'It almost makes me wish I'd stayed married to Paul and we'd had a family of our own.'

Hawk arched mocking brows, knowing that Sarah's marriage to an habitual womaniser had been a disaster from start to finish. 'How much almost?' he derided.

She gave a soft laugh. 'Not much,' she grimaced. 'But I must admit that being here, with the baby up too, makes me feel a little homesick for my own family in the States.'

Holly hadn't wanted to go back to sleep after Leonie had given her a bottle earlier and so he had suggested she join them for a while; the fact that everyone had got to hold his daughter except him made him wish he could just tell them all that she was *his* daughter, and he just wanted to sit and hold her himself.

But he hadn't done anything of the sort. He was enthralled at how much more relaxed Leonie was with the baby tonight. Not that he didn't know why she was, just as he knew why she had agreed to marry him; she had allowed Holly into her heart. He acknowledged heavily that he hadn't been able to get in with her.

'Would you like to take some time off and go see them?' he asked Sarah quietly, still watching Leonie holding Holly as she talked to Jake.

'Heavens, no,' Sarah dismissed ruefully. 'I've never got on with my kid brother, his wife is a pain, and their two brats are spoilt rotten. Besides that, my parents think I'm still ten years old! I only said it makes me *feel* homesick, not that I actually wanted to be with my family. After two days I'd be screaming to be let out!' She grimaced. 'I'd much rather be here with you.'

Hawk laughed softly. 'So that's why you've remained my secretary for the last ten years; it's a good excuse to get away from your family.'

'You guessed it!' She smiled at him.

He returned Sarah's smile, but his attention wandered from the lovely woman at his side as he saw Jake follow Leonie out of the room as she took Holly back to the nursery.

'Did you talk to him about Spencer?'

Leonie straightened from placing the sleeping Holly in her cot, having known this question was coming. 'Not yet,' she dismissed. 'I—The opportunity didn't come up,' she avoided.

Jake frowned. 'He has a right to know your ex-husband is still hanging around.'

She looked at him sharply, wondering if Jake knew Hawk had that right because she had agreed to marry him. Something in Jake's expression told her Hawk hadn't confided in this man.

'I told you I'll tell him,' she said lightly. 'There's plenty of time. Michael won't be back here for a while, at least.' He would never come back here at all if she had her way!

'Leonie, I said I'd let you handle this,' Jake spoke slowly. 'But Spencer worries me——'

'Give me a little more time.' She put her hand imploringly on his arm. 'Hawk and I are just—just starting to understand each other, please don't do anything to spoil that.'

Jake's expression was stony. 'If something happens to you or Holly because I——'

'It won't,' she reassured him hastily. 'I told you, I can handle Michael.'

'Leonie, you *can't* handle him,' he said firmly. 'I doubt if you ever could.'

She sighed as his brows arched pointedly at her blushing cheeks. 'Maybe I couldn't,' she conceded, 'but I can now. Anyway, why should you care what Hawk thinks or feels?' she attacked. 'You're hurting him more by giving in your notice and leaving him after sixteen years than I am not mentioning the fact that my ex-husband occasionally likes to make a pest of himself!'

Jake stiffened, suddenly very distant, although he hadn't moved. 'I don't have any choice,' he said coldly.

'But——'

'I love Hawk as a brother, I always have,' he continued abruptly.

'Then why——'

'Don't ask.' He drew in a ragged breath. 'Just accept that it's better I go.'

'But where will you go? What will you do?' Leonie shook her head in puzzlement.

He gave a harsh laugh. 'Despite the state of employment nowadays, PA's with my experience are still very much in demand. I've already received several job offers that are very tempting.'

'Hawk would double any offer you received from someone else, and you know it!'

'Maybe,' Jake bit out.

'Then——'

'He's given me enough already,' rasped Jake. 'I can't ask him for anything else.' He quietly left the room.

Leonie watched him go with a puzzled frown, turning back with a sigh to feast on the uncomplicated beauty of her daughter as she slept. How untroubled life was at this age, how lacking in emotional pain! She had a feeling Jake wished he could know the same oblivion right now.

To Hawk, watching as Jake finally left the nursery, it seemed he and Leonie had been alone in there for a very long time. If Jake thought he could find one of those 'different things' he wanted to do with his life with Leonie and Holly he was going to be sadly disappointed!

CHAPTER TEN

LEONIE FELT conspicuous sitting alone in the lounge/bar of the Claymont Hotel, but when she had arrived at the hotel half an hour ago and been informed by the receptionist that Mr Spencer had left the hotel mid-morning but was expected back for lunch she had had little choice but to sit and wait for him. Unfortunately the lounge area was also part of the bar in this small hotel, so she sat alone at a table in the corner with a glass of fresh orange juice in front of her as the lunchtime crowd from surrounding businesses began to fill the room.

If Michael didn't arrive back soon she was going to have to leave without seeing him; she couldn't sit in this bar all day waiting for him.

Hawk had invited her out for lunch, but she had told him she was meeting an old friend in town. He hadn't been pleased. He would be even less pleased, she knew, if he were informed that her ex-husband was the supposed 'old friend'!

A friend was something Michael had never been, and it hadn't taken her long to realise she couldn't love the monster he was either. Now that she was going to marry Hawk Michael had to realise he would be wiser, for his own safety, to stay away from her. And Holly. She could still remember her panic of yesterday when Michael had picked Holly up. If he wouldn't agree to leave them alone she would have to go to Hawk and tell him everything.

'Well, well, well!' drawled a mocking voice. 'Become a secret drinker, have you?'

Leonie looked up at Michael unflinchingly, putting her glass down carefully. 'The time to have done that was while I was still married to you,' she snapped.

He raised one brow mockingly as he sat down on the stool opposite her. 'Is it being the mistress of Henry Hawker Sinclair the Second that's suddenly given my little kitten claws?' he taunted.

She could feel the colour leave her cheeks; it hadn't taken him long to find out exactly who 'Hawk' was! 'I'm not his mistress,' she muttered, looking around them uncomfortably. The lounge was full of people munching on the bar-snacks they served out here between twelve and two o'clock.

'Holly is his child,' Michael mocked.

Leonie drew in a ragged breath. 'Could we get out of here?' she said coldly, picking up her bag. 'Go somewhere we can be more private?'

His eyes widened appreciatively. 'Maybe your ice *has* melted a little!'

'What are you doing?' She pulled back as he dragged her towards the staircase.

'Taking you up to my room,' he told her softly. 'It's *very* private up there,' he added suggestively.

Leonie wrenched her arm out of his grasp. 'A walk outside is privacy enough,' she snapped.

He shrugged, following her out into the sunshine, his hands thrust in his trouser pockets. 'So what are *you* doing in Claymont?' he drawled.

'Visiting you,' she said impatiently.

His brows rose. 'You should have called first—

you could have been sitting in that bar all day waiting for me to get back.'

She had come here in the first place on the spur of the moment—she knew Michael had to be dealt with! 'You're here now.' She unzipped her bag, taking out an envelope and holding it out to him. 'This is what you came here for.' She looked at him with dislike. 'Take it and go.'

He ignored the envelope. 'Exactly how many millions do you suppose your rich lover has?' he mused.

She swallowed hard. 'I haven't the least idea— or interest—in how much money Hawk has,' she told him coldly.

'Well, I have,' chided Michael. 'I suppose he could actually be worth *billions*,' he added thoughtfully.

Leonie drew in a ragged breath; she hadn't imagined he would have found out Hawk's identity this quickly. She should have known better; where money was concerned Michael was like a blood-hound, he could always find it if it was there.

Money was one of the reasons he had married her, he had told her shortly after their wedding. She was already earning money from the Winnie Cooper books, more than he was earning as an office worker.

'Don't even think about it, Michael,' she advised wearily. 'Hawk won't be blackmailed.'

'Your friend yesterday gave the impression Sinclair is *very* protective of his mistress and the child your affair has produced,' he taunted.

Leonie sighed. 'He also warned you that Hawk would be a dangerous man to cross. Hawk isn't someone you could bully, Michael,' she warned.

'I didn't think he was,' he mused. 'But I'm sure he wouldn't want the intimate details of his lover's marriage spread across the front page of the newspapers.'

'That's more likely to embarrass *you* than it is me,' she snapped.

His lips quirked. 'Not the way I would tell it!'

She came to an abrupt halt, turning to face him. 'Take what I'm offering you, Michael,' she said softly, holding out the envelope once again. 'And don't be a fool.'

His face darkened angrily. 'The only fool here is you—if you think I'm going to accept the pittance you can give me when Sinclair can give me much more!'

'You really think Hawk would give you anything?' she scorned.

Michael nodded confidently. 'If he cares about you—and I think he does,' he derided. 'And he isn't going to give the money to me; you're going to ask him for it.'

'Me?' she repeated apprehensively. 'I told you, I'm not interested in Hawk's money.'

'But I am,' he drawled softly. 'And I'm sure he could be persuaded to be financially indulgent with the woman who's borne his daughter.' He raised his brows challengingly. 'Or would you rather we all got into a legal battle over your brat's paternity?' he added pleasantly.

Leonie wasn't fooled by the mildness of his tone; she knew just how dangerous the threat was. 'You promised you'd leave Holly alone,' she reminded him sharply.

He shrugged. 'That was before I found out exactly who her father *is*.'

She swallowed hard. 'Hawk could break you,' she choked fiercely.

'But he won't,' Michael dismissed lightly. 'Will he?' he taunted.

Money. That was all that seemed to matter to this man. Never mind that he could be hurting an innocent child with his vicious lies. 'I'll see what I can do.' She turned away.

'In the meantime this will do very nicely . . .' He took the envelope out of her hand. 'I'll call you in a few days,' he smiled confidently before striding back towards his hotel.

Leonie was shaking badly. She always felt ill after an encounter with Michael. She should never have started this, she should have challenged Michael from the first to do his worst. Now it was too late. And it could only get worse once she was actually Hawk's wife.

'Leonie?'

She turned sharply, forcing herself to relax as she faced Stephen Colter. 'Stephen,' she greeted him lightly. 'What are you doing in town?'

He frowned. 'Just looking round. Who was that guy with you just now?'

A flicker of irritation darkened her eyes; did all Hawk's friends protect what was his? And then she chastised herself; Stephen was one of the few people at the house who didn't know she and Holly *were* Hawk's. He was obviously just concerned by the fact that her meeting with Michael seemed to have upset her.

'Just a friend who couldn't make it for lunch,'

she dismissed brightly.

He didn't look convinced, his gaze went in the direction Michael had taken. Then he turned with a dismissive shrug. 'In that case let me offer to be your escort,' he grinned.

'Oh, but——' Why not? Stephen was a likeable enough man, when he wasn't getting drunk after arguing with his father!

He held up his hands defensively. 'I'll behave,' he promised dryly. 'Besides, Dad and I haven't even spoken for a couple of days,' he added with a grimace. 'He still wants me to go back to London to stay until the wedding,' he told her conversationally as they walked along together. 'I know you said it isn't necessary, but having me around just seems to upset him.'

'Oh, I'm sure it isn't that,' she protested. 'He loves you very much, I can tell.'

'Yeah,' Stephen nodded. 'I love him too. But that doesn't mean we have to get along. He has his life to lead and I have mine; and they're totally different.' He shrugged.

Leonie put her arm companionably through the crook of his. 'Let's go and have lunch and you can tell me all about going to college in America,' she encouraged.

He quirked blond brows. 'Did Dad forget to mention that I've dropped out of college?'

What the hell was she doing with Stephen?

Hawk watched from the lounge as Leonie and Stephen arrived back together in her car, scowling as they laughed together as they entered the house. Leonie had gone out to lunch with an 'old friend', she had said, so how had she managed to return with Stephen?

A guilty flush seemed to darken her cheeks as she looked up and saw him standing in the lounge doorway.

'Hiya, Hawk,' Stephen greeted lightly on his way up the stairs. 'Beautiful day.'

Hawk frowned as he watched the young man navigate the stairs, a bedroom door closing seconds later. His censorious gaze returned to Leonie, and he wondered what she had done that could merit that look of apprehension in her eyes.

'Is Stephen drunk again?' he rasped, his hands thrust tensely into his denims pockets.

She shook her head, her hair shimmering like a red-gold flame. 'He only had one beer.'

Hawk's mouth tightened. 'Where?'

'At the restaurant,' she shrugged, giving a nervous smile. 'My friend let me down and so Stephen very kindly offered me lunch instead.'

Was it his imagination, or was her head tilted at a challenging angle? Hell, no, of course it wasn't his imagination; Leonie knew damn well how he would feel about her being with any other man but him. Especially as Stephen was more her age than he was. He didn't like being reminded of the fact that he was nearly fifteen years older than she was!

'The two of you met in town?' he prompted harshly.

'Yes,' she confirmed brightly.

'How convenient,' he drawled.

Her cheeks flushed with anger this time. 'What are you implying, Hawk?'

What was he implying? he asked himself wearily.

It was him she had agreed to marry, after all. 'Nothing,' he dismissed with a sigh. 'But it might have been nice if you'd called me when your friend let you down and the two of us could have had lunch together as I originally planned.' He shrugged.

'I told you, I met Stephen accidentally. I hadn't had *time* to think about calling anyone.' Leonie's eyes were fever-bright. 'If you don't trust me, Hawk, maybe we'd better just forget the whole thing; I've had one unreasonable husband, I certainly don't need another one who's unnecessarily *jealous*!' With a choked sob she turned and ran up the stairs.

Well done, Sinclair, groaned Hawk, you just blew it again!

Leonie bent over Holly as she lay sleeping in her cot, just watching her daughter for the sheer joy of it, letting all the tension of the morning drain out of her.

It was obvious what Hawk had been implying just now, the assumption he had made about her having lunch with Stephen.

But she shouldn't have reacted so emotionally; the tears were wet on her cheeks even now. She didn't like to cry, she never had; she had found it to be a complete waste of time and energy, solving nothing. But Hawk had made her cry just now, with his mistrust of her.

She was coming to care for him. In spite of herself she was *falling in love with Hawk Sinclair*!

He had known he would find her here; he had

instantly realised she would seek peace with their daughter.

She was so lovely as she bent over Holly's cot, her strength and beauty having returned to her almost completely during the last few days, erasing the frail waif he had looked at when he returned to claim her for his own. He didn't fool himself that her recovery had anything to do with him; he knew that it was her love for Holly that had given her the will to regain her strength.

Tears glittered on her cheeks, and he knew he was responsible for *those*, had made her cry with his unwarranted suspicions. Of course Leonie wasn't interested in Stephen, she wasn't even interested in *him*, despite agreeing to marry him.

'Leonie,' he called to her softly, full of self-disgust when she gave a nervous start.

Her eyes were full of apprehension again, and—and fear. My God, he thought—yes, she *feared* him!

He gave a choked groan, crossing the room in long strides, enfolding her in his arms as she straightened warily. 'I am jealous,' he acknowledged gruffly. 'I'm a jealous *fool*. Forgive me!' His arms tightened about her.

'It wasn't just you,' she admitted with a sniffle against his chest. 'I——The morning was a disaster, and then Stephen came along and cheered me up, and——'

'Then I came along and acted like an idiot because you'd had lunch with him and not me,' he said wearily. 'How are you going to like having a fool for a husband?' he added dryly.

He achieved his objective as she gave a watery

smile. 'You aren't a fool, and you know it,' she reproved.

He grimaced. 'Not from anything I've done lately, I don't.'

'Turn around,' she encouraged softly, and the two of them looked down at Holly. 'We must have done something right nine months ago,' she said huskily.

The daughter he loved. And the woman he was coming to love to the point of *insanity*! How else could he explain his uncharacteristic jealousy and possessiveness?

As soon as Leonie was well enough they were going to do that 'something right' again, and they were going to go on doing it for the rest of their lives!

Hawk kept his arm about her waist as they left the nursery, reluctant to let her go when, for once, she wasn't trying to free herself from his touch. And he didn't want to go downstairs either. Hal and Laura were out in the garden together, Sarah and Jake busy working in the study. He wanted the moment of closeness to continue.

'Hawk, there's something I need to talk to you about.' Leonie looked up at him with a frown. 'Privately,' she added earnestly. 'Let's go into my bedroom.' She opened the door.

He had never been invited into a woman's bedroom just to talk before, but then the whole of his relationship with Leonie was unique, always had been. Always would be. He had absolutely no doubts about that.

He felt a moment's regret as she moved away from him, but knowing her need to get away was because she had just realised she had let him get too close.

That was all right—she had agreed to marry him, they had the rest of their lives together for her to get used to him touching her. He just prayed it wouldn't take that long!

Yesterday, loving her, touching her, he had almost gone out of his mind, had lain awake most of the night with an ache in his body only this red-haired sprite could satisfy. He had heard her go in to Holly just after three o'clock this morning, and longed to be with both of them, but he had kept to the promise he had made her. The hours until morning had seemed never-ending. As soon as Hal and Laura were safely married he and Leonie were quickly going to follow their example; at least then he could share Leonie's bed, even if she wasn't ready for anything else!

At the moment she looked uncomfortable just having him in her bedroom, glancing nervously at the bed, as if the intimacy they had shared there was suddenly too vivid in her mind. Good—he never wanted her to forget the beauty they had known together.

Leonie twisted her hands together nervously. 'Stephen said something at lunch that I think you may be interested in,' she frowned. 'It seems he's dropped out of college,' she revealed concernedly.

Hawk was interested, very much so. No wonder Jake was walking around like a bear with a sore head believing himself to be a complete failure. 'What the hell did he do that for?' he asked impatiently, running a hand through the thickness of his hair.

Leonie shrugged. 'He said he'd had enough.'

Hawk sighed. 'Jake had such plans for him——Why the hell didn't he discuss this with me?' he burst out irritably. 'Maybe I could have helped.'

'Jake or Stephen?' she probed gently.

'Both,' he bit out. 'Jake obviously feels this is a reflection on his parenthood, Stephen believes leaving college has all the answers. Both of them are wrong.'

She gave a sympathetic smile. 'I know that Jake and Stephen are like family to you, but——'

'They wouldn't appreciate my interference,' he acknowledged dryly. 'Stephen's made his decision, I don't suppose there's anything I could say to him to get him to change his mind . . .? No, I thought not,' he sighed as Leonie shook her head. 'Then maybe I can help Jake see that this isn't the end for Stephen, that he can change his mind back again and still go to law-school like Jake wants. The two of them are heading for a complete rift in their relationship if someone doesn't make one of them see sense,' he scowled. 'Having almost made the same mistake myself I can assure Jake it isn't worth it!'

'Stephen seemed very adamant that he wouldn't be going back,' Leonie frowned.

Hawk nodded abruptly. 'We're always so sure we know what we want at that age. Jake just has to give Stephen time to realise he can't drift for the rest of his life. Thanks for telling me all this,' he said gratefully. 'Maybe I can even persuade Jake that he isn't the one who needs to change his life—Stephen is,' he added ruefully. 'Hell, changing *his* job isn't going to alter anything.'

'I hope you can help.'

It was a long time since Hawk had confided any of his problems with a woman. It felt good. Real good.

'Thank you kindly, ma'am,' he affected the Texan drawl that had faded from his accent years ago, tipping an imaginary hat, and was rewarded for his efforts when Leonie gave a girlish giggle.

She bobbed a curtsey. 'You're very welcome, sir,' she returned mischievously.

He might have been acting like a fool lately, but he wasn't going to be one any more today, so he left her while the shared warmth still existed between them, a smile still curving his lips as he made his way slowly down the stairs.

He sobered somewhat as he entered the study in search of Jake. Sarah sat alone in the room, looking up with a smile.

'Jake?' he prompted without preamble.

'In the kitchen, I think,' Sarah said lightly. 'There've been several telephone calls for you while you were at lunch——'

'They can wait,' he dismissed; the damn phone had been ringing night and day since the word had got out that he had set up his headquarters here. He wasn't in the mood to deal with any of it right now.

Jake had obviously just finished his lunch, and was sitting across the kitchen table from June, the two of them looking very self-conscious as he walked unannounced into the room. June blushed as she stood up to clear away, while Jake scowled at him for the interruption. Maybe the idea of Jake being attracted to this woman wasn't far wrong after all!

'I need to talk to you, Jake.' Hawk shot June an apologetic smile. The housekeeper was polite enough to him, but she still didn't seem to like him. It could make things a little awkward around here when he moved in permanently—as Leonie's husband.

'If it's about the Alton Hotels——'

'It isn't,' he cut him off softly. 'It's personal. Very personal.'

Jake frowned, his expression clearing as he gave an agreeing nod of his head. 'Let's go into the lounge. Thanks for the lunch, June,' he smiled at her warmly.

The blush that still coloured her cheeks made her look almost girlish. 'You're very welcome,' she murmured huskily.

Hawk grimaced ruefully to himself as he and Jake went into the lounge; June served *his* meals as if she wished she dared add a touch of arsenic to them! He wasn't conceited enough to think that every woman he met had to be attracted to him, but he couldn't remember ever encountering this veiled dislike from a woman before. The problem would have to be settled once he and Leonie were married; he refused to be treated like an interloper in his own home.

Jake turned to him, the sun shining in the window behind him outlining the bulk of his body. 'She told you, then,' he said with some relief.

Hawk frowned. 'Who?'

'Leonie,' Jake supplied impatiently.

Now how the hell had he known——? Maybe Stephen had been to the kitchen and spoken to his father since his return? What the hell, it was all out in the open now, maybe they could deal with the problem.

'Yes, she told me,' he nodded. 'I'm just glad somebody did.'

Jake frowned. 'I know I should have come to you, but——'

'You don't owe me any explanations, Jake,' Hawk cut in softly. 'I have to admit I was a little disappointed you didn't feel you could confide in me, but that was your decision,' he shrugged.

'And Leonie's,' rasped Jake.

'She only found out just now——'

'Is that what she told you?' his friend sighed heavily. 'The little fool!'

Anger burned within him. 'What's that supposed to mean?' he snapped.

Jake shrugged. 'Leonie has known about him for a lot longer than that. I warned her yesterday, but she has some ridiculous idea that she can handle him.' He gave a scathing snort. 'If you could have seen the way he looked at Holly . . .!' He shook his head.

Hawk had the feeling that some of this conversation had been lost on him. Jake made it sound as if Stephen were some sort of threat to Leonie and Holly, and that he couldn't believe.

'Did Leonie tell you he was at the hotel the night you took her there for dinner?' Jake's eyes were narrowed. 'That it's only a matter of time before he realises you're Holly's father and tries to cash in on the fact?'

'Stephen?' said Hawk disbelievingly.

Jake scowled. 'What the hell does he have to do

with this?' He was suddenly very tense.

'I'm not sure.' Hawk shook his head dazedly. 'I wanted to talk to you about the fact that you're upset because Stephen has dropped out of school, and you——'

'*That's* what Leonie told you?' Jake groaned raggedly.

'Yes,' Hawk gave a puzzled frown. 'What did you think I was talking about?'

The other man drew in a harsh breath. 'I don't know. I—er——'

'Yes?' prompted Hawk warily as Jake became suddenly evasive.

'Maybe you'd better go back and talk to Leonie some more,' he grimaced.

Hawk shook his head slowly. 'Why don't you talk to me, Jake?' he asked softly. 'Who exactly was it that was at the hotel that night?' His eyes were narrowed to icy slits.

Jake groaned. 'Leonie's going to kill me for opening my big mouth!'

'Not as painfully as I am if you don't open it again,' warned Hawk softly.

Jake's expression darkened. 'I'm going to tell you because I think you have a right to know, *not* because of any threats you might make,' he said. 'Spencer,' he bit out. 'Michael Spencer saw the two of you together that night at the hotel. He came to the house yesterday——'

'Here?' Hawk ground out disbelievingly; why the hell hadn't Leonie told him that bastard had been creeping about the place?

Jake nodded. 'I saw the two of them talking together in the garden. Leonie seemed—upset, so I went out to make sure she was okay. He seemed to be threatening her in some way, so I warned him off. Then he picked Holly up——Calm down, Hawk,' he advised softly as a murderous gleam flared in Hawk's eyes. 'He put her into my arms— but not before he'd made a couple of veiled threats concerning Holly and Leonie. I——'

'Why the hell didn't you tell me?' Hawk attacked. 'He's the sort of man who likes inflicting pain on a woman!'

And Spencer had been right here, within his grasp! God, what he wouldn't have given to have had his hands on him!

The 'friend' Leonie had been meeting in town for lunch today, the one who had 'let her down'! Why the hell would she have been meeting Spencer? And yet he knew, somehow he just *knew*, that was who she had gone to Claymont to see.

'I could see that,' sighed Jake. 'I wanted to come to you straight away, but—well, Leonie wanted to tell you herself.' He grimaced.

She hadn't mentioned her ex-husband to him, had preferred to meet the other man in secret instead. *Why?*

'If anything had happened to her——'

'I know,' Jake said wearily. 'But she was so adamant about wanting to tell you herself. And— well, she can be damned persuasive,' he added defensively.

'When it comes to her and Holly's welfare you'd do well to remember that you owe your first loyalty to me,' Hawk bit out coldly, turning towards the door.

'Where are you going?'

He gave an angry sigh. 'Back to Leonie to get the full story,' he rasped. 'Don't ever let me down in that way again, Jake,' he warned softly. 'I'll talk to you about Stephen again later.'

Jake stiffened. 'There's nothing to talk about.'

'We'll see,' said Hawk softly, closing the door behind him with forceful anger.

Why hadn't Leonie told him about Spencer's visit? She didn't still care for the bastard, did she? He knew she didn't love *him*, and there were some women who continued to love a man no matter how cruel he might have been to them. He wouldn't have believed that of Leonie, but she had never actually said she *hated* the man who had once been her husband, despite all that he had done to her!

Hawk's conversation with Jake didn't appear to have gone well, Leonie realised as he strode purposefully across the lawn to where she sat with Laura and Hal, his expression thunderous.

She picked up the jug of iced lemonade that stood on the table in front of her. 'Would you like some——'

'I want to talk to you. Now. Alone,' he grated coldly.

Hal made a protective movement. 'Dad——'

'Stay out of this, Hal,' Hawk ordered harshly. 'Leonie and I need to have a little talk about her first husband,' he added gratingly.

Leonie gave him a startled look, her hand shaking badly as she carefully replaced the jug on the table. Surely Jake hadn't——

'First husband,' Laura repeated frowningly, a sudden glow in her eyes as she looked at them excitedly. 'Does that mean the two of you——'

'No——'

'Yes!' Hawk spoke gratingly over her denial, taking a firm grasp of Leonie's arms. 'There aren't going to be any more secrets, Leonie,' he told her softly. 'None at all. You understand?' he prompted in a controlled voice.

She understood only too well; she knew that he would demand the whole truth from her now. And that was something she hadn't told anyone, not even Laura.

She nodded. 'Let's go into the house.'

Hal eyed his father aggressively as he spoke to Leonie. 'Are you sure that's what you want to do?'

'Hal, I asked you to stay out of this,' Hawk reminded him, dangerously soft. 'This is between Leonie and me.'

'But——'

'He's right, Hal.' Leonie put a reassuring hand on his arm, touched that he cared for her enough to want to defend her against his father.

'But if the two of you are getting married——'

'We'll talk to you about that later,' Hawk cut in decisively. 'Let's go inside,' he added, keeping a firm hold on her arm as he walked at her side.

She flinched a little as they faced each other across the lounge. She had seen Hawk angry before, furiously so, but that anger had never been turned directly on her before, his disapproval over Laura and Hal always taking precedence. But right now his anger was focused directly on her, and it was a daunting thing.

'You might well look guilty!' he rasped suddenly. 'Just when were you going to get around to telling me you still have assignations with your ex-husband?'

Leonie gasped at the injustice of the accusation. 'That's a lie!'

Hawk's mouth twisted. 'You met him today, didn't you?' His eyes were narrowed.

Her face paled. 'Stephen . . .?'

'Stephen told me nothing,' Hawk snapped. 'He didn't need to, I was able to guess that all on my own. After Jake told me Spencer was at the hotel that night we went there for dinner, *and* that he also came *here* yesterday morning!' He glared at her angrily.

'I was going to tell you——'

'When?' he scorned.

'When I felt the time was right,' she flared.

'And just when was that going to be?' he challenged. 'You've known almost forty-eight hours that Spencer was in the area!'

'Michael is my responsibility——'

'Not when he threatens you and our daughter he isn't,' challenged Hawk.

'He didn't——' Leonie swallowed hard. 'All right, maybe he did,' she conceded harshly. 'But I would never let him hurt Holly.'

'And what about you?' He was breathing deeply in his anger. 'What sort of price are *you* willing to pay to keep him away from Holly?'

Her face paled. 'What do you mean?' she gasped.

'Did you go to bed with him?' he grated.

Relief flooded through her that he didn't realise just how much she had 'paid' the last year. 'You know I'm not able——'

'There are ways, Leonie,' he reminded her hardly.

Her cheeks burnt. 'Not with Michael there aren't,' she denied with distaste. Making love with Michael had all too quickly become something she merely suffered during her marriage to him. He had soon felt the same way when she wasn't able to respond to him.

Hawk's breath left him in a ragged sigh. Evidence of how much the thought of her and Michael together disturbed him. 'I suppose I should be grateful for that, at least,' he bit out. 'What did he want here, Leonie? And why didn't you tell me he was in Claymont?'

'Maybe because I knew you would react like this,' she attacked. 'Michael is a part of *my* past, and——'

'By coming here like he did he's also part of *our* future,' Hawk said harshly.

She shook her head. 'He's gone now.'

'Why?'

She looked up defensively. 'Why not?'

Grey eyes narrowed to icy slits. 'Did he get what he came here for?'

'He's gone, isn't that enough?' she evaded aggressively.

Hawk slowly shook his head, watching her thoughtfully. 'It depends what you gave him to leave,' he said softly.

Her eyes flashed as dark as emeralds. 'I gave him what I always give him; money!' She faced him challengingly, breathing deeply in her agitation.

Hawk was suddenly still. 'Why would you give your ex-husband money?'

'Hawk——'

'Unless you still care for him?' he accused harshly. 'Is that it, Leonie—are you one of those women who like it when a man's rough with them?'

Her arm arced up with all the force she had, her hand making hard contact with his lean cheek, her fingers tingling from the contact, although Hawk remained unmoving as the livid welts appeared on his skin. Leonie stared at him in horror for what she had done.

'Well?' he challenged in a voice that sounded as if he had cut glass in his throat.

Her eyes widened with renewed fury. 'Oh yes, Hawk,' she bit out caustically, 'I loved it every time something didn't go Michael's way and he would hit out at me.' She ignored the way his eyes narrowed coldly. 'I enjoyed walking around with bruises that prevented me going out of the house for days at a time. But most of all I was in *ecstasy* when he would take my body simply because it was his right to do so. But the best night of all was the night Danny was born, when he——'

'That's enough, Leonie,' Hawk choked.

'Oh no.' She shook her head. 'You wanted to know how much I *liked* Michael's rough treatment of me! The night Danny was born I wasn't feeling well, I'd been in bed most of the day because I felt so ill. But when Michael came to bed he was in the mood to make love, and the fact that I didn't feel well was "my own fault. After all, I was the one who'd wanted the brat!",' she recited bitterly. 'When I refused his lovemaking he—he——'

'Leonie, don't,' Hawk muttered in a pained voice, moving to take her in his arms.

She evaded his grasp. 'When I refused he raped

me,' she finished defiantly. 'After that all I knew was blinding pain. Until they told me that Danny was too small, that they doubted they'd be able to save him.' She looked at him coldly. 'Oh yes, Hawk, I run to Michael's arms every chance I get for more of the same treatment!' she told him contemptuously.

He closed his eyes in self-disgust. 'I'm sorry,' he choked. 'So sorry.' He looked at her pleadingly. 'I just——The thought of your meeting that bastard behind my back sends chills down my spine!'

'What do you think it does to mine?' Leonie snapped unsympathetically.

He drew her hands into his. 'Tell me why you give him money,' he prompted huskily.

She gave a ragged sigh, knowing the time for prevarication was over. And maybe once Hawk knew the truth he could help her. She suddenly needed very badly to lean on someone, and Hawk had such broad shoulders, gave her a sense of security. She was so tired of going on alone.

'I give Michael money because,' she drew in a ragged breath, 'because I was still married to him the night Holly was conceived and he threatened to claim paternity of my unborn child!'

CHAPTER ELEVEN

'WHAT?'

That bastard, that weak son-of-a-bitch who beat up women because he wasn't man enough to go against someone of his own strength, had dared to threaten claiming paternity of *his* child? He would see the other man in hell first!

Hawk watched as Leonie sank weakly into an armchair, all the worry and pain she had gone through alone during the last months reflected in her shadowed eyes.

He had helped do this to her, as surely as if he had been Michael Spencer's accomplice. Without his child growing inside her Leonie wouldn't have been vulnerable to the other man.

He went down on his haunches beside her chair, taking her hand in his, amazed at how cold it was when the weather was so warm. 'I'm here now, Leonie,' he told her gruffly. 'I'm not going to let him near either you or Holly again,' he promised grimly, knowing it was a promise he would keep at all costs; Michael Spencer was going to receive another visitor today, and he wasn't going to find this one at all cowed by his bullying tactics!

Leonie sat back in the chair, her eyes closed. 'He'd been to see me several months before, asking me for money because he was out of work again.' She shook her head. 'I refused to help him. Then— then you and I—met.' She gave a pained frown.

'And the next time Michael pressed me for money I was very obviously pregnant—with someone else's child.'

Hawk sat at her feet, gently caressing the back of her hand with his thumb. 'I believed the two of you were already divorced, you know,' he told her gruffly, knowing it was no excuse for the way he had decided he wanted her and brooked no refusal to his desire.

She gave a bitter smile. 'We were about to be. We were actually at a meeting between our lawyers discussing the final terms when I fainted, and the doctor they called to examine me diagnosed my pregnancy. Michael was livid at first, furious that I could have found someone else to care about enough to have their child.' Her eyes were a dull green. 'Then he saw a way he might be able to make the knowledge pay off for him. I refused to drop the divorce proceedings and return to him as his wife, so he asked for money to keep quiet about not being the baby's father instead.' She shook her head. 'He threatened a court case for the custody of my child if I didn't give him what he wanted.'

Now wasn't the time to berate her, to tell her what a fool she had been to give in to any of Spencer's demands; Leonie knew exactly what a mistake she had made.

'You could have come to me,' Hawk prompted softly.

She gave a ragged sigh. 'I knew you'd find out about Holly some time, but I had hoped it would be after Laura and Hal were married. Maybe then we would all have been able to weather the scandal Michael was—is *still*—threatening,' she added with a shiver of apprehension.

'I'll take care of him,' Hawk told her grimly.

'You don't understand,' she said shakily. 'Michael knows who you are now, and——'

'If he doesn't he very soon will,' rasped Hawk. 'Don't worry about him any more, Leonie,' he advised huskily. 'Spencer is my concern from now on.'

He wished she could have looked more reassured by the statement, but she still looked worried. Hell, of course she was worried, she'd had that bastard messing up her life for so long it was going to take time for her to realise it was over.

And it was over for her. She was his now, the woman he loved above everything and everyone else, and he would protect her with his last breath.

If Sarah hadn't made the mistake about Leonie's divorce already being a fact he would never have pushed for that night with her, he never went near married ladies, but he couldn't exactly blame Sarah for the mistake she had made. He had demanded results immediately, and considering the divorce was on its way through the usual channels, and that Sarah had had no idea that his interest in Leonie was purely personal and not just in the sister of the woman he had believed was out to trap Hal, she had done the best that she could in the time he had given her.

Looking at Leonie, a woman who was so tiny he felt as if he could put her in his pocket and carry her about with him always, he wasn't so sure that even knowing she and her husband were *happily* married could have kept him away from her that night!

'He told me to ask you for money,' Leonie told him dully.

His eyes narrowed thoughtfully. 'And what did you say?'

She shrugged. 'That I'd see what I could do.'

'You *were* going to tell me about him?'

Her eyes flared brightly. 'Of course I was going to tell you about him!' she snapped. 'I told you I was.'

'Yes,' he acknowledged softly, thinking fast. 'Is he still at the hotel at Claymont?'

She shook her head. 'I would doubt it. Once he has what he's come for he doesn't usually hang around,' she said harshly.

'You gave him money this morning?' he prompted.

'Yes,' she confirmed defensively. 'Enough to keep him happy for a while.'

'Does Laura know he blackmails you?' His eyes were narrowed.

Her head went back. 'I never told Laura everything that Michael did. If I had Laura would have felt she had to defend me, and I couldn't put her through that.'

Laura's reluctance to argue once again? 'Why not?' he encouraged gently.

A shutter came down over her emotions. 'My marriage was my mistake, mine to deal with.'

Hal was right, Laura didn't like to argue with people. Oh, she had defended Leonie rather heatedly a couple of times to him, but she and Leonie had a closeness that surpassed all boundaries, even those of a lover or a husband.

Maybe he was seeing something that wasn't

really there. Twins were always supposed to be that much closer than other siblings, and Leonie and Laura had also lost their parents at an early age too, a situation that was sure to draw them even closer together.

And yet that didn't explain Laura's reluctance to argue.

Maybe once he and Leonie were married she would start to open up to him. As he intended sharing his every waking thought with her she was going to find it hard not to reciprocate.

'Our marriage isn't going to be a mistake,' he told her lightly. 'It's also going to take place as soon as I can get the special licence,' he added firmly, watching her warily.

'It's only two more days until Laura and Hal are married,' she instantly protested, as he had known she would. 'Besides, I can't be a proper wife to you yet.' Her cheeks were fiery red.

'I want *you*, not sex,' Hawk dismissed scathingly. 'I know I enjoy making love to you, but it isn't *all* I want from you!'

'No, there's Holly too,' she accepted quietly.

Was she ready to know he loved her? Whether she was ready or not, he couldn't keep the emotion to himself any longer.

'I'm not marrying you because of Holly either,' he bit out firmly, giving a wry smile as her eyes widened disbelievingly. 'I asked you yesterday if you were ready to hear about Leonie, and you obviously weren't.' He grimaced at the panic he had caused her yesterday. 'But today I'm going to tell you anyway,' he added firmly.

She still didn't want to hear it, he could see that

by the way she wouldn't meet his gaze. But dammit, he needed to tell her, and she couldn't go on hiding from emotion for the rest of her life!

'I'm forty years old.' He gave an acknowledging inclination of his head as a glimmer of mischief lightened her eyes. 'And contrary to what some people might think,' he added dryly, 'that does not make me half senile!' He relaxed slightly as she smiled. 'What it does make me,' he continued seriously, 'is mature enough to recognise a second chance when I'm given one. Leonie, my first wife died, and with her all the boyish dreams I had of a happy-ever-after. That's why, when love entered my life a second time, I knew to hang on to it for all I'm worth. I love you, Leonie, with a love that's all the deeper because I know what it is to have loved and lost.'

He meant it. She could see that he meant every word. But Michael had meant it too once, and his love hadn't lasted. Not that she thought Hawk was anything like Michael; she knew he wasn't. But although Hawk believed he loved her today he might not feel the same way tomorrow. She daren't risk her fragile dreams on such uncertainty.

She shook her head, extricating her hand from his. 'I don't love you—I'm sorry.'

She had hurt him, she could see the pain in the darkness of his eyes. The last thing she wanted to do was to hurt anyone, especially this man who was usually so strong and invincible, but how much more would both of them be hurt later on if they found their love was only because of Holly after all?

Hawk drew in a ragged breath, giving a curt nod of his head. 'Maybe that was too much to hope for,' he accepted dryly. 'But you *are* marrying me, and as soon as it can be arranged.'

'But——'

'And I want that bastard's ring off your finger *now*,' he added harshly.

Leonie looked down at the thin gold wedding band she wore on her left hand. It had been the hardest thing she had ever done in her life to divorce Michael; she had always believed until then that marriage was for a lifetime, the way her parents' marriage had been. Even after the divorce she just hadn't been able to remove her wedding ring.

She drew it slowly off her finger now, wordlessly handing it to Hawk, her eyes widening as he moved to open the window, reaching back to launch the ring as far away as he could throw it.

There was a look of immense satisfaction on his face as he turned back to her. 'Tomorrow we'll go shopping for our rings, and *that* one you'll never take off,' he promised gruffly.

Our rings? That must mean Hawk intended wearing a wedding ring too. Somehow she had never envisaged him as a man who would like to wear such a positive sign of belonging to a woman.

'We'll be married the day after Hal and Laura,' he continued briskly.

'We can't——'

'We're going to, Leonie,' he told her firmly. 'I want you as my wife and Holly officially as my daughter so that I have the right to show Spencer just how little his threats mean to us.'

She grimaced. 'He thinks I'm your mistress.'

'I should be so lucky!' Hawk gave a rueful grimace.

Leonie couldn't help but return his smile. 'I don't think I would make a very good mistress,' she mocked. 'Michael didn't call me the Ice Maiden for nothing,' she added hollowly.

Hawk scowled. 'Spencer didn't know what the hell he was talking about. Besides, when a man takes a virgin bride—as I'm sure you were,' he said softly, 'she can only be guided by what her husband teaches her. How the hell could he expect you to be anything but unresponsive when he didn't give a damn about your pleasure?'

'Did you find me a—disappointment?' It was important that the single night they had known together should mean as much to him as it had to her at the time. It was only later that the guilt had come, and when it came it was with a vengeance; she hadn't been able to explain her responses to this man' to herself.

He gave a gentle smile. 'Honey, disappointments don't haunt my dreams and fill my every waking moment,' he said dryly. 'I haven't been attracted to any woman since I met you. In fact, my life has become divided into two distinct times, before Leonie and after Leonie.'

Her life was the same, although in her case it was also before and after Holly. She had agreed to marry this man, why shouldn't it be sooner rather than later?

'All right, Hawk, I'll marry you in three days' time,' she decided. 'But Laura and Hal aren't going to be too happy about missing the wedding.'

His mouth twisted. 'I don't think they would particularly care, as long as we *are* married. And they don't have to miss the wedding at all if they don't mind delaying their honeymoon twenty-four hours.'

'Would you want to delay the first twenty-four hours of your honeymoon?' She smiled, remembering Laura and Hal's complete absorption with each other since he had arrived from Acapulco.

'Leonie, I'm delaying the start of my honeymoon for a couple of weeks,' he said softly. 'And I don't mind in the least!'

God, she was lovely when she blushed! Hawk mused. He wanted to sweep her up in his arms right now and carry her off to bed for a week. His restraint was out of necessity, not choice.

'The honeymoon can wait but the wedding arrangements can't,' he reminded her briskly. 'I have a licence and the rest of the arrangements to see to, and I'm sure you'll want to drag Laura off to the shops as you "don't have a thing you could wear",' he teased.

Her smile was something he would never grow tired of seeing. and he wasn't unaware of the fact that that smile was returning more and more easily each day. He was personally going to make sure that continued, starting with a little visit to Spencer!

'I think our little bridesmaid should have something extra pretty to wear too, don't you?' She wrinkled her freckle-covered nose prettily.

Holly. At a time when he considered that all he had left in life was his business and eventually being grandfather to Hal's kids, this beautiful woman had given him a whole new start in life.

Plenty of time later to tell her there wouldn't be any more children, that he wasn't going to risk losing her. He was hoping that by the time he had to tell her that the two of them would be so close they wouldn't need anyone else but each other and the child they already had.

Maybe it was a futile dream when Leonie had all but rejected his declaration of love, but no matter what happened there would be no more children. Maybe it was as well that they had these few weeks before they could make love, it would give him time to do what had to be done.

'Something really lovely,' he nodded agreement. 'Although she'll never be as beautiful as her mother—she doesn't have her red hair, for one thing!' he added teasingly.

Leonie gave him a look of affected indignation. 'My hair isn't red, it's titian, like the Duchess of York's.'

'Forgive me, Your Highness,' his mouth quirked, 'Holly doesn't have *titian* hair.'

'She will have,' Leonie said with certainty. 'Laura and I both had fair hair as babies.'

Another red—*titian*-haired little minx to watch over and protect. He couldn't imagine a more fulfilling lifetime occupation.

'I realise you probably won't want to wear white on Tuesday,' he said quietly. 'But maybe something close to that?' he prompted.

Leonie looked rebellious. 'I have no intention of discussing my wedding dress with the bridegroom,' she told him primly. 'It's bad luck.'

His mouth twisted. 'And we need all the good luck we can get, hm?' he guessed ruefully.

She shrugged. 'You have to admit this won't be an—orthodox wedding.'

'It will be *our* wedding,' he told her firmly. 'The only one either of us will ever have, so I want it to be perfect.'

'In that case, I'm sure it will be,' she smiled.

'Facetious witch,' he drawled.

'Having second thoughts?' she taunted.

His gaze steadily held hers. 'Never!' It was a promise as much as a denial.

He could see by the flicker of panic in her eyes that Leonie was still wary of marriage, to any man. He would have to go slowly with her, much more slowly than he had been doing. The trouble was he forgot everything but holding her in his arms and proclaiming her his when he was with her.

'I don't want you to give Spencer another thought,' he instructed harshly. 'He's my problem now.'

Leonie looked upset. 'What are are going to do?'

'Don't worry.' His mouth twisted. 'Nothing illegal.'

She sighed. 'Somehow that doesn't reassure me.'

Hawk gave a hard smile. 'It shouldn't,' he drawled, bending to give her a quick kiss, moving back before she had time to protest—or respond, if she was going to. Sometimes he wished they could be like other couples, like Hal and Laura, the affection between them completely spontaneous. Maybe in time they would be. 'I'll go and talk to Jake about being my witness,' he added dryly. 'He's far from happy that we've taken so long to decide to get married.'

She nodded. 'He seems convinced that Holly will

be a teenager before her father and mother are married!'

It was testament to how much Jake liked Leonie that he had held his silence about Spencer when she asked him to. But Hawk didn't feel jealous of that affection any more; he knew, after several heated conversations with Jake, that the other man liked her, not desired her. Not that the other man didn't still have some questions to answer about Spencer!

No wonder Leonie had turned to him so brokenly on the drive back from the hotel the other night. And did Spencer's visit to the house yesterday morning have anything to do with the way Leonie had responded to him on that blanket beside the river? What did it matter *why* she responded to him, as long as she did!

'Three more days should satisfy even him,' Hawk said hardly. 'Do you want me to come with you when you put Laura and Hal out of their misery,' he derided, 'or can you handle that alone?'

'I'll tell them,' she said lightly. 'You'd better go and talk to Jake.'

He found the other man back in the kitchen again when he went in search of him; he and June broke off what seemed to be a rather heated conversation as Hawk entered the room. He looked at the two of them searchingly; what *was* going on between these two?

He shot them a puzzled frown. Jake was looking rebellious now, while June seemed upset. 'I need to talk to you, Jake,' Hawk told the other man slowly.

'Sure,' snarled Jake, marching over to the door,

halting to turn abruptly and face the woman across the room. 'I'm sorry, June,' he bit out abruptly, his expression bleak. 'But you're interfering in something you just don't understand.'

She shook her head sadly. 'Oh, I understand, Jake, I understand only too well,' she added softly.

Jake's eyes narrowed. 'How——I'll talk to you again later,' he rasped, shooting Hawk an impatient glance.

Hawk slowly followed the other man out of the room; he was certainly starting to feel like an unwanted third around those two! June seemed like a very nice woman—apart from her unexplained dislike of him!—so why was Jake fighting the attraction? Oh hell, he and Jake had enough tension between them without him interfering in his relationship with June Gaynor.

Sarah was in the study working when the two men entered the room, and Hawk tersely sent her off to the kitchen for a break, apologising ruefully when she gave a pained frown.

'What is it?' Jake demanded impatiently, sitting on the edge of the desk.

The other man looked weary, as if he hadn't been sleeping at all well. And if this added strain was because of the attraction he felt for June . . . 'If it's any consolation, I think she likes you too,' Hawk drawled.

Jake's eyes narrowed. 'Who?'

'Well, I certainly don't mean Leonie,' he snapped.

Jake stood up. 'If you're going to start those insane accusations again——'

'I'm not.' Hawk ran a weary hand over his eyes before thrusting his hands into his trouser pockets.

'Shall we talk about Leonie first, or Stephen?' he said softly.

Jake stiffened. 'There's nothing about Stephen to discuss,' he bit out coldly.

'He's dropped out of college——'

'That's my problem, not yours,' the other man retorted.

It was true, and yet he and Jake had always been such friends that very often they had shared the bringing up of their two sons. He couldn't turn off his concern for Jake—and Stephen—just because he was told this was none of his business.

'Make it mine too, Jake,' he encouraged huskily.

The other man shook his head. 'There's nothing more to say about it. Stephen has dropped out of college. He's over twenty-one,' he shrugged. 'It's his decision.'

'It's a decision you can't condone——'

'Of course I don't condone it!' Jake flared furiously, his eyes glittering. 'I think he's an idiot, that he's wasting his life, but there isn't a damn thing I can do about it!'

'Would you like me to talk to him?' Hawk suggested gently. 'An outsider who can see both points of view?'

Jake's mouth twisted. 'Stephen isn't in the mood to listen to anyone just now—especially the man he knows is my best friend!'

Hawk had doubted that closeness lately; it felt good to know it was still there, no matter what his and Jake's differences were at the moment. 'I could try,' he offered softly.

'No,' Jake argued. 'It wouldn't do any good. Besides, Stephen isn't here any more,' he added challengingly.

Hawk frowned. 'What do you mean?'

The other man shrugged. 'He's gone to London until the wedding.'

'Why?'

'Because I sent him there!' flared Jake. 'His behaviour has been disgraceful since he got here. A few days to think things over alone won't do him any harm,' he added grimly.

Hawk wasn't convinced of the wisdom of that, but he could see by Jake's challenging expression that he wouldn't welcome the criticism. And Jake should know his own son better than anyone else. He had some idea now how Jake had felt when he had to stand by the last nine months and witness his completely wrong handling of Hal; he felt like banging Jake and Stephen's heads together to get them to see sense.

But for now he had a wedding to announce, and he knew that would please Jake if nothing else he had done lately had.

And then he had a visit to Michael Spencer to arrange. That would please *him* immensely!

CHAPTER TWELVE

THE RINGING of the telephone sounded ominous.

It had been a morning of non-stop activity, all the last-minute rush and bustle preparing Leonie for what she would have to go through tomorrow morning before her own wedding.

Hal hadn't wanted to wait for a church wedding, but Laura had decided she would have everything else that a church wedding should have had, including the small luncheon reception for the guests at the house. Besides helping Laura get ready for the wedding Leonie had also helped June in the kitchen.

And now, with only ten minutes to go before they all left for the register office, the ringing of the telephone was very unsettling.

She picked up the receiver mere seconds before Hawk reached it, her eyes widening appreciatively on him in his grey morning-suit; this man looked good in anything!

'Yes?' she spoke breathlessly into the receiver.

'Laura?' Hal said immediately.

'Certainly not,' she mouthed Hal's name to Hawk as he raised his brows questioningly. 'She isn't allowed to *speak* to you before the ceremony either,' she reproved. Hal had spent the night at a hotel in town, intending to meet them at the register office.

'Leonie!' he greeted her in some relief. 'Laura isn't about, is she?'

She frowned at his almost desperate tone. 'No, she's upstairs,' she replied slowly. 'Hal, you haven't changed your mind, have you?' She evaded Hawk's reaching hand as he would have furiously taken the receiver from her.

'Of course not,' Hal scoffed instantly. 'I just—— Stephen hasn't arrived!' he revealed in a panicked voice.

'Oh no!' she groaned.

'What the hell is it?' Hawk demanded tersely. 'What's wrong?'

Leonie put her hand over the mouthpiece. 'Stephen hasn't turned up,' she explained with a frown. 'Hal sounds frantic.'

'Hell,' scowled Hawk. 'This is all Jake's fault,' he sighed. 'Okay, tell Hal I'll stand up as the other witness,' he instructed tersely. 'In the meantime we'll just have to hope Stephen arrives before the ceremony.'

'What's happening?' Hal demanded down the telephone line. 'Leonie?' He sounded more desperate than ever.

'Don't worry about a thing,' she soothed him. 'Your father will deal with it.'

'Oh, good.' Hal sounded relieved to have the problem taken out of his hands. 'I've been calling the hotel in London all morning, but they haven't seen him at all today,' he added worriedly.

'Your father said he'll be the other witness,' Leonie calmed again. 'I'm sure Stephen is on his way,' she encouraged.

'Maybe,' Hal said tersely. 'Thank Dad for me.' He rang off.

Leonie turned to a scowling Hawk. 'Maybe you

should have stayed in town with Hal,' she said lightly. 'He sounds a little panicked without anyone there to reassure him.'

'Jake and Sarah are there,' he dismissed vaguely. 'If Jake hadn't sent Stephen to London none of this——'

'I think a panicked bridegroom is enough for one day,' she reproved gently, moving to straighten his grey tie. 'Don't you?' She quirked one mocking eyebrow.

He relaxed slowly, looking down at her with warm eyes. 'I wish today were our wedding day,' he murmured gruffly.

Leonie moved back abruptly, suddenly very self-conscious. 'I don't think we should tell Laura about Stephen,' she said briskly. 'She'll only worry, and it could all be for nothing.'

'Okay,' he dismissed absently, still gazing down at her. 'You look beautiful, did you know that?'

Her cheeks felt warm. 'Wait until you see Holly,' she evaded responding to the compliment.

The pale green and cream full-skirted floral suit, with its tiny fitted jacket and wide belt at her waist in the same material, was something else she and Laura had purchased during their shopping trip yesterday for her own wedding outfit. Her hair was loose about her shoulders, and she felt almost carefree. It was only when she thought of her own wedding tomorrow that she panicked a little.

'I'd rather look at her mother,' Hawk murmured huskily, his hand gentle beneath her chin as he tilted her face up to his. 'You're so beautiful, Leonie,' he told her softly before his lips descended on to hers.

'Leonie, I——Oh!'

Leonie pulled hastily away from Hawk to turn to a red-faced June, the other woman looking completely flustered as she witnessed their closeness.

'Tell her,' Hawk instructed gruffly, his arm possessively about Leonie's waist.

Leonie swallowed hard, knowing what he was asking. Hawk had meant it when he had said there were to be no more secrets, but she had managed to get him to wait until the end of the reception today before announcing their own wedding tomorrow. She was hoping the same friends and family would be able to attend their wedding too, although she had preferred the idea of a small luncheon party afterwards for a few close friends, with Laura and Hal leaving for their honeymoon straight after lunch. June was one of the people still to be told of their arrangements.

Hawk's expression was suddenly teasing. 'You do realise June's been resisting the impulse to poison my food ever since I moved in?' he drawled.

June blushed deeply red. 'Oh, I haven't——'

'Don't be silly, Hawk,' Leonie dismissed impatiently.

'Am I being?' He quirked dark brows at a still flustered June.

Her chin went up challengingly. 'I can't stand people who pass judgements on other people,' she announced stiltedly.

'June . . .?' Leonie eyed the other woman dazedly.

Hawk frowned. 'What judgement did I pass?' he asked softly.

June shook her head. 'I prefer not to discuss it.'

'But I think we have to,' Hawk cajoled. 'You see, after tomorrow I'm going to be moving in here permanently.'

June gasped, looking uncomprehendingly at Leonie. 'Surely——'

'As Leonie's husband,' he finished softly.

'Husband?' June repeated in a high-pitched voice. 'But I thought—I thought——'

'Yes?' Hawk encouraged.

Leonie had no idea what was wrong with the woman who had become such a good friend the last six months; she had been so occupied with other problems that she hadn't noticed any friction between her and Hawk. Obviously Hawk had been well aware of June's dislike of him.

June looked uncomfortable. 'You seemed to disapprove of Leonie because she had a baby but no husband. I——Well, I——'

'That was my fault,' Leonie realised with a groan. 'That first day you saw Holly,' she explained to Hawk as he turned to her questioningly, 'when you left so abruptly. I told June that perhaps you didn't approve of unmarried mothers,' she revealed with a self-conscious grimace.

She had spoken out of self-defence that day, she hadn't realised the housekeeper would take the remark so much to heart.

To her relief Hawk's mouth quirked with amusement. 'You were right, June,' he drawled. 'I *don't* approve of this mother being unmarried—especially when it's *my* child she's the mother of!'

Leonie closed her eyes with a self-conscious groan, afraid to open them again as June gave a disbelieving gasp. Trust Hawk to blurt out the truth in that way—and to sound so proud of it too!

'I had no idea,' poor June began to splutter, 'or I wouldn't——Oh dear,' she groaned awkwardly. 'If you'd like my notice, Mr Sinclair, I quite understand——' She broke off as Hawk roared with laughter.

Both women turned to stare at him, Leonie with rising anger. There was nothing in the least funny about having June hand in her notice!

'June,' he finally sobered, although a grin still lightened his features, 'you can be as nasty to me as you want when I know it's in the cause of protecting Leonie.' He sobered completely, looking down at Leonie with dark eyes. 'You see,' he murmured softly, 'I don't ever want anyone to hurt her either.'

Leonie blushed at the possessive intent in his voice, but she didn't move away as she normally would have done, knowing she was completely safe in the haven of his arms.

'I really am sorry,' June grimaced uncomfortably. 'And—congratulations,' she added awkwardly. 'I actually came to tell you that it's time we left for town,' she told them with a frown. 'I know it's customary to be a little late, but even so . . .!'

Leonie gave a hasty glance at her watch. 'Heavens, yes!' she gasped. 'I'll go and get Laura——'

'And *I'll* get Holly,' Hawk announced determinedly. 'Yes?' he prompted huskily at her sharp look.

'Yes,' she agreed slowly, accepting that she would have to relinquish quite a lot of her daughter—*their* daughter, to this man.

June halted her as she turned to go up the stairs. 'I really am sorry,' she repeated contritely. 'You just seemed so upset that day he came here, and I——'

'It's all right, June.' Leonie squeezed her hand consolingly, gazing after the man who had caused all the trouble as he tactfully went up the stairs ahead of her. 'Hawk likes to indulge in the melodramatic,' she dryly derided his method of announcing himself as Holly's father. 'But it is the truth, and we're going to be married tomorrow.'

June nodded. 'I'm surprised you got him to wait that long,' she said wryly.

Leonie laughed softly. 'So am I!'

'I'm glad that's settled.' Hawk was waiting for her at the top of the stairs. 'I wasn't sure which one of us you would choose if it came to that!' He eyed her derisively.

'Why, June, of course,' Leonie came back pertly. 'You can't cook, can you?' Her eyes gleamed mischievously.

'I have other, much more useful talents as a husband.' He wiggled his eyebrows and twiddled an imaginary moustache.

Leonie gave him a scathing look. 'One of them isn't a believable impression of Groucho Marx!'

He chuckled. 'Because I wasn't *doing* Groucho Marx!' he said disgustedly. 'Don't you recognise a lecher when you see one?'

'Unfortunately, no,' she gave him a pointed look.

Hawk groaned. 'Will I ever win one of these verbal battles with you?'

Leonie eyed him speculatively. 'Do you want to?'

He looked at her appreciatively. 'No,' he acknowledged indulgently. 'Boredom is something I'm never going to fear being married to you!'

She affected a haughty look. 'Can I say the same, I wonder?'

His mouth quirked. 'Ask me the same thing on our first wedding anniversary!'

He was so self-confident, and he had reason to be. No woman could ever be bored with this man, not if she lived with him for a thousand years. He was so dimensional, so complex—eternity wouldn't be long enough to learn all there was to know about this man. But she suddenly so much wanted to try!

'I have to get Laura.' She moved away from him. 'Otherwise Hal will really start to panic,' she grimaced.

He nodded. 'I want this to be a happy day for all of us.' He drew in a ragged breath. 'Leonie, Spencer is the last person I want to mention today, but I have to if I'm to reassure you that it's all over with him.' He looked at her intently.

Leonie had felt her cheeks pale at the mention of her ex-husband, but she looked at Hawk uncertainly as he finished the statement. What did he mean? What had he *done* to Michael? Not that she was concerned about Michael, she had given that up long ago, but she didn't want anything to happen to Hawk.

He grasped her arms. 'I'm not going to go into

details, suffice it to say my lawyer and I have made sure Spencer will never come near you again.'

She looked up at him searchingly, knowing that above all else she could trust him. If he said Michael had gone from their lives then she believed him.

'Thank you,' she said huskily, tears in her eyes. 'This *will* be the happiest day of my life.'

Hawk shook his head. 'That's tomorrow,' he told her huskily. 'Laura and Hal's wedding is just a practice run!'

Leonie was still smiling as she went into Laura's bedroom, although the tears actually started in her eyes as she saw how beautiful her sister looked in her frothy white dress of satin and lace.

Laura took one look at her and her own tears started to fall. She stood up to cross the room, and the two sisters hugged each other tightly.

'Everything will change after today,' choked Laura.

Leonie's arms tightened about her twin. 'We all have to go forward,' she comforted her. 'It isn't as if we aren't going to see a lot of each other,' she cajoled. 'And you do love Hal, don't you?' she prompted softly.

'Oh yes,' Laura replied without hesitation, straightening, but still maintaining a hold on Leonie's hands. 'We are doing the right thing, aren't we?' she said uncertainly.

Leonie smiled encouragingly. 'You're just suffering from a bride's rightful attack of nerves,' she soothed. 'As soon as you see Hal you'll *know* you're doing the right thing.'

'You thought you loved Michael too once,'

Laura said worriedly.

Leonie frowned. 'I'm not sure that I did, not the way you love Hal. I just—I *wanted* to fall in love like other people did, and he—well, he knew a good thing when he saw it,' she conceded bitterly, remembering the way Michael had decided she earned enough for both of them and had instantly given up his job. 'It wasn't the same, Laura,' she insisted.

'And Hawk?' asked Laura. 'How do you feel about him?'

To stand by and let her answer that would be to destroy the tentative friendship that had sprung up between them the last couple of days. Hawk didn't like feeling vulnerable, but where Leonie was concerned he surely was.

The bedroom door stood slightly ajar, allowing him to have overheard part of the conversation between the two sisters, and he pushed the door completely open to stand in the doorway. 'You two might not mind keeping Hal waiting,' he said lightly, 'but this young lady isn't going to remain quiet indefinitely.' He looked down at Holly as she moved restlessly in his arms, wearing a pretty pale green dress that seemed to hint at a slightly red shading to her hair. Leonie was right, their daughter was going to be another redhead.

He watched the two sisters often as they sat in the back of the car together as he drove them all into town, June by his side, obviously still a little embarrassed at the mistake she had made as she gazed out of the side-window. He was relieved *that* problem was out of the way, anyway.

Leonie still worried him, however. From what he had overheard her say to Laura a few minutes ago she had had trouble falling in love even before her disastrous first marriage and the death of her son. What other reason could there be for her sounding so desperate about *wanting* to fall in love—she had only been twenty, for God's sake, hardly old enough to have considered herself an old maid.

He didn't understand the woman he loved at all, but he was going to. And this time he would do his investigating into her past himself; he was going to leave nothing to chance.

It was a beautiful ceremony, the love that openly surrounded the bride and groom as they gazed at each other making it so.

Stephen hadn't arrived, so Hawk had acted as the other witness, and Leonie had seen him have a few harsh words with a stony-faced Jake before the ceremony, the two men having studiously avoided each other since then.

Holly behaved perfectly, sleeping through the whole thing, much to Leonie's relief. But how would Holly dare do anything else when she was held so firmly by her father!

'Let me take her,' offered Sarah as they all posed for photographs outside.

'No, let me,' Hal offered mischievously. 'It'll give our grandchildren something to think about when we show them our wedding photographs!' He and Laura posed with the baby held between them.

Leonie insisted on taking Holly so that they

could have some more traditional photographs taken, standing to one side with Hawk until it was their turn to pose with the bride and groom.

'Did Jake have any idea where Stephen could be?' she asked Hawk softly.

'No,' he grated, his eyes narrowed. 'He didn't seem overly concerned either!'

'Oh, I'm sure you're wrong,' she protested. 'I know he's angry with Stephen just now, but——'

'Leonie, I've known Jake almost half my life, and I know something of the way he feels; he seemed almost relieved Stephen hadn't turned up today.' Hawk shook his head.

Leonie sighed. 'It seems such a pity, they're both such nice men. And I meant that quite impersonally,' she added quickly, aware of how frayed Hawk's temper had been concerning Jake, especially over the last few days.

His mouth quirked. 'I know that,' he gave her a wry smile. 'Loving someone makes you vulnerable.'

She was all too aware of that vulnerability, that was why she feared expressing her love for Hawk. Maybe one day she might feel brave enough, but not yet. She just wasn't ready to open herself to that sort of pain again just yet.

'Come on, you two!' Hal stood grinning in front of them, obviously relieved the trauma of the ceremony itself was over. 'Laura and I want to have a family photograph with just the five of us, and then just the three of you together.'

They couldn't have made a more public declaration of their relationship, and yet as Hawk posed at her side Leonie felt proud of the fact that she and Holly belonged to such a man. She smiled brightly into the camera, she and Hawk laughing together as Holly chose that moment to give one of her windy smiles, giving the impression that she too was happy with the day.

There were only thirty or so guests invited back for the buffet luncheon, but even so the house seemed very overcrowded.

Hawk swore beside her as the telephone began ringing almost as soon as they entered the house. 'It's either Stephen phoning to explain why he didn't make it, or it's a business call for me,' he grimaced. 'And neither one of them is welcome just now!'

'I'll go and answer it,' Sarah offered with a smile. 'You're due to give your speech any time now.'

Hawk didn't look pleased by the reminder as his secretary hurried from the room. 'I don't like speaking in public,' he confided to Leonie as she gave him a puzzled look.

Her eyes widened. He always gave the impression that he was so self-confident, so composed, so this disclosure came as something of a surprise to her.

'I know,' he grimaced. 'It doesn't fit in with the image. Nevertheless, it's true.'

Leonie rested her hand on the crook of his arm. 'Holly and I will be rooting for you,' she encouraged.

'I——What is it?' he frowned at Sarah as she made her way back to his side.

'Bob Norman is on the phone——'

'The Chairman of Alton Hotels,' Hawk told Leonie softly.

She turned to the other woman, having become interested in this deal that was taking up so much of Hawk's time.

'He wants to talk to you,' Sarah shrugged. 'He says it's urgent.'

Hawk scowled. 'Didn't you tell him my son got married today?' he rasped.

'Of course,' Sarah said calmly. 'He said he only wants a few minutes of your time,' she added regretfully.

'Okay,' Hawk agreed impatiently, giving Leonie an apologetic look. 'This should only take a few minutes. Tell Hal to start the speech without me if I'm delayed,' he drawled.

She laughed softly. 'Oh, I'm sure we'll all manage to wait for you!'

'Witch!' he muttered before turning to stride confidently across the room.

Sarah looked uncomfortable. 'I really didn't mean to interrupt this time for him, but Bob Norman *did* sound in a panic.'

Leonie gave the other woman an understanding smile. 'It doesn't matter,' she dismissed, soothing Holly as she began to fidget, her blue-grey eyes wide open.

'Feeding time again?' Sarah guessed indulgently.

'It seems like it always is,' Leonie grimaced, sitting Holly up so that she could have a look around. 'I'd better go and warm a bottle for her,' she excused herself with an apologetic smile.

'Let me hold her while you're gone,' Sarah offered. 'I've never particularly wanted one of my own,' she admitted, 'but I don't mind borrowing someone else's occasionally.'

'You can give them back that way,' Leonie acknowledged with an understanding laugh, leaving Holly with the other woman as she went out to the kitchen.

She hesitated outside the study, aware of Hawk's raised voice, wondering whether she should go and see what was wrong with him or if she should just mind her own business. As she heard him swear she decided on the former.

'——For God's sake, Bob, it isn't only my son's wedding today that's holding me back,' he rasped down the telephone line, his back towards the study door. 'I'm getting married myself tomorrow. Don't be clever, Bob,' he growled. 'My bride might be willing to wait, but I'm certainly not!'

Leonie smiled at his vehemence, pitying the poor man on the other end of the line for daring to suggest such a thing; it had taken all Hawk's patience to get him to wait this long before marrying her. He had come to her only yesterday and suggested they elope to Las Vegas instead of waiting until tomorrow!

She gently touched his arm. 'What is it?' she prompted as he turned to her sharply.

'Just a minute, Bob,' he snapped tersely to the other man, putting his hand over the mouthpiece. 'He wants me to go over and complete the deal immediately,' Hawk explained impatiently. 'The shareholder who has the balance of power in my favour is seriously ill and not expected to last more than a couple of days, and his son isn't in favour of selling to me.'

'You'll lose the deal,' she frowned.

'It doesn't matter——'

'You'll lose the sale,' she nodded. 'Tell him you'll be there tomorrow.'

'But——'

'Hawk, if I'm going to be a business man's wife then I'd better start acting like one,' Leonie told him firmly. 'From what I can tell you've been planning this business deal for months, so waiting a few extra days for our wedding isn't going to matter.'

Hawk looked rebellious, not liking that idea at all, obviously. Then his face lit up with suppressed excitement; Leonie doubted if he would ever lose *complete* control. 'Come with me,' he suggested eagerly. 'We could spend a few days in New York finalising the deal and then go on to Las Vegas the way I wanted to.'

It was impetuous, mad, it would completely upset the plans they had already made. 'And then a few days in Los Angeles to see how the Winnie Cooper series is going?' she prompted pertly.

Hawk gave a rueful grimace. 'That *has* to be part of the deal?'

She shrugged, her eyes glowing mischievously. 'It seems a pity to go all that way and not pop into the television studio.'

'Los Angeles isn't just around the corner from Nevada, you know,' he said dryly. 'Oh, all right,' he gave in as she looked disappointed. 'Calm down, Bob,' he ordered the other man as he went back on the line. 'My fiancée thinks she'd like to be married in Las Vegas.' He winked at her as she gave an outraged gasp. 'I don't blame her for that,' he answered a remark the other man made in return.

'Blame me for what?' Leonie demanded in a whisper.

Hawk put his hand over the mouthpiece once again. 'Not wanting to let me out of your sight long enough for me to change my mind about the wedding,' he revealed with a challenging glint in his eyes.

Leonie glared at him as he returned to his conversation with the chairman of Alton Hotels. They both knew very well that *he* would never change his mind about marrying her!

Going to America with him was madness. It wasn't as if their wedding couldn't have waited another week or so, she couldn't even be a proper wife to him yet because of——Oh, goodness!

She pulled on the sleeve of Hawk's jacket. 'We forgot all about Holly,' she burst out at his frowning look.

'We'll take her with us,' he decided instantly. 'No, Bob,' he drawled as the other man heard his half of the conversation, 'not my mother-in-law! We were just deciding to bring our month-old daughter with us,' he explained.

And make of that what you will, Bob Norman, Leonie thought with a groan.

'Thanks,' Hawk accepted the other man's obvious congratulations. 'We're rather pleased about it too.'

Maybe she was the only one who found it odd that she was marrying the father of her child when that child was already five weeks old! Everyone else seemed to think it was perfectly normal.

And only Hawk could have so calmly suggested they take along a month-old baby on such a trip.

He could have no idea of all it would entail, the special arrangements they would have to make taking such a young baby with them. But of course he did, she remonstrated with herself, he had already been the father of a baby before. Well, if he thought they could cope with it, why not?

Hawk was just bringing his call to an end when Sarah came quietly into the room with Holly, quite capably feeding her the bottle she held.

'I'm so sorry,' Leonie closed her eyes apologetically, 'I completely forgot!'

'Don't worry about it,' Sarah assured her with a smile. 'My brother has two kids that I've practised on a little. I guessed you must have been tied up,' she shrugged dismissively.

'Ah, Sarah.' Hawk turned to her briskly, his telephone conversation over. 'Don't worry about that.' He took Holly into his own arms, feeding her absently. 'Phone the airline and get two seats booked to New York for tomorrow.' He looked down at the baby he held. 'Oh, and include an infant in that booking,' he added with satisfaction. 'Leonie and I are going over to complete the Alton Hotel deal.'

Sarah looked up from her shorthand pad. 'Just the two seats?' she arched blonde brows.

He grinned. 'Well, I think Holly is a little young to need a seat of her own just yet!'

'No, I meant——'

'I know what you meant,' he smiled. 'But you and Jake might as well stay here, I can meet up with the lawyers in New York. Come on, Leonie, we'd better go and tell Hal and Laura about our change of plans,' he told her briskly, striding from the room with Holly still held in his arms, feeding her with an ease born of habit.

Leonie shot Sarah a rueful grimace before following Hawk from the room.

No announcement was made of their own wedding plans after all, but Leonie knew that no one at the reception could be in any doubt of Hawk's proprietorial claim to her as he continued to feed Holly in front of everyone, maintaining that hold on his daughter even when she had fallen asleep after all the excitement of the day. Not that it mattered what anyone thought; Leonie would be Mrs Henry Hawker Sinclair the Second by the time she returned from America. That title was going to take some living up to.

Hal's idea had been a good one. The four of them relaxed together over a candlelit dinner before Hal and Laura left the next day for their honeymoon and he and Leonie left for the States.

Leonie had protested that the newly married couple should be alone on their first evening as husband and wife, but Hal and Laura had been adamant that they join them for this private celebration now that they weren't going to be present at their wedding after all.

Hawk was glad they had insisted; he had never seen Leonie as relaxed as she was tonight. She finally seemed to have come to terms with the fact that they were a couple, that nothing was ever going to part them again. That didn't include loving him, but seeing her almost as sparkling and carefree as she had been the first time he met her was reward enough for him at the moment.

This time alone with her and Holly in the States was going to——'Oh, my God!' he groaned suddenly, and three pairs of eyes turned to him anxiously. 'Holly doesn't have a passport,' he said frantically. 'And——'

'Calm down!' Leonie patted his hand just as if he were an over-anxious little boy. 'Holly is on my passport; Laura and I intended taking a trip over to the States ourselves next month at the invitation of the television studio.'

Hawk had forgotten all about that promotional visit his executives had planned for the Brandon sisters. Hell, he had forgotten everything lately except this temptress whose hand still touched his.

Hal chuckled softly. 'I wish the two of you had got together sooner,' he grinned. 'I think I like seeing my always-in-control father in a panic.'

He realised it was probably a condition he was going to have to become accustomed to now that he had Leonie permanently in his life; as he had known, boredom was *not* going to be a problem with Leonie as his wife.

'Very funny,' he drawled, meeting Hal's amused gaze. 'Might I remind you that this little witch's twin is now your *wife*!'

He listened appreciatively to the husky sound of Leonie's laugh, wanting her new relaxation around him to go on for ever.

But all too quickly the evening had to end, and he and Leonie shared a smile of silent amusement at Hal's over-acted displays of tiredness. Hell, he wouldn't even have bothered with the act if he and Leonie had been married today; he would have spent the entire evening in bed with her sharing the delights they *could* have together. Only another week or so and Leonie would be able to know all the pleasure he wanted to give her. He hoped she realised they weren't going to remain celibate until then!

Hal and Laura excused themselves as soon as they entered the house and he and Leonie once again shared a smile of complete understanding, although Hawk sobered slightly as the bedroom door closed upstairs seconds later followed by complete silence.

He gave a start of surprise as a tiny hand crept into his, looking down at Leonie as she gazed back up at him.

'I understand, Hawk,' she said softly.

And he knew she did, that she had known he had just realised the loss of his son, that Hal was completely a man now, with the responsibility of his own wife.

He gave a rueful smile. 'Let's think of it as: I've gained a daughter and you've gained a brother.'

'Let's,' she agreed encouragingly.

June stood up as they entered the lounge together. 'Did you have a nice evening?' she greeted warmly.

One thing about June Gaynor, when she forgave and forgot, she did just that. The other woman had completely accepted Hawk's new role as Leonie's husband-to-be, and was starting to treat him with the same clucking concern as she did the two sisters.

'Very nice,' Leonie was the one to answer her. 'Has Holly behaved?'

'She's been a little restless since I gave her her

bottle an hour ago,' June frowned. 'So I should leave it a few more minutes before you go in to check on her.'

Leonie faced Hawk nervously across the lounge once the housekeeper had gone up to her bedroom, the ease they had known with each other all evening completely gone. And he suddenly knew why; Leonie was unsure about whether or not he intended kissing her goodnight!

His gaze dropped to her lips; just the way her top lip was fuller than the bottom was enough to arouse him. Oh God, *how* he wanted to kiss her, but not goodnight!

The last few days had been full of frantic activity as they prepared not only for Hal's and Laura's wedding but for their own, and there hadn't been a lot of time for them to be alone together. Consequently their contact had been brief too, the merest brushing of his lips against hers, which she seemed only to tolerate. Now they had the chance to be alone for more than a few minutes, and how he wanted to make full use of them!

Leonie's hands moved nervously together. 'I suppose I should go up and make a start on my packing for tomorrow. I didn't realise there'd be quite so much to do, and——'

'Leonie,' he gruffly cut off her nervous speech, standing so close to her he felt as if he were drowning in the sweetness of her perfume. 'Leonie, let me love you,' he encouraged intensely.

Let him love her. She knew he meant physically, and for that she was glad; allowing him to love her in any other way was something she was still frightened of.

But Hawk hadn't touched her in an intimate way since she had realised she was falling in love with him, and she had no idea how she would react in his arms now that she knew she loved him so deeply.

He had been a tower of strength to her for the last three days, always there to help when she needed him. She had even allowed him to proof-read the work she had finally been able to do on the Winnie Cooper book everyone was waiting so anxiously for, something she and Laura had never allowed before a book was completed before. She still smiled when she remembered Hawk's admission to having become a Winnie Cooper fan! So much for those 'fourth-rate detective novels' he had once spoken of so scathingly.

If he touched her now was she going to go up in flames? Soon he was going to have the right to touch her whenever he chose to, and she wasn't going to be able to hide her feelings then. Nevertheless, she baulked at having her emotions laid bare.

'Please, Leonie,' he urged huskily as he saw her hesitation.

Hawk wasn't a man who begged for anything; he had known the full power of being Henry Hawker Sinclair the Second too long for that. And yet he felt no qualms about pleading with her, of showing her just how vulnerable he was where she was concerned. She owed their relationship the same honesty, at least.

'I'd like that,' she told him breathlessly, and was rewarded with the sudden blaze of desire that burned brightly in his eyes.

His mouth was gentle against hers, his hands on her shoulders drawing her against the hardness of his chest. Her lips parted beneath his, her senses leaping at the hard probe of his warm tongue, engaging in the duel he seemed to want, her breath catching in her throat as she felt the caress of his hand as it moved ever closer to the throbbing peak that instantly knew the touch of its master.

The silky material of her dress was no barrier to his questing hand; he pushed the material aside as he bent his head to draw the pulsing nub into the warm caress of his mouth.

Watching him was an eroticism in itself, long dark lashes fanning his flushed cheeks as he took the fullness of her breast in his mouth. Her breathing became ragged as she suddenly found herself looking straight into his darkened eyes, the raw desire there making her tremble anew.

He watched her as his tongue laved the dusky-rose tip of her breast, drawing it into his mouth before slowly caressing it once more with the tip of his tongue.

Her heart was leaping, her pulse racing, her whole body shaking with a need that evoked a burning ache between her thighs. She could feel herself already moist there, and felt feverish, crying out as Hawk transferred his attention to the other nipple while his fingers tugged against the aching hardness of the other.

Her hand moved up of its own volition, cradling his nape as she held him against her, pressing him into her, shuddering uncontrollably as he eagerly accepted the invitation, using his teeth too now as he caressed the nipple that needed his loving so badly.

Leonie needed his loving badly, she acknowledged that, knowing only wonder and beauty in Hawk's arms, needing more than they could share here.

'Let's go to my room,' she gasped as his hand played over the flatness of her stomach to curve over the mound that ached so badly for his touch. 'Hawk, I'm going to explode if you don't soon love me completely!' she cried out her desperation.

He slowly released her. Leonie felt faint with a hunger of her own; she was shaking so badly she wasn't sure she would be able to make it up to her bedroom.

'Hawk,' she looked up at him with big green eyes, 'are you going to let me love you tonight?'

He became suddenly still, his eyes fevered at the images her words projected. 'If it's what you want,' he answered gruffly. 'But only if it's what you want,' he added tensely.

She had felt his desire throbbing against her as he made love to her, vividly remembered the feel of him, the steel encased in velvet, and she wanted more than anything to give him the same pleasure he gave to her so unselfishly.

'More than anything,' she confirmed shakily. 'But you'll have to teach me, show me what you like——'

'Teach you?' he repeated softly, very still.

She nodded. 'Hawk, I know I'm not technically a virgin; I couldn't possibly make that claim when I've been married and have a child,' she acknowledged ruefully. 'But the only pleasure I've ever known was with you, the only pleasure I've ever wanted to bestow has been with you. I want so much to please you, Hawk,' she added huskily. 'But I'm afraid I won't know how!'

His arms went about her as he pressed her face against his chest. 'Just being with you pleases me,' he told her gruffly.

She shook her head. 'I want to make love to you.'

He trembled. 'You will, Leonie,' he assured her shakily.

She looked up at him with pleading eyes. 'You'll help me?'

Hawk released his breath raggedly. 'I'll help you,' he agreed. 'Although just thinking about it's driving me insane!'

She smoothed his hair back from his brow. 'It makes me feel hot and weak,' she said softly.

'That too,' he acknowledged with a tiny shudder.

They stared at each other for long timeless minutes, their eyes saying all that needed to be said. Finally Hawk was the one to break the tension, putting his arm about her shoulders as they went slowly up the stairs.

'I'll go and check on Holly,' Leonie said softly as they reached the nursery door.

Hawk smiled. 'I'll come with you. I'm finding it's one of my greatest pleasures just standing over her cot watching her sleep.'

Leonie eyed him pertly. 'And here was I convinced *I* was one of your greatest pleasures!'

His mouth quirked. 'You're the *ultimate* pleasure!'

Her cheeks were burning as she entered the

nursery, her bravado leaving her as she shyly avoided Hawk's teasing gaze.

Then her shyness turned to panic as she moved to Holly's cot and found it empty!

CHAPTER THIRTEEN

LEONIE TURNED frantically back to Hawk. 'What——'

'Now calm down,' he told her firmly. 'Maybe she woke up and June or Laura took her in with them as we were still downstairs.'

She pushed past him out of the room, knocking sharply on June's door and walking in before she had time to receive an answer, her face ashen as she backed back out of the room, knocking on Laura's and Hal's door this time, waiting slightly longer than she had outside June's room, then going in as she heard the murmurs of muffled surprise inside the room. Laura and Hal stared back at her from their bed just as dazedly as June had from hers seconds earlier.

And Holly wasn't with either of them!

Leonie felt the nausea washing over her as she turned to face Hawk. 'She's gone,' she gasped weakly. 'Holly's gone!'

Hawk caught her as she fell, knowing as June came to her door belting her robe, and Hal and Laura got out of bed to do likewise, that Leonie had told the truth; their precious daughter wasn't in the house!

Pain such as he had never known before pressed down on his chest, and he would have sunk to the floor with Leonie still in his arms if Hal hadn't

251

hurried forward to help hold him up.

Holly was gone! Oh, dear God, what did it mean? Who could have done this to them? *Why?* *How?* Who would have dared come into the house in this way?

Hawk turned accusingly to June as she stared at them with stricken brown eyes. 'You said she was sleeping. That——'

'Dad,' Hal cut in reprovingly, 'you know June had nothing to do with this.'

Yes, he knew. June cared for Holly as if she were her grandchild. Then *who*? Only one name came instantly to mind, and if Spencer had harmed one hair of Holly's head he was going to regret it for the rest of his life. Which wouldn't be for long once Hawk got his hands on him.

'I can manage,' he rasped at Hal as he would have taken Leonie from him; no one was ever going to take her from him. 'You'd better see to your own wife,' he ordered with a worried frown at Laura.

Laura sat on the edge of the bed rocking backwards and forwards in silent agony, tears streaming down her pale cheeks. She cringed as Hal approached her, moving to the back of the bed so that he couldn't touch her.

'Laura——'

'I told Leonie she was wrong.' She still rocked backwards and forwards, her arms wrapped about her bent knees. 'I told her you have to love or you shrivel up and die.' Her voice was so lacking in emotion it was painful to listen to. 'But she was right.' She shook her head, her eyes dull. 'We both loved Holly, and now she's been taken from us too. Don't touch me!' she told Hal shrilly as he would have reached for her. 'Don't touch me or you'll die too!'

Hal turned to him beseechingly, completely at a loss with how to deal with the situation. Hawk was filled with a burning anger. 'Holly isn't dead, Laura,' he said harshly.

For a moment she looked at him as if she didn't recognise him, and then there was the merest glimmer of memory in her eyes, those green eyes that were so full of pain it was like looking into the depths of hell. 'Isn't she?' she said flatly.

He drew in a ragged breath, holding Leonie easily in his arms. 'June, call the police and then a doctor. Tell both of them that it's urgent,' he added grimly, carrying Leonie into her bedroom, placing her gently down on the bed and looking down at her with pain-filled eyes. 'I'll get her back, Leonie,' he promised. 'And once I do neither of you will ever leave me again!'

As he continued to stare down at her he could hear a strange noise, something like an animal in pain, and turned round expecting one of the cats to be in the room with them. And then he remembered that the six of them were shut up in a room downstairs for the night.

He also realised that the pained sound was coming from him, and that the tears were falling against the hardness of his cheeks.

'Damn you, Spencer!' he cried out his anguish. 'Damn you for doing this to her.' He looked down at Leonie. 'Damn you for doing this to me! And damn you for daring to so much as *touch* our daughter!'

He would find the other man if it was the last thing he ever did!

Leonie woke slowly, her mind feeling foggy, completely disorientated for a moment.

Goodness, she must have slept deeply, she realised with a pained wince as she sat up, guessing by the sunlight filtering in behind the curtains that it was already eight or nine o'clock in the morning. Strange, she didn't recall getting out of bed to feed Holly during the night. Perhaps the baby had slept right through for the first time, she thought excitedly. It could certainly——

The memory of last night flooded sharply back to her—the empty cot, the searching for Holly, the sudden blackness. And then later, the agonising pain, the torment, of knowing someone had taken her beautiful baby, the crying out for Holly, for the child she loved so deeply. And then the sharp sting in her arm before the blackness closed in once again.

'It's all right,' June soothed as she moved into her line of vision. 'You're all right, Leonie,' she calmed her.

'Holly?' choked Leonie, knowing by the way June's gaze slid away from hers that Holly was still missing. She slumped back against the pillows. 'Where's Hawk?' she asked dully.

June moistened her lips. 'He and Hal left straight after the police had finished their questioning——'

'The police?' Leonie's sharp gaze swivelled to the other woman.

June shrugged, looking much older than her forty-five years this morning. 'They had to be informed,' she explained gently.

'Of course,' Leonie nodded abruptly. 'Where did Hawk and Hal go?'

The other woman swallowed hard. 'I'm not really sure,' she shook her head.

Michael. Hawk had gone to find Michael. She knew without being told that Hawk also believed Michael was responsible for—for Holly's disappearance. And he wouldn't wait for the police to find the other man. And Holly.

She squeezed her eyes shut as the sweet memories of her baby washed over her, the tears escaping through the tightly closed lids. She had only just begun to show Holly how much she loved her, she couldn't possibly lose her now.

'Laura?' she prompted abruptly.

'She's—resting, too,' June supplied with an awkward grimace.

'Resting?' Leonie echoed sharply.

June shook her head. 'The doctor had to sedate her too. She——Well, she——'

Leonie straightened too quickly, feeling dizzy for a moment, and closed her eyes to shut out the spinning of the room. 'What happened?' she demanded firmly.

She listened with an increasing heaviness as June told her of Laura's reaction to Holly's disappearance.

'I've never seen her like that before,' June finished huskily.

'Do the police have any idea who—who——' Leonie couldn't go on, just the thought of someone else having her beautiful daughter was making her tremble. 'Have they heard from anyone?' she choked.

She knew what the answer was going to be even before June shook her head. If it was Michael—and who else could it be!—he would enjoy letting her suffer a little before asking for what he really wanted: money. In the meantime, if he harmed Holly in any way he would have more than Hawk's wrath to contend with.

'Hawk and Hal should be back soon,' June added encouragingly. 'Maybe they'll know something.'

Knowing Michael as she did Leonie knew they would never be able to find him. And he had no idea how to take care of a baby, no idea what to feed Holly, or how to change her, or—or *anything*! But only he would dare to enter the house and take Holly in that way.

'Can I get you anything?' June offered as she saw the utter despair on her face.

Leonie shook her head. 'I think I'll go and sit with Laura for a while.' She stood up unsteadily, not surprised to find that she was wearing a sheer cream nightgown, sure that Hawk would have undressed her before putting her to bed last night.

What was all this doing to him? He loved Holly just as much as she did, she was sure of that, and he had known her a much shorter time to love.

Oh God, she should never have denied Holly her love, should never have held herself aloof from her own baby for the first three and a half weeks of her life. She might never get another chance to show Holly how much she *did* love her . . .

Laura looked so peaceful as she lay asleep in

her bed, but Leonie knew it was only an illusion, that as soon as her sister woke up her pain would begin again—Laura, who had refused to accept that love *meant* pain.

Leonie stood up restlessly, her heart beating rapidly as the room across the corridor drew her like a magnet. The nursery . . .

The room looked as it always did when Holly had been got up for the day, the tiny quilt not pulled back as it had been when she gazed uncomprehendingly into the empty cot the night before, but neatly tidy, the teddy bears they had received as presents when Holly was first born lined up along the bottom of the cot, the clown-patterned quilt seeming to be laughing up at her. And the laughter seemed to be getting louder, and louder, making her head feel as if it were about to burst, as if——

'Stop it!' June's hand landed painfully against Leonie's cheek and she sank to the carpet, her body racked by anguished sobs. 'Leonie, don't,' June knelt down beside her, taking her in her arms. 'Please don't. Oh God, it's all my fault,' she choked. 'If I'd kept a closer eye on Holly none of this would have happened!'

They were all so filled with guilt, a guilt that wasn't going to do a thing towards bringing Holly back. June certainly wasn't responsible for what had happened, and she couldn't allow her to believe she was.

'No,' Leonie said firmly. 'None of us could have stopped what happened last night,' she realised with certainty. She gave a deep sigh. 'I'd better get dressed.'

June frowned. 'Are you sure you feel up to it?'

Leonie rose unsteadily to her feet. 'I have to be strong, for Holly's sake. I have to——' She turned sharply as she heard the front door open and close. 'Hawk!' she cried expectantly, running from the room.

One look at Hawk's haggard face and Hal's desolate one and she knew they hadn't brought her daughter back to her.

Oh, God, Leonie looked as if she were about to shatter into a million pieces, Hawk thought brokenly.

They had gone to Spencer's home, where his disgruntled landlady had told them what she had already informed the police: that Spencer had left late yesterday afternoon and hadn't been back since. They had pressed the sleepy woman for names of his friends, anyone else they could question about where he could have gone. She had finally told them to try the female tenant in the flat opposite Spencer's, a lead that had also proved fruitless. The woman had been obviously eager to get back to the man who *was* sharing her bed for the night. And so they had got the landlady out of bed again, stressing how important it was that she remember any of Spencer's friends. She had finally come up with the name of a man who lived a few blocks away. Another dead end—the man was too high on something to be of any help to anyone.

The police were looking for Spencer now; he could only hope they would have more luck.

In the meantime he had to tell Leonie that Holly was still missing.

She turned to Hal with pained eyes. 'Laura is still sleeping, so you might as well have breakfast before going up to her.'

She knew. She had taken one look at his face and she knew their darling daughter was still with Spencer somewhere.

Why didn't she rant and rave at him, remind him of the assurance he had given her only yesterday that Michael Spencer would never bother them again! He couldn't bear the quiet calm that hid so much pain.

Hal shook his head. 'I couldn't eat a thing. I—I think I'll just go up and sit with Laura.' He came to an abrupt halt at the bottom of the stairs. 'I'm so sorry about this, Leonie,' he choked, turning blindly towards her.

Hawk almost broke down and cried again himself as he watched Leonie comforting his son, the bulk of Hal's body totally eclipsing her as she held him in her arms.

Hal left them with a wrenching sob, running up the stairs as if he were pursued by demons.

Leonie looked at Hawk with tears swimming in her eyes. 'Would you like some breakfast? You must be exhausted, and——'

'Leonie!' he groaned, opening his arms to her, sighing his need as she instantly moved into them, burrowing her face against his chest.

She had never seemed more like a child to him, a lost and lonely child who didn't understand why anyone would want to hurt her, and keep on hurting her.

'Oh—I'm sorry,' Sarah said awkwardly as she came out into the hallway.

Hawk looked at her sharply, bent protectively over Leonie as she still clung to him. 'Get Jake, and tell him——'

'But he isn't here,' Sarah shook her head, her expression one of deep concern. 'He doesn't seem to have been at the hotel all night,' she shrugged worriedly.

Hawk's eyes narrowed, and he wanted to pursue the subject further, but not now. Right now he had to get Leonie back up to her bedroom.

'Let me.' June appeared at his side, putting an arm comfortingly about Leonie. 'And I think you'll find Jake in the kitchen,' she said huskily.

He bent to kiss Leonie gently on her brow. 'We'll find her,' he said with more conviction than he actually felt. He could have sworn when he had met Spencer two days ago that the other man wouldn't bother them again; and look how wrong he had been about that! He daren't even think of what would happen to Leonie if he didn't get Holly back for her.

He stood at the bottom of the stairs watching Leonie and June until they disappeared into the bedroom before turning briskly to Sarah. 'Cancel all my arrangements for today,' he ordered. 'And then find out anything you can about Michael Spencer,' he added grimly. 'And I mean everything!'

'Isn't he——'

'The bastard who has my daughter,' he bit out harshly. 'And I want him!' His hands clenched into fists at his sides.

Jake rose slowly to his feet when Hawk joined him in the kitchen, and if anything he looked more haggard than Hawk felt, his face pale, a dark-blond growth of beard on his chin, his clothes giving the impression that he had slept in them.

'No news?' he rasped.

Hawk shook his head. 'Where the hell have you been all night?'

Jake gave a guilty start—or did it only look guilty to him? What could his friend and assistant have to be guilty about? Hell, Holly's disappearance was making him suspicious of everyone!

'I went to look for Stephen,' explained Jake, shrugging awkwardly. 'I didn't find him.'

Hawk's eyes were narrowed. 'No?'

Jake gave a ragged sigh. 'He hasn't booked out of his hotel room or anything like that, his clothes are still there, but he just——Forget about Stephen,' he dismissed harshly. 'What can we do to get Holly back?' His gaze was intent.

Hawk drew in a shaky breath and sat down heavily. 'Find Spencer,' he bit out angrily.

'You think it's him?' Jake gave a puzzled frown. 'But I thought you'd settled——'

'So did I,' snapped Hawk. 'But obviously I was wrong. Now it's a question of either finding the bastard or waiting for him to make the ransom demand. Knowing what a cruel son-of-a-bitch he can be I would say that won't be too quick in coming!' His eyes glittered coldly. 'If I don't get her back soon, Jake, this could destroy Leonie,' he added raggedly.

'You think he did this for money?' Jake said slowly.

Hawk nodded tersely. 'And to hurt Leonie and me as much as possible,' he said grimly. 'He should get some cheap thrill when I go on television tonight asking him to return Holly to us! I'm having the telephone number here broadcast too.'

'The police are allowing that?' Jake frowned.

Hawk shrugged. 'She's my daughter, Jake,' he said tersely. 'I'll give everything I have to get her back.'

The other man shook his head. 'You'll get all the mental cases coming forward as well.'

'It's a risk I have to take,' Hawk said heavily. 'I want my daughter back, Jake, and I'll do anything I can to achieve that!'

'Wouldn't it be better to wait——'

Hawk shook his head firmly. 'Someone out there may have seen Spencer with Holly. If they have, I and the police want to know about it. Once we've received a ransom demand the police have insisted on a media black-out.'

'You're agreeable to that?' prompted Jake.

'I said I'd do anything, Jake,' Hawk bit out. 'And that means anything *Spencer* demands!'

Leonie was in control again now, regretting the lapse when she had almost collapsed in Hawk's arms. She was stronger than any of them now, had faced the pain of loss enough to know that grieving didn't help anything, that they had to sit and wait for whatever came next.

She had just finished dressing when she heard Laura's raised voice coming from her bedroom, and she quickly ran out to be with her sister now that she had woken up; possibly she the only one who understood the reason Laura had fallen apart so completely.

Hal was trying to take the distraught Laura into his arms, and Laura was fighting him for all she was worth!

'Leave her to me.' Leonie deftly took Hal's place, and Laura at once fell into her arms, sobs racking her body.

'I was good, Leonie,' she choked. 'I was *so* good. Why am I being punished? *Why?*'

Leonie glanced up at Hal, sympathising with his complete inability to deal with something he didn't even understand. 'Let me talk to her for a while,' she suggested gently. 'Just for a while,' she encouraged as he would have protested.

'You'll call me if she needs me?' he said uncertainly.

She gave him a gentle smile. 'I promise,' she nodded, waiting until he had left the room before turning back to Laura and softly beginning to talk, telling her sister all the things she knew she needed to hear, slowly feeling the tension ease from Laura's shaking body, watching as total awareness returned and her sister softly began to cry.

CHAPTER FOURTEEN

IT HAD been the longest day of Hawk's life.

He, Jake and Hal had spent the afternoon and evening visiting every person Spencer had ever spoken to, with only the briefest of breaks in between when he had made his appeal on television. As Jake had predicted, it seemed every crackpot in the country had either seen or had Holly. The police were monitoring all the calls, and none of them had been from Spencer. He would know when the real ransom demand was made, he was sure of it.

Leonie had spent the time with Laura, a still strangely withdrawn Laura, although she had lost the look of hell from her eyes.

And Leonie—dear God, he had no idea what she was thinking any more. The vulnerability had gone, and in its place was a strength that nothing seemed able to pierce. She had become the comforter, not the comforted. And he knew that was the only reason she had come to his bed tonight.

He had sat up with the two policemen who were monitoring the telephone for several hours, but it seemed only the real crazies called at that time of night, and he had grown sickened by their warped minds, eventually coming wearily up to his room.

All had been silent upstairs, and he wondered briefly how Hal and Laura were faring together.

Laura was treating her new husband rather like a stranger she had to be polite to.

Leonie's door was firmly closed against him. Not that he could blame her; he had promised to get Holly back, and so far he had failed miserably. He had told her she would never know another day's unhappiness, and yet her heart had been broken because he hadn't recognised how dangerous Spencer was.

He had turned sharply into the nursery, moving about the room touching everything that was Holly's, wondering if her golden head would ever rest inside the cot again, tightly gripping the cot sides as thoughts of his beautiful daughter took him through a nightmare of broken images that were too unbearable to contemplate. Those bastards, with their sick warped minds, had conjured up the images he had been fighting all day. They would get Holly back, they *would*.

He had staggered blindly into his bedroom, almost falling down on to the bed in his agony of grief.

And then the door had opened and a slight figure in a pale nightgown moved amongst the shadows the moonlight cast over the room.

Hawk had sat dazedly as Leonie came down beside him to take off his shoes and lay them neatly to one side, completely still as she deftly unbuttoned his shirt and stripped that from his shoulders with coolly impersonal hands, offering no resistance at all as she helped him back on the bed until he leant back against the pillows, her tiny hands dealing with the fastening of his denims before they too were gently eased off his body.

And she hadn't stopped there, black undershorts joining the neat pile of clothes before she pulled back the covers and arranged them over him.

He had watched as she moved about the room putting the clothes in their appropriate places, shirt and underwear in the laundry basket, his trousers neatly hung in the closet. And through it all she hadn't said a word, neither did she speak as she moved the covers slightly back before climbing into the bed beside him.

She lay there still, her head resting against his shoulder, her hand on his chest, and they were farther apart than if they had been in separate rooms.

And neither of them had any intention of falling asleep tonight.

They both lay in the darkness, eyes wide open, living in their own individual hell, more like strangers than lovers. Because Leonie like this was a stranger to Hawk, the same stranger who had offered to let him take Holly away with him when he left. He hadn't realised just how far that woman had receded during the last few days until she appeared once more. And this time he didn't have the strength to reach her.

But he had to *find* the strength, because no matter what happened, Leonie was going to be his. He *loved* her, damn it; he couldn't live without her!

'No, Hawk,' Leonie stared at him in horror. 'Send him away!' She shook her head in frantic denial of the suggestion he had just made.

He remained unmoving. 'Do you know the effort it took to actually get him to come out to the house this afternoon?'

'I don't care,' she choked. 'Send him away! How can you even contemplate the two of us getting married *now*, when our daughter is missing?'

'Why not?' he shrugged.

Because Holly could be lying dead somewhere, her beautiful eyes closed for ever, or maybe they would just never know what had happened to her; Michael seemed to have done a good job of disappearing—why shouldn't he make Holly just disappear too? And Hawk had brought a man here to *marry* them!

He was a monster, a cold, unfeeling——No, he wasn't, she realised brokenly, he was the man who loved her so much he had been willing to do anything to break her out of the cold shell she retreated to so that the pain shouldn't touch her.

But she had to feel that pain if she were to love, and she did love Holly and Hawk so very much.

He was watching her now, trying so hard to appear unaffected by what he was forcing on her, but now she could see the anguish in his eyes, the utter despair he was trying to keep from her.

She held out her arms to him. 'I still think Las Vegas sounds a romantic place for a wedding. Will you take me there when this is all over?'

They held each other so tightly it was painful, and Leonie wasn't sure if the tears she tasted on her lips were Hawk's or her own.

'I love you, Hawk,' she choked, feeling a sudden freedom that gave her heart the lightness of having wings. 'I love you so much,' she repeated raggedly.

His hands cradled each side of her face. 'Enough to marry me even if—even if it's just going to be the two of us?' His gaze was intent.

If Holly were dead. She knew that was what he was trying to say. She refused to accept that anything that final had happened to Holly, but she knew she would marry Hawk anyway, that to be without him now would mean returning to being only half alive. It might be safer that other way, but she needed Hawk to make her truly alive.

She needed to tell him that, and there was only one way for him to be really sure. 'Ask your Mr Simpkins to come in and marry us now,' she told him softly.

His breath left his body in a raggedly relieved sigh, his arms tightening about her. 'There is no Mr Simpkins,' he admitted brokenly. 'Just the man who loves you very much trying to reach you in the only way I knew how!' He stared down into her eyes. 'Tell me again that you love me,' he encouraged huskily.

'I love you, Hawk,' she repeated obediently. 'And that's the last time you can meekly expect me to do your bidding,' she added with some of her old spirit.

He gave the ghost of a smile. 'There's still so much I need to know.'

Leonie knew he was thinking of the way Laura had become withdrawn too. Her sister was so distant from Hal today that he might have been a stranger to her and not the man she had loved enough to wait a year for.

They needed to get Holly back as much for Laura's sake as for their own and Holly's.

'I——'

'Hawk, I'm sorry to interrupt,' Jake said harshly,

'but I need to talk to you.'

They turned to looked at the other man, Leonie's eyes widening at how drawn and totally beaten Jake seemed, with dark shadows beneath his eyes, as if he too hadn't slept for some time, his face pale, his cheeks hollow.

He didn't seem able to look at her, his attention was concentrated on Hawk. 'I went back to London to look for Stephen again last night and this morning,' he revealed stiltedly.

Hawk nodded. 'Any luck?'

The other man swallowed hard. 'No.' He drew in a ragged breath. 'You see, the thing is——' He looked as if he were in torment.

'What is it?' Hawk demanded sharply. 'Has something happened to Stephen?'

Jake's mouth tightened. 'If he's the one responsible for taking Holly I'm going to kill him!' he stated flatly, his eyes blazing.

Hawk's sudden tension was also her own. What on earth did Jake mean? Of course Stephen hadn't really got Holly. The younger man hadn't had that much to do with the baby, but she was sure he had no reason to harm her.

Hawk felt as if someone had punched him in the chest. Stephen had Holly? He couldn't imagine what had caused Jake to even think that, let alone that it might be true!

'It's because of the money.' Jake collapsed on to the sofa, his face in his hands. 'If I hadn't told him he wouldn't get any more money from me none of this would have happened!' His shoulders began to shake as he sobbed.

Hawk put Leonie firmly to one side, going down on his haunches beside Jake. 'What the hell are you talking about? Stephen wouldn't do a thing like this for *money*,' he shook his head.

'You don't know what he's capable of.' Jake too shook his head. 'None of us really do.'

'*What are you talking about?*' Hawk's control snapped as he grabbed hold of Jake's shirt-front and shook him. 'Why do you think Stephen might have taken Holly for money?'

'Because Stephen is a drug addict.'

Hawk released Jake slowly, turning to look at June as she stood in the doorway, aware of Leonie's stricken gaze on him as he shook his head disbelievingly.

'It's quite true,' June said softly as she came into the room and closed the door behind her. 'I should know—my son died of a drugs overdose,' she added quietly.

Hawk heard Leonie give a pained gasp, as nausea washed over him. 'Jake?' he prompted harshly, his breath catching in his throat as the other man slowly nodded. 'Stephen?' he said disbelievingly. 'Surely he isn't stupid enough to have——'

'It's the intelligent ones who always believe they can experiment with drugs and then just give them up any time they care to.' Once again it was June who answered him, sitting beside Jake now, her hand resting sympathetically on his. 'They believe that right up until the day they realise that it isn't fun any more, that they *need* the drugs so desperately they'll do anything to get them. If you can realise and accept that while the drug possesses them they're no longer your child you stand a chance of helping them, of understanding them; my husband couldn't, and he died of a heart attack at only thirty-eight.'

And Amy had died because one of those doped-up bastards had been so high they didn't know what they were doing!

But accepting that Stephen, a boy he had been so close to he had almost been like his own son, was also one of those mindless addicts, was impossible. Memories of the fair-haired angel he had looked as a child as he had enticed Hal into one piece of mischief after another flashed into his mind. Not Stephen—he couldn't believe it!

And if he couldn't believe it how much more painful it must have been for Jake.

He looked at the other man, at the way he stared sightlessly in front of him, all trace of the teasing flirt he had always been completely erased. Because he knew that everything June had said about Stephen was true.

'Why?' he groaned. 'Stephen didn't *need* drugs!'

'He does now,' Jake said dully. 'And he does anything to get them. He even had me bring some through Customs for him once from a friend of his in Mexico.'

Hawk's eyes narrowed. 'When?'

Jake gave a ragged sigh. 'About a month ago. Hell, I know more accurately than that,' he said bitterly. 'It was exactly four weeks ago.' He looked up at Hawk with darkened eyes. 'Yes, the day before I gave you my notice,' he acknowledged. 'The package got damaged in my case, and when I realised what was in it I confronted Stephen with what he'd made me do. He didn't care that I'd broken the law, betrayed a friend, he just wanted the drugs so that he could shoot up again! He won't go into a clinic, refuses to accept that there's anything wrong with him. He dropped out of college because he would rather be in his flat pumping drugs into his body. I tried, I really tried to help him,' he choked, his hands clenched tightly together. 'But I finally had to admit that there's nothing I can do, that he won't let anyone help him.'

'He has to want to help himself,' June put in quietly. 'It's the only way.'

Hawk was finding it almost as difficult as Jake must have done to come to terms with Stephen's addiction. He had always despised people who took drugs, hated them because one of them had taken Amy's life. But he had never known one personally before.

And from what he had been able to tell of Stephen since his arrival here he was becoming recklessly careless, mixing drugs and alcohol. He was going to kill himself if he didn't stop soon.

And he might have Holly!

Leonie had always known June's husband and son were dead, she had been drawn to the other woman because of the tragedy, but she hadn't realised just how much of a tragedy it was until now. Poor June!

But what if it was Stephen who had Holly, a drug addict who could become desperate enough to do anything?

'Hawk, you have to find him!' Leonie clutched frantically at his arm.

He turned to her like a man in a daze, and after the shock he had just received she could understand the emotion, made all the more traumatic because his first wife had been killed by a drug addict, a fact she was sure Jake was well aware of, his guilt about Stephen extending much further than the drugs he had unwittingly taken into America illegally. Jake had to be fully aware of how unsympathetic Hawk would be about Stephen's plight.

How unsympathetic they would *both* be if Stephen did have Holly and she were to be harmed!

'Oh, I'll find him,' said Hawk in answer to her plea. 'And if he has Holly, I don't care how much I cared for him in the past, he'll regret the day he ever crossed me!'

Jake stood up. 'I'll come with you.'

'No, I—Okay,' Hawk accepted tightly as the other man looked determined. 'You can tell me the places you've already tried!'

'Jake's been through hell since Stephen turned up here with Hal.' June spoke softly once the two women were alone. 'He blames himself, of course. We all do.'

'Sorry?' Leonie gave a pained frown, still caught up in thoughts of Stephen having Holly.

'Parents,' June explained sadly. 'When a child becomes an addict like Stephen or my Robert did we always think there must have been something we could have done to prevent it, that something we did must have caused our child to turn to drugs.'

Jake's need to change the way he had been living his life? But Leonie wasn't interested in hearing this now, she just wanted to think positive thoughts about having Holly safely back with her!

'It isn't usually that way at all,' June shook her head.

'June, I'm really not——'

'Interested,' the other woman acknowledged softly. 'I can understand that. I just wanted you to realise that Stephen is sick, that his actions aren't ones he would normally make. Drug addicts aren't normal. Stephen needs help——'

'I *need* my daughter!' cried Leonie in an anguished voice. 'I need her back with me safe and well. I need her with me so that I can watch her grow up, to see Hawk's eyes gleam with pride when she takes her first steps, calls him Daddy for the first time, begins school, brings her friends home for tea, meets the man she wants to marry! That's what *I* need!'

June got up wearily. 'I know you do, love. I know you do,' she choked. 'I really don't believe Stephen has her,' she shook her head.

'You don't think he's that dangerous yet?' Leonie pounced desperately.

'All drug addicts are dangerous,' June said heavily. 'But if Stephen was so desperate for money he kidnapped Holly you would have received a ransom demand by now.'

That was true, it had been thirty-six hours now since Holly had been taken; if Stephen were that desperate for money to feed his habit then he would have contacted them hours ago. That brought her right back to Michael again. *He* wasn't desperate for money, just to enjoy making her suffer, as he had always done.

God, she couldn't bear this! How was she supposed to *live* until the time Michael called them with his ransom demand!

Hawk stared grimly into the unlit fireplace, absently stroking Tulip as she lay on his legs, barely conscious of the two policemen who had been at the house ever since that first night, only the loud ticking of the clock sounding louder and louder in his head. Time. Surely it was something that had to be running out?

He hadn't mentioned it to Leonie, but he knew she had to realise they should have heard from *someone* by now.

His expression softened as he glanced at her, her head resting against his arm as she dozed restlessly, the first sleep she had had in almost forty-eight hours. She looked like a child herself; she wasn't strong enough to take any more pain.

And yet here they sat, waiting for the telephone call that would bring their daughter back to them.

He and Jake had spent the afternoon trying to find Stephen, barely talking to each other, both filled with a grim purpose. Hawk didn't doubt for one moment that if they had found Stephen with Holly Jake would have been the one to go for the younger man's throat.

As the afternoon dragged on he had become more and more convinced that Stephen knew nothing about Holly's disappearance, and with that acceptance had come his compassion for Jake, the realisation that it could so easily have been Hal in Stephen's condition. As Jake had said to him so long ago, there *were* much worse things

Hal could have told him than that he was in love with a woman who was older than him and whom he had only known for three weeks!

If only someone would call! Most of the crazies had had their cheap thrill by now, and all that was left was the loud tick-ticking of that damned clock!

He and Leonie had kept close to the telephone all day, one or both of them taking every call, although he had tried to spare Leonie from the really sick ones. What was wrong with people, that they had to twist a knife that was already deeply buried in their hearts!

But Leonie was sleeping now, and for that he felt grateful. He knew that——

He stiffened as the telephone rang again, and Leonie came instantly awake. Both of them were on their feet within seconds, waiting for the policeman's nod of assent before grabbing up the receiver.

The muffled voice on the other end of the line could have belonged to anyone, and Hawk wondered if this weren't just another of those sick calls. Then he tensed.

'——the tiny mole on her right shoulder,' the hollow-sounding voice taunted.

Hawk nodded frantically to the two listening policemen, clutching Leonie's hand in a grip that must have been painful but which didn't even make her wince, her whole attention riveted on his telephone conversation.

'What do you want?' he demanded harshly.

'So you believe I have her,' the muffled voice jeered.

His hand tightened about the receiver. 'I *know* you have her,' he conceded raggedly.

'Very well,' the voice was briskly impersonal now. 'I want her mother to bring——'

'No!' he rasped, shaking his head in fierce denial. 'I'm not letting you near Leonie!'

'Hawk——'

He shook his head at Leonie as she would have cut in. 'I'll bring you whatever you want,' he spoke savagely into the receiver.

'Not good enough, I'm afraid,' that hollow voice taunted. 'It has to be your precious Leonie.'

Hawk drew in a harsh breath. 'I said no.'

'You aren't in a position to argue,' the voice insisted. 'Now listen to me closely, because I'm only going to say this once—I'm not about to make myself a gift to those nice policemen you have listening in on this call,' it mocked.

Hawk was barely aware of the demand for a million pounds in exchange for Holly's safe return, agreeing to everything that was asked of him, knowing that the police were taping the call. He was more concerned with the fact that Leonie was the one who was going to have to deliver the money, that they were going to have no choice but to agree to that very positive demand.

There were no guarantees that Leonie taking the money would give them back Holly, and there was every chance that Spencer would take delight in causing Leonie more suffering.

They had no choice but for Leonie to take the money Spencer demanded, but God, he couldn't stand it if he should lose Leonie too!

CHAPTER FIFTEEN

LEONIE listened to the tape of the conversation once more, knowing that neither she nor Hawk could help identify the caller, that the voice was too muffled and hollow for them to positively be able to do that. But they were nonetheless both still convinced that it had been Michael.

A million pounds. He wanted a million pounds. She was sure Hawk had that amount of money, but could he get it in time for tomorrow night, the time the caller had told them they could do the exchange at a busy underground station in the heart of London?

Hawk seemed to sense her worry. 'I've had my bank standing by since it happened,' he told her gruffly.

'Sir,' one of the policemen stood up, a fresh-faced young man who looked too young to be in the position of responsibility he obviously had. 'We don't advise that you——'

'I don't give a damn what you advise!' Hawk turned on him savagely, his eyes blazing. 'That's our daughter that maniac has!'

The young policeman glanced uncomfortably at Leonie. 'We understand that, Mr Sinclair, but you have no proof that——Well, it's going to be difficult to have Mrs Spencer watched in a place like——'

Leonie was no longer listening. What the young policeman hadn't finished saying was that they had no proof that Holly was *still alive*! Her hopes had been raised, only to be dashed again by the stark truth of that.

Hawk's furious face swam dizzily in front of her, the startled exclamations of the three men sounding distant to her as she fainted for the second time in two days.

She opened her eyes to find herself in her bedroom, the bedside lamp burning softly as Hawk sat grimly beside the bed waiting for her to wake up, having once again helped her into her nightgown. She smiled at him wanly. 'I'm sorry.'

He sat forward, clasping her hands in his. 'I can't let you be the one to go tomorrow, Leonie.' His eyes were shadowed with pain.

'I have to,' she reproved gently. 'You heard him—it's me he wants.'

'What does it matter who it is as long as he gets the money?' snapped Hawk.

She smiled sadly. 'We both know it isn't just the money he wants.'

'I'm not going to let him hurt you any more, damn it,' he said harshly. 'I promised you——'

She put a gentle hand against his rigidly clenched jaw. 'I love you, Hawk. I love you very much!'

He closed his eyes as if in pain, coming down on his knees beside the bed, his head resting against her breasts. 'God knows I love you more than life itself,' he choked. 'If anything happens to you——'

'It won't.' She lightly caressed the dark thickness of his hair. 'Hawk, make love to me,' she requested intently.

He raised his head to look down at her dazedly. 'It's too soon after—after——'

'No, it isn't,' she said quickly as both of them threatened to break down again at the painful memory of *why* it was too soon. 'Another week and Doctor Fulton will pass me medically fit for anything,' she continued in an over-shrill voice. 'Hawk, I need to be close to you, as close as we can get, I need to be a *part of you*!' she added intensely.

'I need you too,' he said raggedly, his face pressed against her breasts once more. 'But I'm afraid of hurting you,' he admitted gruffly.

'You're hurting me by denying me,' Leonie told him shakily, wondering if she would actually have to beg to get this sensitive man to make love to her, knowing she would if she had to.

The last thing Hawk felt like doing was making love, not knowing if he possessed the gentleness tonight that Leonie would need during her reintroduction to lovemaking.

But he needed her desperately too; he wanted to be buried inside her, to stay that way until she had to leave to get their daughter.

But what if he should hurt her, what if he should unleash the savagery he felt inside on this beautiful witchchild?

He daren't take the risk.

He was going to refuse her, Leonie could see it in his eyes. Not because he didn't want her, she was sure of that.

'Come and hold me.' She folded back the bedclothes invitingly. Hawk stood up, about to join her on the bed, when she stopped him. 'Not like that,' she said huskily, touching his denim-clad thigh. 'I want you to hold me in your arms like you did last night.'

Uncertainty flickered in his eyes, and she could clearly see the battle he fought within himself before reluctantly unbuttoning his shirt and then removing the rest of his clothes.

His body was warm, so very warm, and she snuggled against him, feeling his tension increase, casually draping one of her legs over his, knowing by his sharply indrawn breath that the contact had affected him as deeply as it had her.

He wanted her—she needed no further proof of that as she ran her fingertips lightly across the hard wall of his stomach down to the velvet shaft that pulsed at her softest touch.

She had never seduced a man before, never wanted to, but she knew that they could only live through the pain of uncertainty tonight by belonging to each other, completely and utterly.

Hawk's breath was sucked in in a gasp as she trailed kisses down his throat to his chest, suddenly gripped with curiosity to know if those flat brown nipples were as sensitive to her lips as hers were to his, flicking her tongue across the hardened nub, knowing by the way one of Hawk's hands clenched in her hair that he was just as aroused by the caress as she was.

Her hair trailed tantalisingly across his chest as she laved the other nipple with the hardened tip of her tongue, Hawk's breathing harsh above her as those kisses moved down his flat stomach, hovering at his full arousal, feeling his tension mounting, finally moving to encase his warm velvet, cupping him beneath that shaft as she heard him cry out his agony of desire.

He lay rigidly beneath her, fighting for control, moist against her lips as that control threatened to break.

His hand was rough in her hair as he dragged her head up and away from him, rising above her to become the aggressor, pinning her arms above her head as he captured first one breast between his lips and then the other in fevered torment, inciting a frenzy of desire that quickly had her writhing beneath him.

'I want you inside me,' she choked.

'Not yet.' His gaze was heated as it swept over her body. 'Oh God, not yet!'

His lips were hot against her, his tongue flicking and laving until an aching spasm of completion arched her hips high off the bed.

And still he held her beneath him, the ache becoming an agony that quickly rose up again, sobbing as the fiery completion claimed her once again, but knowing that Hawk still wasn't satisfied, bringing her to that point again and again until he pushed her legs wide apart and thrust into her with one smoothly fluid motion, her softness claiming all of him as he slowly sank that throbbing shaft full-length within her.

Some of the tortured desire left his eyes as he stared down at her heaving breasts, a fine sheen of perspiration dampening his body. 'Am I hurting you?' he groaned.

Leonie lifted her hips high off the bed, her softness moving against the long length of him before gently pulling away, repeating the action, moving up and down as he held himself above her, all the time her gaze holding his.

He gave a choked groan as his mouth swooped down to claim hers, his movements matching hers now as he thrust heatedly within her, arching to kiss her breasts as she groaned her release once more, seconds later pumping his seed hot and fierce within her.

Leonie cradled his head against her breasts as he breathed raggedly, feeling his tears hot against her.

And then she began to talk. 'Sixteen years ago we lived in a small community on the outskirts of London.' She felt him stiffen in surprise, slowly raising his head to look at her, satisfied with what he saw as he once again rested against her. 'My mother liked to get out of London every chance she could—she loved to go down to the coast. At first it was okay, but by the time Laura and I got to ten we considered ourselves a bit old to go on to a beach and play with our buckets and spades.' She gave a sad smile at the memory of how grownup she and Laura had considered themselves to be.

'It was a Sunday,' she continued flatly. 'My parents wanted to go for a drive, which we knew would end up at the coast somewhere, but Laura had arranged to go skating with one of our cousins. I wasn't all that keen on skating,' she grimaced, 'so I said I would go with my parents. Mummy thought Laura should come with us, but Laura said she didn't want to, that she wanted to be with her friends.'

'She argued?' Hawk prompted softly.

Leonie gave a ragged sigh. 'Yes.'

He nodded. 'What happened?'

'My aunt said Laura could stay with them for the day, and so reluctantly my parents agreed. It began to rain almost as soon as we set out,' she frowned at the memory. 'Rusty was with us, and——'

'Your dog?' Hawk guessed correctly again.

'Yes,' she confirmed shakily.

'Leonie, you don't have to tell me this.' His hands cradled either side of her face as he gazed down at her intently.

She nodded. 'If we're to help Laura, I do.'

'And what about you?' he groaned. 'Is this going to help you?'

She met his gaze unflinchingly. 'I want to share all that I am with you, Hawk,' she said huskily. 'And to do that I have to share the past too.'

He rested his forehead briefly against hers, kissing her lightly before gently resting against her breasts once more.

'Rusty loved to go to the coast with us,' she began again. 'But he hated the rain, and he whined almost continually as it continued to pound on the car.' She swallowed hard. 'I don't know if that distracted Daddy or not, but suddenly the car gave a sharp lurch and we—we'd left the road. The car went over and over, finally—finally coming to a halt on its roof.'

Hawk's only reaction was the tightening of his arms about her.

Leonie drew in a harsh breath. 'I'd been screaming and screaming as it happened, and then suddenly there was silence, complete and utter silence, not even Rusty was barking any more,' she remembered clearly. 'And then I knew why.' Her voice broke emotionally. 'He lay lifeless on the crushed roof of the car, either his neck or his back broken, I'm not sure.' She shuddered at the memory, her nails digging into Hawk's back, although he gave no sign of complaint.

'And then——' She moistened her stiffly dry lips. 'And then the silence came to an end,' she choked. 'My parents were still alive, trapped by the crushed front of the car. My mother regained consciousness first, screaming in agony——'

'Don't go on,' Hawk groaned, his arms painful about her.

'I have to, Hawk,' she choked. 'I have to tell you all of it so that you understand.'

'All right,' he moaned, her pain his pain.

'Mummy's legs were trapped in the crushed and ragged metal, I could see she was bleeding, but the way the car was lying and the way the roof had been forced down almost to the level of the seats made it impossible for me to go to her. And then Daddy regained consciousness too. He must have been in just as much pain as Mummy, but he tried not to show it—he spoke soothingly to my mother until her screams faded to a painful rasp, comforting me in the only way he was able, by telling me over and over again how much he and Mummy loved both Laura and me.'

'Were you hurt?' Hawk grated.

'No more than a few scratches,' Leonie revealed heavily. 'You'll never know how much I wished Rusty's fate had been my own as the hours dragged on and on with my parents dying before my eyes!' Her eyes were fever-bright with the memory.

Hawk sat up to look at her sharply. 'No one rescued you?'

She swallowed hard. 'We always went by a country route, Mu—Mummy always enjoyed the country. It was a wet Sunday morning, a time when most people were still tucked up in bed. No one saw the car leave the road because there was no one else but us on the road!'

'Oh, dear God!' Hawk's pain increased.

Leonie nodded abruptly. 'My father talked to my mother and me for what seemed like hours—I learnt later it was probably three or four. He talked about everything he could think of to try and keep us calm, he was so wonderfully brave, until—until he realised Mummy was no longer listening,' she revealed in a choked voice. 'I don't know how long she'd been dead, maybe only minutes, but it could have been hours.' She began to shake, tears falling unchecked down her cheeks. 'She was only thirty-two, so—so beautiful and kind. And she was dead!' Leonie began to sob at the vividness of her memories.

'I don't want you to go on,' Hawk told her emotionally.

As she looked at him she knew all the tortures of hell were in her eyes. 'I have to, Hawk,' she groaned. 'Can't you see that?'

'Yes.' His expression was fierce. 'Yes, damn it, I can!' He closed his eyes as he crushed her to him with steely arms.

Leonie clung to him. 'Once Daddy realised—realised Mummy was dead he seemed to lose what little strength he had. He'd lost so much blood, and we'd been trapped down there for so long, I think he just lost hope. I tried to talk to him, to make him see that he had to live for Laura and me, but——They said later that they didn't know how he managed to survive as long as he had with the way his legs were—were injured.'

'How long were you alone in the car with them?' Hawk prompted softly.

'About another three hours, I think.' Leonie moved restlessly at the memory. 'The windows were completely crushed down, the doors wouldn't open, and by the time my aunt had raised the alarm because we hadn't called them as we'd promised to do it had been over eight hours since the accident happened. I was in deep shock——'

'I'm surprised you survived at all!' said Hawk with feeling.

She nodded. 'You can imagine what it all did to Laura, why she——'

'I understand completely about Laura,' he assured her. 'And we'll explain to Hal so that he understands too. But it's *you* who concerns me.'

'I was all right, in time,' Leonie dismissed abruptly.

'How could you be after all that you suffered?' Hawk said scathingly.

She shrugged. 'They sent me to an excellent psychiatrist——'

'Who did?' he demanded.

'My aunt and uncle.'

He frowned. 'The ones you and Laura went to live with?'

She swallowed hard, moistening her lips. 'Actually—there were two aunts and two uncles.'

Hawk's frown deepened. 'You mean you were

moved about between your relatives?'

'No.' She avoided his probing gaze. 'Laura went to live with one uncle and aunt and I—went to live with another,' she revealed in a rush.

'They *split you up*?' he thundered.

'Try to understand, Hawk——'

'But I don't,' he exclaimed furiously. 'You and Laura had just gone through the worst trauma of your lives, *you* had actually lived through that trauma for eight hours, and Laura had been left with such a guilt complex that she's never got over it—and they *separated the two of you*!'

Leonie sighed. 'They didn't have any choice unless they actually put us into care. And none of them wanted to do that. Hawk, both aunts had children of their own, they couldn't cope with two emotionally disturbed ten-year-olds!' she reasoned sharply.

'So they coped with one each!' he said disgustedly. 'And what did that do to you and Laura? Hell, don't answer that,' he dismissed harshly. 'I've seen what it did to you! How long did that go on?'

She shrugged. 'Until we were old enough to move out and get a place of our own together.'

'Too damned long,' he rasped. 'And this was why you *wanted* to fall in love with Spencer!'

Leonie gave him a puzzled frown, remembering her conversation with Laura before her sister's wedding. 'You heard that?'

He nodded abruptly. 'Not intentionally,' he defended. 'And I certainly didn't want to give you the opportunity to tell Laura how you felt about me!'

She gave a gentle smile. 'If you had you would

have heard me tell her I love you very much. I think I always have. I was certainly filled with an uncharacteristic lust that first night we met!'

His eyes flickered with uncertainty. 'But you said——'

'I know what I said,' she acknowledged softly. 'But I'd been hurt so many times in the past that I was afraid to trust what I did feel. Especially when a certain man woke me the next morning hurling all sorts of insulting accusations at me,' she recalled heavily.

God, he had, hadn't he, had destroyed the gentle bud of their love before it had even had a chance to bloom.

He recognised that it had been difficult for Leonie to care for anyone again after what she had gone through, first with her parents, the separation from her twin, then her marriage to Spencer and the loss of her son. He felt emotionally moved that he should be the man lucky enough to receive the precious gift of her love. He was also sure that she had never entrusted anyone with the tragedy of her past before.

He wanted to make sure she never knew another moment's pain, wished he could make that possible for her. They had to get Holly back before they could even think about being completely happy.

It was achieving that that still worried him. He ached at the thought of Leonie being the one to confront Spencer, more concerned than ever now that he knew of all the pain Leonie had suffered in the past, pain that could have totally destroyed a less strong woman.

He had no idea what would happen to that strength if they didn't get Holly back!

He didn't even want to think about that, daren't think about it. And he knew, as he began to make love to Leonie through a night-time of love, that he daren't give her the time to think about it either.

CHAPTER SIXTEEN

LEONIE FELT so conspicuous standing on the busy platform. Not that there was anything about her appearance to draw attention to her; there were plenty of other women getting on and off the underground trains wearing similar outfits to her grey business suit, also plenty of other women carrying briefcases.

But none of them had a million pounds inside their briefcase!

And none of them had been standing on the same platform for almost an hour waiting to hand that money over for the return of their baby.

Five o'clock had been the time for the meeting, and she had arrived here shortly before that time. And she had waited and waited and waited . . . If Michael was here she certainly hadn't seen him.

Neither had she seen the police who were keeping a watchful eye on the exchange, but if she couldn't recognise them she also hoped Michael couldn't either. He wasn't likely to show himself if he thought he was about to be arrested.

She hadn't wanted the police here at all, especially as they doubted, because of the location, that they would be able to work to full efficiency. But Hawk had insisted; he had wanted her to have some protection. Waiting impotently in the background for the outcome of the meeting was almost killing him, she knew. He was a man who always liked to take charge. She didn't doubt that Michael had known exactly how Hawk would feel about that when he made the condition that she had to be the one who brought him the money.

Another train came into the station, and Leonie anxiously searched the faces of the people getting off and the ones milling about to get on. None of them was Michael.

She glanced up towards the clock; five fifty-seven. An *hour* late. What had happened? Had something gone wrong, or had Michael just wanted to make her suffer a little longer? She knew that anyone capable of creeping stealthily into her home to take Holly as they had had to be capable of anything.

She had been told that she mustn't hand the money over until Michael had either given her Holly or told her where she was; she hoped it was the former. Although she couldn't see Michael carrying a baby about with him.

Her palm felt damp where she clutched tightly to the handle of Hawk's briefcase, her heart sinking as she realised Michael might not turn up at all.

He *had* to turn up. None of them could go through this a second time!

But he was an hour late. Where could he be? Why didn't he just take the money and go away!

She turned sharply as someone knocked her from behind, smiling wanly at the woman with the pink spiky hair and black garish make-up as the woman apologised. For a moment she had thought Michael——God, she was so tense she felt as if she was about to snap in two!

There was another train due in a few minutes,

and the people who worked in the heart of England's capital were hurrying down the stairs to escape the rush and bustle there at the end of the day.

Leonie once again searched the sea of new faces, starting to tremble badly as once again she recognised none of them. Where *was* Michael?

No doubt this all appealed to his warped sense of humour as he envisaged her rising panic!

How much longer was she supposed to wait? She would wait all night if she had to, but would it do any good? Could it be that Michael had never had any intention of picking up the money at all, that he was just showing Hawk that the threat he had made to bring charges of blackmail against him if he dared to ask Leonie for money again or so much as hinted at any scandal attached to Holly's birth meant less than nothing to him? Hawk had told her of his warnings to Michael, with his lawyer as a witness; Michael had made a serious mistake not heeding that warning!

The next train came into the station, but as fast as the platform emptied it filled up again with people waiting for the next train. Wherever the policemen were it had to be virtually impossible for them to even be able to keep sight of her, let alone be able to pick out Michael! He had chosen his spot well.

To ease her tension Leonie thought of her dark-eyed sister as she had looked before she left home. Laura would be all right in time, she was sure of it. Hawk had told Hal the full story of the past, and Leonie didn't doubt that with her husband's help Laura would eventually allow her love to flow again.

Once they had Holly safely back home.

Leonie closed her eyes as she envisaged a life without her daughter. She had promised Hawk they would go on together if that should happen, but she didn't know how either of them would do it!

Hawk had to be going through a worse kind of hell than her right now; at least she had searching for Michael to keep her from going insane.

She felt tears prick the back of her eyes at how futile that now seemed to be. She had arrived full of hope and anticipation; an hour of watching trains come and then go again had shattered almost all that hope.

She could hear another train coming, people were moving forward to take their places ready for boarding. Lights blazed as the train came towards the end of the tunnel, and Leonie once again turned her attention back to the people waiting on the platform, still more coming quickly down the stairs. For a moment she caught sight of a windswept fair head that could have been Michael's, and then it was lost to her view as the crowd surged forward, vying for a place close enough to get on the train, knowing not all of them would get on, since the train was already crowded from previous stations.

Leonie craned her neck trying to see that blond head once more, but her lack of height and the number of people made it impossible for her to see more than those immediately around her. Maybe she would get a better look once the crowd had thinned out a little.

The rush of cold air told her the train was rapidly approaching the station now, the noise was becoming deafening. And then suddenly, just as her eyes widened incredulously on Hawk as he stood halfway down the stairs, holding up a tiny shawl-wrapped bundle for her to see and recognise, she felt a sharp push in her back and felt herself falling forward, straight into the path of the glaringly bright lights of the train!

To Hawk, watching in silent horror, what happened next seemed to take place in slow motion.

One second Leonie's face had been bathed with glowing happiness as she saw Holly in his arms, the next her expression had turned to fear as she began to fall, and fall——

And then suddenly strong arms came out to stop her, pulling her backwards just as the train engine tore by them to come to a halt further up the platform.

And then Hawk was running, Holly held protectively in his arms, running to be with the woman he loved.

Leonie's arm hurt where she had been pulled back with such force, but the pain was nothing to the agony she would have known if she had fallen into the path of the speeding train.

She turned to her rescuer, about to thank him, when she saw people staring curiously at the struggling woman with the spiky pink hair as someone else held her a few feet away, the woman kicking and swearing as she fought her captor.

Leonie was still too numb from her close shave with death to be able to puzzle out what was happening, but she did understand that she had seen Holly alive and well in Hawk's arms just seconds before she felt herself falling. She turned frantically to search for him, her face lighting up with gladness as she saw it hadn't been an hallucination. Hawk was almost at her side now.

She looked eagerly up into his face as he gently handed her their daughter. Holly was gazing up at her with widely enquiring eyes.

A choked sob caught in her throat as she buried her face in her daughter's neck, breathing in the scent and feel of her as if she never wanted to stop holding her and looking at her.

'How the hell did you——Why, Hawk?' demanded a grating voice. 'She's mine, Hawk. You're *both* mine!'

Leonie looked up slowly, recognising the voice, but not the woman with that pink hair and dark make-up. 'Sarah?' she said disbelievingly, looking for some sign of the beautifully elegant woman beneath the garish disguise. 'Sarah, is that you?' she stared incredulously.

Blue eyes blazed at her contemptuously. 'Don't look so surprised,' sneered Sarah. 'It's me Hawk loves, me he's always loved!'

Leonie looked dazedly at the other woman, turning to Hawk as he gazed pityingly at his secretary.

Sarah Ames loved Hawk, had probably done so for years.

Hawk pulled Leonie tightly against his side, sorrow in his eyes as he looked at the woman who had worked for him for eleven years. 'I love Leonie, Sarah,' he told her gently.

'Of course you don't,' she dismissed impatiently. 'I was the one you were taking out until we came here—the only one,' she announced triumphantly.

'To business dinners,' he reminded her softly. 'Sarah, Leonie and I are going to be married.'

'Only because she had your child,' scorned Sarah, looking as if she was wearing some hideous mask with her face covered in that lurid make-up. 'But now *I* have—had——' She looked uncertainly to where Leonie held Holly in her arms. 'Give her to me!' She tried to pull free of the policeman's restraining arms. 'Once she's mine and you're out of the way Hawk and I can be together again. Give her to me, I said!' Her eyes flared with fury as Leonie's arms tightened protectively about her daughter.

The policeman standing beside Leonie shifted uncomfortably. 'Mr Sinclair, I think Mrs Ames should go to the station now——'

'Hell, yes,' confirmed Hawk with a pained groan, shaking his head as he looked at Sarah, her face contorted with hate as she glared at Leonie. 'Sarah, I don't know what to say——'

'Tell them it's me you love,' she prompted harshly. 'Tell *her*——'

Hawk shook his head. 'I can't do that,' his voice was filled with sorrow, 'because it wouldn't be true. I'm sorry——'

'You're lying!' Sarah pulled ineffectually against the hold on her. '*She* means as little to you as all those other women.' She looked at Leonie scornfully. 'You just feel obligated to her——'

'I love her,' Hawk told her again firmly.

Sarah was still denying the truth of that as she was led away, and Leonie knew how stunned Hawk had to be that someone he had trusted and called friend, as he had Sarah, could have done such a thing in the name of what she called love.

They emerged into the sunshine with their daughter just as the police car with Sarah in it drove off down the street.

'Go with her, Hawk,' Leonie encouraged impulsively. 'Try to help her in some way.'

He looked down at her with pained eyes. 'I don't know if I'm capable of helping her after what she did,' he groaned. 'Do you know how they found Holly?' he grated. 'Because the maid at the hotel who was cleaning the rooms became concerned about the baby that kept crying in room 319! Sarah had just left her there unattended—and God knows how many times she'd done the same thing since she took her!' he added harshly. 'She'd put the "Do Not Disturb" notice on the door and just left her!'

Leonie shuddered to think what could have happened to Holly all those hours Sarah had spent at the house with them and left the baby alone in her room; she hated the thought of the other woman anywhere near her precious daughter, and her arms tightened protectively about Holly as she searched the tiny body for any signs of harm.

'She's fine, Leonie,' Hawk reassured her gruffly as he correctly interpreted her worry. 'A doctor checked her over immediately. It's when I think what could have happened, to Holly, and to you just now——'

'I feel the same way,' she nodded. 'But Sarah's sick, not really responsible for her actions. I—I hate her for what she did, but I—I pity her too.' She shook her head.

He put a hand up to his eyes. 'I never guessed—never had any idea——She was always just my efficient secretary. God, I didn't even see her half the time!' He shook his head bewilderedly. 'Maybe if I had I would have seen this sick possessiveness she seems to feel towards me.'

Leonie put her hand on his arm. 'And maybe you wouldn't. You have to go with her, Hawk,' she encouraged again. 'No matter what she's done, you're all she has just now.'

He gave a low groan. 'I almost lost you——'

'I know, Hawk.' She moved into his arms. 'I know!'

She couldn't know, couldn't possibly realise how helpless he had felt as he watched her falling into the path of that train! The memory of it would haunt him for the rest of his life. He doubted if a day would pass when he wouldn't think of it.

And she wanted him to help the woman who had almost been responsible for her death, who *had* been responsible for taking Holly from them.

He hadn't been able to believe the miracle of it when the police brought Holly to him as he waited tensely for Leonie to hand the money over to Spencer. He was shocked when they told him that Spencer was in Monte Carlo, apparently gambling recklessly—Hawk hoped he was trying to make the fortune he could no longer acquire from him or Leonie! Hawk had been completely stunned when the police told him that a Mrs Sarah Ames occupied the room where they had found Holly.

He had realised then that something was wrong, although Sarah had certainly had the opportunity to get into the house and take Holly. But he hadn't been able to understand the demand for money.

He had arrived on the stairs leading down to the platform just in time to see some pink-haired clown pushing Leonie towards the train. He was hardly able to believe the woman could be his usually impeccable secretary, but recognised that the disguise and the location had been her means of escape. After killing Leonie . . .

They were all drinking coffee in the lounge together when Leonie heard Hawk's car in the driveway. He had been at the police station with Sarah for over three hours, but he had called a short time ago to let Leonie know he was on his way home.

She paused to look down at Holly as she slept. Hal had brought the carrycot in here for her so that she didn't have to be parted from the baby even for a moment, and she was certainly not eager to put her upstairs in her room. It would be a long time before she felt comfortable doing that again.

Hawk looked haggard as she went out into the hallway to meet him, taking her silently into his arms to just rest his head against hers.

'It was bad,' Leonie prompted after several minutes.

He drew in a ragged breath. 'She's convinced that I love her, that you tricked me into bed and are now tricking me into marriage.' He gave a shaky sigh. 'It was like seeing a complete stranger.

She really believed that if she could get rid of you I would turn to her.' His arms tightened.

Leonie had already guessed that the ransom demand was just a way of getting her on her own, that the underground station had deliberately been chosen as a way of Sarah ridding herself of the person she believed stood in the way of her dreams, obviously sure she could escape during the mayhem she left in her wake, without ever being recognised.

What was more difficult to accept was that it was *Sarah* who had done these terrible things. She hadn't got to know the other woman that well, but she had always seemed friendly and warm when they had spoken. It must be even more difficult for Hawk to accept after knowing Sarah all these years!

'The others are in the lounge,' she told him. 'Would you like to go into the study and talk?' she suggested softly.

'Holly?' he frowned, glancing up the stairs. Their daughter's disappearance was a nightmare they were *both* going to have to live with for a long time!

'She's in the lounge with the others,' Leonie assured him softly.

He nodded. 'Then that's where we'll go. Has Jake heard anything from Stephen yet?' he frowned as they went through to the lounge.

Jake looked up as he heard the tail-end of the question, sighing deeply. 'He's admitted himself to a clinic for treatment,' he told them. 'His doctor telephoned this evening to let me know he's all right. I can't see him for a while but——Hell, I'm just glad to know where he is and that he's trying to help himself,' he groaned, his hand tightly squeezing June's as she sat beside him.

Leonie could see how moved Hawk was by the information, standing beside him as he paused to gaze down at his daughter before answering the other man.

'I'm glad, Jake,' he said gruffly. 'Very glad,' he added warmly. 'Now perhaps you'll reconsider your resignation?' he added lightly.

Leonie smiled at Hawk's ability to comfort the other man without an outward show of affection that Jake just wasn't up to coping with tonight. They had all been in the room when Jake received the call about Stephen, had all witnessed his emotional relief. They knew he had been close to breaking down then, that he would have done so now if Hawk had handled the situation differently; and Jake certainly wouldn't have thanked him for that!

Jake glanced at June. 'I'll let you know,' he answered Hawk softly.

Hawk grinned his satisfaction at Leonie, both of them hoping that June and Jake would remain drawn to each other once the trauma they had both known had faded and their emotions were allowed to come forward; from the way Jake was looking at the blushing woman at his side it certainly seemed as if it was a possibility!

Leonie watched as Hawk glanced at Laura. Her sister was still badly shaken by what had happened to Holly, but Hal was being marvellous with her, and they had managed to persuade Laura to see the psychiatrist she should really have seen after their parents' death and whom only Leonie had visited.

'Don't look so worried, Hawk,' Laura drawled suddenly. 'I'll soon be arguing with you over working Hal too hard when he should be with me!'

Hawk grinned his relief. 'I'll look forward to it!' he teased.

Laura returned his smile, snuggled up against Hal. 'I should check with Leonie about my temper before sounding too pleased about it,' she taunted.

Laura had the reputed redhead's temper—the two of them had fought incessantly when they were children; Hawk might find his work cut out trying to win an argument against a fully armed Laura! Not that he looked too worried at the prospect.

'What's going to happen about Sarah, Dad?' Hal gave a pained frown. 'She had to be insane to do what she did!'

Leonie looked anxiously at the man she loved, knowing the last hours had to have been a tremendous strain for him.

He shrugged, 'That isn't for me to decide. But she is very ill,' he added harshly. 'I can't believe she actually tried to *kill* Leonie,' he groaned huskily. 'That Holly's kidnapping was all a ruse to achieve just that. And she did it all because she *loved* me!'

Leonie could see exactly how much all this had upset him on top of Holly's abduction, knowing how shaken she had felt when she got home, needing to be close to the people she loved and who loved her. But Hawk was different from her, and she recognised that he needed to be alone for a while to come to terms with Sarah's warped idea of love.

'You must be famished,' she said brightly, knowing food was probably the last thing on his mind. 'Let's go into the kitchen and I'll get you some supper.'

'As long as June doesn't threaten to quit because you've taken over her kitchen,' he drawled, giving the housekeeper a teasing smile.

June smiled. 'Once you've tasted Leonie's cooking for a while you'll be begging me to stay!' she told him confidently.

'I'm marrying a woman who can't cook?' said Hawk disgustedly as he followed Leonie from the room as she wheeled the carrycot in front of them to park it just inside the kitchen, both of them wanting their daughter near.

She turned to give him a mischievous smile. 'I can write fourth-rate detective novels!'

Hawk sat down at the kitchen table with a groan. 'Are you still going to be reminding me of that when we're eighty?'

'When *you're* eighty, my dear man,' she said lightly, putting steak on to cook while she got out the salad from the fridge, '*I'll* still be a spritely sixty-six!'

His mouth quirked. 'I bet I'll still be able to match you in stamina.'

'As you chase me around the bedroom?' she teased.

'Probably,' he grimaced. 'Walking stick and all!'

They both needed this ridiculous sense of fun after the tension of the last few days, and Hawk especially needed to relax.

'I'll probably be chasing you,' Leonie said dryly.

'You won't hear me complaining!' He grinned.

Leonie placed a cup of coffee in front of him. 'Just plain ordinary coffee, in your honour,' she said. 'June bought some last time she went shopping as she's been getting rumblings of disapproval from the men in the house!' she told him pertly.

He took an appreciative sip of coffee. 'I won't tell you what Jake said about the decaffeinated sort!' he smiled.

'I can imagine,' she drawled. And she could imagine; the decaffeinated coffee definitely lacked the boost ordinary coffee gave to the adrenalin.

Hawk leant on his elbows on the table, his cup held in his hands, his expression suddenly haggard again, and Leonie realised the time for teasing had passed.

'It's all right, Hawk.' She stood behind him, her arms about his neck, her hands resting against his chest, her cheek against his. 'Holly and I are both fine. It's all over now.'

She could feel him tremble as he drew in a ragged breath. 'Seeing you falling towards that train will haunt me for the rest of my life,' he shuddered.

Her arms tightened about him. 'I know.'

Hawk shook his head. 'Sarah said that she's loved me for years, that she knew I was attracted to her too when I was so supportive during her divorce.' He sighed. 'She was upset—I would have done the same for anyone. But Sarah didn't see it that way, and all these years she harboured the idea that we were somehow a couple. Then six months ago I stopped dating other women and took her to social functions that I had to attend.' He sighed. 'After making love to you over nine months ago I couldn't get you off my mind, and dating other women became something that just didn't interest me. Sarah was my secretary, I thought she realised I only took her out because of business.' He looked up at Leonie with pained eyes. 'Once we moved in here and I couldn't take my eyes—or my mind—off you, you—you became a threat to her, to what she thought we had together!'

Leonie let him continue to talk as she held him, knowing he needed to tell her—and that she needed to hear.

'She saw us together that night we had dinner at the hotel, although she didn't realise why I'd been so interested in knowing about you all those months ago until Hal held Holly for the wedding photographs. Then she saw the resemblance.' He shook his head. 'She finally broke when I told her that I was taking *you* back to New York with me instead of her. From what I can tell she hated you, blamed you for taking me away from her. She wasn't able to recognise that I loved you long before you loved me!'

Leonie moved then, coming round to sit on his knees, holding his face cupped between her hands as she gazed into his eyes. 'I told you I began to love you that night we first made love,' she said softly. 'If you hadn't jumped to the wrong conclusions about Laura's and Hal's absence the next morning I believe I might have let myself love you sooner than I did.' She kissed him deeply before snuggling against his chest. 'None of it matters now, Hawk. What does matter is that we're together, we have a beautiful daughter—and the rest of our lives to show our love to each other. We have a lot to be grateful for,' she added with feeling.

Hawk gazed down at the tiny woman he held in his arms, knowing he had more reasons than most never to take their love for granted. He *had* lost Amy, and he had almost lost Leonie; Leonie would never ever doubt his love for her, he would make sure of that.

'I love you, Mrs Sinclair-to-be,' he told her gruffly.

'Please,' she said in mock disdain. 'The name will be Mrs Henry Hawker Sinclair the Second. And I love you too,' she added mischievously.

He barely had time to respond to her kiss before she got lightly to her feet to check on the steak he knew he didn't want—even if it was perfectly cooked. He just wanted to be with Leonie.

He watched her moving gracefully around the room, his woman-child who also happened to be a witch; she had certainly bewitched him. She was the most lovely creature he had ever seen, almost not quite real; it was like being in the presence of a beautiful sprite. He was going to spend the rest of his life besotted with this witchchild!

He frowned a little as she took a plate of chicken from the fridge and began to cut it up into small pieces. 'I thought I was having steak?' And from the burning smell coming from the grill it was going to be far from *perfectly* cooked!

Leonie looked up to give him a pert smile. 'Oh, this isn't for you,' she shook her head. 'Whenever Laura and I have reason to celebrate—and we certainly have tonight!—then the cats always get a dinner of boiled chicken.'

The *cats*. He should have known! Leonie would have been burned as a witch a couple of centuries ago!

He stood up to switch off the cooker, picking up Holly's carrycot to pause at the doorway. 'While you're taking the cats their supper I'll be waiting for you upstairs, contemplating a way *we* can celebrate,' he told her huskily.

Her delight with the suggestion glowed in her eyes. 'Are you sure you wouldn't rather have dinner first?' she teased.

'Nectar and honey will do me just fine,' drawled Hawk, chuckling softly as she began to blush. 'And hurry up, woman,' he growled. 'I *am* famished!'

And when Leonie joined him a few minutes later they shared a banquet, celebrating in life, their love, in all the years they had ahead of them.

EPILOGUE

'WELL, my darling,' Leonie looked up at her husband with glowing eyes, 'it's our first wedding anniversary; have you been bored so far?'

Hawk gazed back at her across the candlelit table. 'I believe I was supposed to ask you that?' he drawled.

She gave a happy laugh. 'How could I possibly be bored with a man who drags me and our daughter around half the world with him on business trips? How could I be bored with the man who has made such a success of the Winnie Cooper series that the public is crying out for more? How could I be bored with the man our daughter calls "Hunk"?' She chuckled softly at the embarrassment Holly had caused her father on several occasions when she had called out to him across a crowded room. *They* all knew it was Holly's version of Hawk, but no one else did! 'Last of all,' she lowered her voice seductively, 'how could I possibly be bored with a man who's *so* inventive in bed?' She batted her eyelashes at him flirtatiously.

'I believe you were the one who came up with the idea that we should——'

'Hawk!' Damn, he still had the power to make her blush like a schoolgirl!

He laughed throatily. 'I *loved* your idea, Leonie!'

The last year had been such a happy one, so filled with love and laughter. And they had so many more years yet to come, all of them as good, she was sure.

She stood up to move seductively around the table. 'Maybe you should refresh my——' She broke off as a cry from upstairs interrupted the silence of the evening. 'Maybe later,' she ran her fingertips lightly down his rugged jaw.

'The story of my life,' groaned Hawk as he too stood up.

Leonie turned to him with glowing green eyes. 'Don't I *always* remember?'

He gave a sensual smile. 'Always.'

They went up the stairs together. The cry was a little louder now, so Leonie quickly moved to pick up her baby son before he woke up his brother.

Twins. Boys. Born exactly ten months after Holly had been born.

She gave Mark Daniel to Hawk while she prepared herself for feeding him. 'Now aren't you glad,' she drew in a little gasp as Mark latched eagerly on to her breast, sucking enthusiastically, 'that I talked you out of having that vasectomy until we were sure I wasn't already pregnant again?' she said warmly.

Hawk sat on the bed to watch her, as he always did if he was at home when his sons needed feeding.

There had been no complications with this pregnancy, or the birth, although Hawk had been more than a little shaken when the doctor told him after Mark Daniel's birth that there was another baby on the way. David John had been born a few minutes later.

Both boys had silky baby blond curls, and at

two months old their eyes were already turning the grey of their father and much older brother, Holly's eyes having fooled all of them and turned the green of her mother.

Leonie's greatest joy had been in being able to feed her sons herself, finally able to share that closeness with her child.

'It would have been a waste, yes,' Hawk drawled.

'And the doctor says we can have more children if we want them,' she reminded him. Mark had almost finished his supper, which was perhaps as well because David was starting to stir as he began to feel hungry. They were very tactful, her sons, rarely waking up at the same time for their food.

Hawk's eyes widened. 'Isn't three enough?'

Leonie gave him a slow smile. 'Nectar and honey?' she taunted, laughing softly as his cheeks were the ones to colour this time.

'Hmm,' he murmured, lightly touching his tongue to his lips. 'Wouldn't they be perfect names for twin daughters?'

As usual when he turned the tables on her, her cheeks were burning. 'Laura telephoned today,' she firmly changed the subject, the intimacy of their conversation making her shift uncomfortably. 'She doesn't want to go to Paris, she likes it in Florida.' Laura and Hal had travelled extensively the last year, and as Laura had promised, she and Hawk had had several arguments about where he sent them.

'Doesn't everyone?' he returned unsympathetically. 'Wait until she's had a few moonlit walks in Paris and she won't want to leave there either.'

'She's threatening to make you a grandfather if

you move them again,' Leonie warned.

He grinned. 'All the more reason for them to go to Paris.'

She returned his smile. 'That's what Hal said!'

His smile deepened. 'Hal's getting more and more like me as he gets older, isn't he?'

And wasn't he proud of the fact! But why shouldn't he be? As far as Leonie was concerned there wasn't a finer man in the world than the man who was her husband.

'Maybe they'll have the twin girls,' she suggested lightly, knowing how much her sister and Hal wanted a child of their own. It seemed she and Hawk only had to make love once and she became pregnant, but Laura and Hal were having a little more difficulty. But Laura had confided in her today that she was very hopeful at the moment, was pretty confident that the test she had had would prove positive. Leonie had a feeling it would too.

'As long as they don't give them the names of flowers I don't care,' Hawk said dryly.

'You were the one who gave me a kitten wearing a diamond bracelet for our anniversary,' she reminded him as she placed David at her breast, gently smoothing his silky hair as he indulged a little more slowly than his brother.

'I didn't name it Sunflower!' he scorned.

'It looks just like a sunflower with that lovely orangy fur,' she defended.

'It *looks* like a ginger tabby to me,' jeered Hawk.

'That's because you have no imagination, no poetry in your soul——'

'I don't?' he said softly, his silver gaze holding hers.

'You—you——*You*!' Leonie groaned with feeling, the ache between her thighs becoming a burning torrent. 'Oh, Hawk, I want you,' she told him raggedly.

He moved to kneel in front of her, lightly cupping the breast his son wasn't latched on to. 'Believe me,' he rasped, his hand caressing, 'you're going to have me!'

He hadn't known life could be this wonderful. This last year with Leonie had been the best he had ever known, and each day he seemed to fall a little more in love with her, until he was sure he couldn't love her any more than he already did. And then he would know that he did.

Watching her now as she tended their sons he was glad she had become pregnant again so soon after Holly. He knew that if she hadn't he would have insisted on denying them both the wonderful experience of knowing she once again carried his child, of watching those children being born. It was something he knew both of them would have deeply regretted missing.

The day that Sarah had tried to take Leonie from him now seemed a lifetime away, and he knew that his life had been different then, completely empty without Leonie and the children they shared. Rather than pushing the trauma of that day to the back of their minds they occasionally talked about it, both accepting that Sarah had been ill, that she still was. The doctors were not sure how long it would be before—or if—she would ever get over this obsessive love she had for him. But she couldn't hurt them now, and she was receiving treatment for her own safety.

'June and Jake also phoned today to wish us well.'

Hawk came back from the past to the present, to his wonderful witchchild.

'I invited them over for dinner tomorrow.' Leonie added huskily, 'I hope that's all right.'

He nodded. 'How's Stephen doing?'

Jake and June had been married six months ago, and when Stephen had decided to go back to law school the three of them had moved to London so that Jake and June could give him the support he needed. So far it seemed to be working out for all of them.

'Fine,' Leonie answered without hesitation. 'He's bringing a girl-friend along with him tomorrow.'

Hawk pulled a face. 'Holly will be upset!'

Their tiny daughter idolised Stephen, had done from the time he began to visit them again nine months ago. Somehow Holly had seemed to know that he needed her childlike innocence to help heal him.

His wife smiled. 'I'm sure Stephen will still find time for her; he loves her as much as she loves him. It's as well you aren't a jealous father,' she teased, settling David back in his cot.

'Just a jealous husband, hm?' laughed Hawk, his arm about her waist as they gazed down at their now sleeping sons.

Completely identical to look at, the boys were already beginning to show signs of a different temperament. Mark was obviously the leader of the two, already displaying signs of a temper, whereas David was more placid, quite happy to wait in line behind his brother. They were sons for any man to be proud of. And Hawk was very proud.

Holly had grown into a lovely little girl the last year, fiery-red curls surrounding her angelically beautiful face as she slept in her cot with her bottom sticking up in the air, a slight smile on her lips, completely confident of her rôle as big sister to the boys she called 'bubbas'. It was going to be a great shock to her when she got older and realised there was only ten months in age between her and those 'babies'!

Hawk still trembled when he thought of all he had almost lost because of one very sick woman!

Leonie felt him tremble against her, and knew that the memories still haunted him as they haunted her. But today was the first of the many anniversaries they would share, and she wasn't going to let anything spoil it.

'Hawk, let's go to the bedroom and . . .' She stood on tiptoe to describe the delicious variation she had been anticipating on the theme they both loved so much.

Hawk drew back to look down at her with widened eyes. 'Is that possible?'

'According to Laura it is,' she nodded. 'But if you'd rather not——'

'Laura?' he gasped—as Leonie had known he would, ushering her out of their daughter's bedroom to close the door softly behind them. '*Laura* told you about that?' he said disbelievingly.

'Your demure sister?'

She nodded again, her eyes glowing. 'Apparently she isn't demure with Hal,' she giggled.

'Obviously,' drawled Hawk. 'Okay, Mrs Henry Hawker Sinclair the Second, let's go and try out this interesting proposition.

'Don't you mean position?' she teased.

'Probably,' he said dryly. 'I was just trying to approach the subject delicately.'

'That should be a first,' she laughed, opening their bedroom door, bathing the room in a warm glow. 'To bed, Hawk Sinclair,' she told him firmly. 'And now! I've been waiting hours for you to make love to me!'

She felt feverish with wanting him, knowing it had always been, and always would be, this way between them.

'I love you, Henry Hawker Sinclair the Second,' she told him with feeling.

'And I love you, Mrs Henry Hawker Sinclair the Second,' he returned intensely. 'I always will!'

'Love me, Hawk,' she gasped her need. 'Love me!'

'I intend to,' he assured her huskily. 'And while I do you can explain to me how Laura says we manage to . . .' The bedroom door closed softly behind them, followed by a giggle, and then silence.

Harlequin Superromance

Here are the longer, more involving stories you have been waiting for... Superromance.

Modern, believable novels of love, full of the complex joys and heartaches of real people.

Intriguing conflicts based on today's constantly changing life-styles.

Four new titles every month.
Available wherever paperbacks are sold.

Harlequin American Romance

Romances that go one step farther...
American Romance

Realistic stories involving people you can relate to and care about.

Compelling relationships between the mature men and women of today's world.

Romances that capture the core of genuine emotions between a man and a woman.

Join us each month for four new titles wherever paperback books are sold.
Enter the world of American Romance.

Harlequin Intrigue

Two exciting new stories each month.

Each title mixes a contemporary, sophisticated romance with the surprising twists and turns of a puzzler...romance with "something more."

Because romance can be quite an adventure.

Intrg-1

Romance, Suspense and Adventure